Truth & Bright Water

Thomas King

———

TRUTH
&
BRIGHT WATER

Atlantic Monthly Press
New York

For my mother.

The dissertation was never enough.

Originally published in 1999 by HarperCollins Publishers Ltd.,
Ontario, Canada

Printed in the United States of America

FIRST AMERICAN EDITION

Library of Congress Cataloging-in-Publication Data

King, Thomas, 1943–
    Truth & Bright Water / Thomas King.
        p. cm.
    ISBN 0-87113-818-2
    1. Boys—Fiction. 2. Friendship—Fiction. 3. Canada—Fiction.
I. Title: Truth and Bright Water. II. Title.

PR9199.3.K4422 T78 2000
813'.54—dc21

                                            00-038618

Atlantic Monthly Press
841 Broadway
New York, NY 10003

00 01 02 03   10 9 8 7 6 5 4 3 2 1

PROLOGUE

The river begins in ice.

Grey-green and frozen with silt, the Shield shifts and breaks out of the mountains in cataracts and cascades, fierce and alive. It plunges into chasms and dives under rock shelves, but as the river leaves the foothills and snakes across the belly of the prairies, the water warms and deepens, and splits the land in two.

Truth and Bright Water sit on opposite sides of the river, the railroad town on the American side, the reserve in Canada. Above the two towns, the Shield is fat and lazy, doubling back on itself in long silver loops as it wanders through the coulees. But as the river comes around the Horns, it narrows and drops into the deep chutes beneath the bridge. It gathers speed here, swings in below the old church, and runs dark and swift for half a mile until the land tilts and the water slows and drains away towards Prairie View and the morning sun.

At a distance, the bridge between Truth and Bright Water looks whole and complete, a pale thin line, delicate and precise, bending over the Shield and slipping back into the land like a knife. But if you walk down into the coulees and stand in the shadows of the deserted columns and the concrete arches, you can look up through the open planking and the rusting webs of iron mesh, and see the sky.

The church sits on a rise above Truth, overlooking the river and the bridge. Built at the turn of the century, it is a plain, squarish building with a raised porch, high windows, and a dark steeple that leans slightly to one side. Instead of being long and sharp with a hard pitch like the steeple on the big Presbyterian church in Prairie View, this steeple is squat and flat with a set and angle that make it look as if a thick spike has been driven through the church itself and hammered into the prairies.

The church was built by the Methodists as a mission to the Indians. The Baptists owned it for a while in the forties. They sold it to the

I

Nazarenes, who sold it to the First Assembly of God, who sold it to the Sacred Word Gospel, who left the church standing empty and moved down the river to Prairie View just after construction on the bridge stopped.

By then, the roof was missing most of its shingles, and the clapboard siding was cupped and pitted. The north side had been completely stripped by the cold and the wind, leaving an open wound of wood that had scabbed over grey and brittle. To the west and the south, the paint that was left had blistered and split and curled up in twists like pigs' tails.

But on days when the sky surges out of the mountains, gun-metal and wild, and the wind turns the grass into a tide, if you stand on the river bottom looking up at the bluff, you might imagine that what you see is not a church gone to hell but a ship leaned at the keel, sparkling in the light, pitching over the horizon in search of a new world.

The Horns, like Truth and the old church, are on the American side of the river, twin stone pillars that rise up from the water and meet to form a shaggy rock crescent that hangs over the river like the hooked head of a buffalo. It is an old place, silent and waiting, and from the high curved shelf of the outcrop, you can turn into the wind and feel the earth breathing or watch the Shield glow black and bright, as the evening shadows run out across the land like ribbons in a breeze.

In daylight, the river valley is bright and dry, wolf willow and cottonwood. Seagulls crowd the tops of the coulees, thrown up into the air like kites, while between the cutbanks, squadrons of pelicans skim the face of the river, single file, searching for their reflections in the shoals and the deeper pools.

At night, the light goes to ground and gives the world up to the insects and the stars. Bats flood the river bottom and tumble in swirling eddies over the water. Coyotes come out of hiding and range the coulees chasing rabbits and the moon, and everywhere the air is warm and sweet.

But beneath the bridge, trapped between the pale supports that rise out of the earth like dead trees and the tangle of rebar and wire that hangs from the girders like a web, the air is sharp, and the only thing that moves in the shadows is the wind.

CHAPTER ONE

Soldier and I relax on the side of the coulee and watch Lum lengthen his stride as he comes to high ground. His skin glistens with sweat, but he moves as if there is no more to the run than the effort of breathing. His arms stay close to his side. His body leans in slightly at the hips.

"Come on!"

Only his legs are in motion. They stretch out across the ground in long, gliding strokes and carry him over the last rise. Soldier barks and charges over the side of the coulee as Lum slows to a lope and circles back. I look at the stopwatch.

"How was it?" There are white lines down the sides of Lum's face and across his back where the heat has dried the salt against his skin.

"Twenty-six minutes, fourteen seconds."

"All right." Lum stops moving and braces himself on his knees. His eye isn't black anymore. It's purple now, and yellow, and doesn't look as if it hurts too much. "I can go faster," he says. "But you don't want to go all out when you're in training."

"That's right."

"Otherwise, when you get to the big race, you're wasted." Lum reaches into his pack and takes out his cigarettes and his gun.

"Thought you were going to give up smoking."

"Toughens your lungs so the dust doesn't bother you." Lum cracks the cylinder and slips a bullet into each chamber. "You think that Cree guy is going to show his face?"

"Can I shoot it?"

"He was lucky." Lum closes the cylinder. "Last year I was sick."

"I'll be careful."

Lum tosses me the gun and lights a cigarette. "All he's going to see of me this year is my ass."

Lum began carrying the gun a couple of summers ago. I figured he had borrowed it from his father, but Lum said he found it out at the landfill. The gun was dull silver with a black handle and a red dot on the front sight. It looked too good to throw away, but Lum said I'd be amazed what shows up at the dump.

The gun was a lot of fun. We'd buy a box of shells at Tucker's Sporting Goods across from Safeway, go down to the river, throw cans in the water, and shoot at them as they floated along. When Lum first showed up with the gun, I was worried that he might try something dumb like Russian roulette. We had seen a really long movie about a bunch of men from a small town in the States who go to the Vietnam War and wind up sitting in a bar with a gun, drinking and sweating and looking tough and bored, taking bets on who is going to live and who is going to die.

One of the men would put a single bullet in a chamber and spin the cylinder, and then another guy would put the gun to his head and pull the trigger. When someone blew his brains out, the film slowed down so you could see the dumb expression on his face, as if the whole thing were a big surprise.

Lum pushes a stream of smoke out of his nostrils and lets it curl around his head. "See if you can hit the bridge from here."

The gun is heavy and cold. I hold it the way the cops hold their guns on television, one hand on the butt, the other cradling the first hand to keep everything steady. I lower the gun slowly until the top of the red dot is in the middle of the rear sights, take a deep breath, and let half of it out.

"The Indian Days long-distance champion." Lum holds his arms over his head. "You know what I'm going to do when I hit the finish line?"

I squeeze the trigger slowly. The sound of the first round is no more than a sharp snap like something cold breaking. The sound of the second round is caught in the wind and blown away.

"I'm going to keep on going. When I hit the tape and everyone is cheering, I'm going to keep on running. And I'm not going to stop until I feel like stopping."

4

We didn't play Russian roulette. We had our own games and some of them were pretty stupid. Once, Lum tried putting the barrel of the gun down a ground squirrel hole and pulling the trigger. Neither of us knew where the bullet went, but the explosion scared the hell out of me and blew dirt into our eyes.

A better game was one where you shot at your own feet and tried to come as close as you could without hitting anything. Sometimes we took our shoes and socks off so we could see exactly where the bullet went, and so we could feel the ground blow up around our toes.

But the best game of all was climbing up into the girders of the bridge and skipping bullets off the concrete and steel. We worked on the angles, and after a little practice, we got each shot to bounce at least once and sometimes twice. Three times was hard, and four was impossible, because by then the only thing left of the bullet was the sound of the ricochet.

With each shot I take, I jerk the gun up, pretending it's a heavier weapon than it is and has one hell of a kick. Sometimes I make an explosion sound under my breath. Sometimes I blow on the barrel.

"If I wanted, I could get one of those running scholarships at a big university." Lum takes the gun and fires a quick round into the dirt next to my foot. "Hell, I'm as good as Tom Longboat already."

"Try hitting the bridge."

Lum has a long drag on the cigarette, cocks the hammer, and smiles. "Don't move."

The evening sun angles out of the clouds for a moment, lighting the sky and setting the prairie grass ablaze. Then it slips behind the mountains and the air turns deep blue and purple, as if the land is slowly being pulled down into a lake.

"You ask your father about jobs?"

"Why don't you ask him," says Lum.

Lum's father and my father are brothers, but you would never know it to look at them. My father is tall with small hands and long hair. Prairie clay and willow. Franklin is shorter, all chest and shoulders, with a crewcut. River rock and fast water.

"I'm not afraid to ask him," I say.

5

"Don't forget to duck," says Lum.

My father drinks from time to time, and every so often, when he's been drinking too long, he'll come by the shop to tell my mother that he's sorry he left us. Sometimes he gets sad and wants my mother to take him back. Sometimes he gets angry and swings at things. But he doesn't really mean it, and he always gives us plenty of time to get out of the way.

Franklin doesn't drink, and he doesn't joke around like my father, so it's hard to tell if he's angry or in a good mood. Lum tells me that you have to watch his eyes, that you're okay until they stop moving.

"Saw the Cousins." Lum grabs the fur at the back of Soldier's neck and pulls it into a wad. "Up by the church."

"No way!"

"Looks like they decided to come home."

"Was he up there?"

"Who?"

"Monroe Swimmer. At the church."

"How should I know," says Lum. "Why don't you ask the Cousins."

Soldier's ears perk up and a hard quiver runs through his body. I figure all this talk about the Cousins is getting him tense. But then I see it, too.

A car. It comes across the prairies, its headlights swinging from side to side. In the dusk, they look like stars moving across the evening sky.

"Headed for the church," I say as I watch the car ride the ridge. "Maybe it's Swimmer."

"You ever see the big-time artist?" Lum holds the gun out at arm's length and follows the car. "Anybody you know ever see him?"

The car stays on a straight line for the church, and I'm beginning to think that it just might be Monroe Swimmer when the lights angle off towards the river and the car drops into a long swale and disappears.

"Tourists?"

"There's no road." Lum turns his head as if he can hear the car moving in the grass. "Tourists need a road."

"Not necessarily," I say. "Remember that German couple?"

Lum stands up. "They're heading for the Horns."

Soldier dances around Lum's legs, his tongue lolling out of his mouth, his jowls hung with chains of slobber. He's hoping there's a game to play and wants to let us know that he's ready.

6

"Maybe we should leave the mutt here." Lum digs a dirt clod out of the ground with his toe and picks it up. "Remember what happened last time."

"That was bad luck."

"Trying to catch a skunk isn't bad luck."

"He wasn't trying to catch it."

Lum drops the clod on Soldier's head. "Next time, you can clean him up all by yourself."

Lum is right. The car is heading for the Horns. It wades out of the bottom of the coulee slowly, like a cow in thick water, and pulls itself up onto the hard plate of the outcrop.

"If I had a car," I tell Lum, "I sure as hell wouldn't bring it out here."

"Truck." Lum shades his eyes as if he can see something more than the shape of the land and the motion of the river. "It's a pickup."

We stand on the bluff. The truck sits on the Horns, its lights pointing across the Shield into Canada.

"Okay," I say. "So, what are they doing?"

"Only a couple of things you can do out here." Lum turns and smiles at me. "You want to sneak down and watch?"

We're too far away to see much of anything, but the sound of the pickup's door opening carries across the prairies like a shot, clear and sharp, and a figure steps in front of the truck.

"It's a woman," says Lum. "You see the guy?"

"What guy?"

"Come on, cousin," says Lum. "She didn't drive all the way out here just to be by herself."

I'm trying to think of other reasons why anyone would risk their tires and their oil pan over broken ground at night. "Maybe she's lost," I say.

"Nobody gets lost out here," says Lum, and he reaches down and scratches Soldier's head. "Just bored."

The woman seems to float in the lights. She turns and weaves her way across the hard ground, her hair streaming, her arms spread wide as if she were a bird trying to catch the wind. Lum moves sideways along the coulee and Soldier follows him.

"She's dancing."

"Great," says Lum. "Maybe she'll take her clothes off."

7

"In your dreams," I tell Lum, but I keep my eyes on the figure in the distance in case I'm wrong. There's always the chance that she might be drunk. When my father has had too much to drink, he likes to joke around and do silly things. Just before he gets angry, he can be really funny.

The woman doesn't dance for long. She slows down by degrees, stops moving altogether, and leans against the truck, her back to the lights. The inside of the truck is dark and lifeless, and the more I watch, the more I'm sure she's come to the Horns alone.

"Show's over," I tell Lum. "Let's check out the church."

Lum grabs my elbow. "Not so fast," he says.

I guess I expect that after the woman catches her breath, she'll get back in the truck and drive off. Instead, she walks to the side of the truck and takes something out of the back.

"What do you think?" says Lum.

"Looks like a box."

"It's a suitcase, cousin," says Lum. "Pay attention."

The woman carries the suitcase and follows the headlights out to the edge of the Horns, where the rock cap rises and curls under itself like a lip and plunges into the river below. You can see Bright Water right across the river, the lights of the townsite, the band office, and the silhouette of the water tower. It's nice, I guess, but I wouldn't drive all the way out here just for the view.

So, Lum is wrong about the guy, and I'm trying to think up other reasons why a woman with luggage is standing on the Horns in the middle of the night when she squats down and opens the suitcase.

"What's she doing?"

"You see that?" Lum thumps me on the shoulder. "She threw something into the river."

"Where?"

"There," says Lum, "she did it again."

A lot of junk winds up in the river this way. Some of it gets washed out of the Bright Water landfill and some of it gets blown off the prairies by the wind. But most of the garbage — car tires, glass bottles, oil drums, shopping carts — comes from people who figure that rolling an old washing machine down the side of a coulee or tossing plastic bags and roofing materials off the bank isn't going to hurt anything.

8

I'm thinking we should walk over to the Horns and tell the woman to throw her garbage somewhere else when she gets up and moves out onto the rock face. She goes all the way to the edge of the cliff until she can go no farther, and then she spreads her arms. And waits. In the cold lights of the truck, against the night sky, she looks like a diver frozen on a board. Or a stone cross.

"She's going to jump."

The woman does look as if she might be *thinking* about jumping, but I'm betting that people who dump garbage into a river aren't going to jump in after it.

"No, she's not."

No matter what, I wouldn't like to be standing that close to the edge. A hard gust of wind could come off the river or a piece of rock could shift under your foot. Looking down too long could also make you lose your balance, so I'm relieved when the woman finally drops her arms and steps away.

"See?" I say. "She was just fooling around."

The woman picks the suitcase up and heads for the truck. I figure she's going to drive off and that will be that, but when she gets there, she reaches into the cab and turns on the radio instead. And as Lum and Soldier and I watch, she steps back into the lights. It's all a little weird. The music coming across the coulees on the wind. The truck lights slicing through the darkness. The woman standing in the glow, her long hair crackling as if she were on fire.

I turn to see what Lum wants to do, but he's looking straight ahead. "You hear that?" he says.

"The music?"

Lum doesn't take his eyes off the woman on the Horns. "It's my mother's favourite song."

I move back a bit just in case Lum is in one of his moods. The song is okay if you like sad stuff that sounds like rain and cloudy days. "Yeah," I say, "it's one of my mum's favourites, too."

The woman begins walking back across the rocks, slowly at first, but as she goes, she gathers speed, the music and the lights pushing her forward, sweeping her along like foam on a current. She doesn't slow down and she doesn't look back, and before either Lum or I can call out or do anything to save her, she is picked up as if on the crest of a wave and washed over the edge of the cliff.

For that first instant, caught at the limits of the truck's lights, the woman appears to float on the air, her body stretched out and arched, as if she's decided to ride the warm currents that rise off the river and sail all the way to Bright Water. But this is nothing more than illusion. Instead, she plummets down the long spine of the Horns and vanishes into the night. There is no sound, no flashing ripples on the water, nothing to mark her fall.

"Holy!" Lum is the first to move. He quickly crushes the cigarette and bends down and ties his shoes. "Time me," he shouts, and he hands me the stopwatch. Lum drops down the side of the slope and heads for the base of the bridge. I'm right behind him for the first fifty yards, but there's no way I can keep up the pace. Soldier charges past me and crashes through the chokecherries and the greasewood as he chases after Lum. I'm not slow, but by the time I get to the bridge, Lum is already up one of the concrete abutments.

"Get on the ladder," Lum yells to me. "Tell me when you see her coming."

There's a safety ladder on one of the columns. I climb it until I can see both the bend in the distance and Lum moving out along a beam below me.

"You see her?"

"No!" I try not to look down. The water is nothing but a dark blur. And as it slides off the rock plates and is forced around the thick footings of the bridge, you can hear it hiss.

"Anything?"

"No!"

The moon comes out, and I watch the light dance on the water. Now and then, a shadow is caught in the current, and for a moment, I think I can see a head or an arm. But it is never anything more than a standing wave or the water tumbling over rocks.

It is late when Lum finally stands up and makes his way back, and I come down the ladder.

"She must have gotten by us," I say.

"No way."

"So, where is she?"

We stand by the river in silence and listen to the water plunge into the channel.

"How was my time?"

I hand him the stopwatch. He looks at it for a moment and nods.

"Where's Soldier?" I listen to see if I can hear him.

"Who cares," says Lum. "Come on."

The way along the bank is a dark twist of willows, mud, and undercuts, and at points, we are forced to retreat up into the coulee and come around from above. Or we have to drop into the river itself and walk the shallows. It would be easier to climb back up to the bluff and follow the road around and out to the Horns. But if the woman has survived the fall and floated to shore or has gotten hung up in the bushes, we'd never see her from the ridge.

"Maybe Soldier has found her."

"That mutt couldn't find his butt with his tongue."

We walk the river all the way to the flat below the Horns. Every so often, we stop to search the water, looking for clues. We even try shouting just in case she's injured, so she'll know that rescue is close at hand.

"Lady!"

"Hey, lady!"

By the time we get to the flat, fog has started to form low on the water. Our runners are filled with mud and sand, and we have to sit on the bank and empty our shoes.

I'm starting to get cold. "Maybe she's dead."

"Off the bridge, she'd be dead for sure," says Lum. "But we've gone off the Horns before, and we're not dead."

"We don't go off the top. We go off the lower ledge."

"I go off the top," says Lum. "I go off the top all the time."

I'm sure we're not going to find anything in the dark and the fog, but I know telling Lum isn't going to do any good. "So, what do we do now?"

"Look for footprints," says Lum. "Current could have brought her in here." Lum reaches into the water and comes up with a rubber glove and a couple of those sticks that doctors shove down your throat to make you gag. "How about this?" He blows up the glove until all the fingers are swollen and white, and taps on it with one of the sticks. It's a dead, hollow sound.

"Christ," I say. "Don't touch it."

"Landfill drum." He ties the glove off and sets it afloat on the current. "Come on. Let's go check out the view."

The climb from the river bottom up to the Horns is long and slippery. In some places, we can grab clumps of grass and pull ourselves along. In other places, we have to dig out handholds and kick our toes into the side of the hill. Behind us, in the dark, I can hear the small avalanches of dirt and gravel rattling down the slope.

By the time we get to the top, we're both tired. I lie down on my back in the moonlight. Lum picks up stones and skips them across the grass.

"You notice anything, cousin?"

I don't move. "Like what?"

"No truck." Lum skips another stone into the grass. "No music."

The truck is gone. It had been sitting on the Horns with its lights on when the woman jumped into the river.

"Maybe we should tell the cops."

"Sure," says Lum. "They love a good Indian joke."

"We didn't do anything."

"Remember what happened to Eddie Weaselhead?"

"That was a mistake."

"Doesn't make Eddie any less dead."

Lum wanders out towards the high shelf. I lie back in the grass and watch the moon in the sky. The song is playing in my head and I'm trying to get rid of it when I hear Lum yell. I look up just in time to see him pull the gun out of his waistband and fire into the grass. The shot skips through and clatters across the rock outcrop. Somewhere in the darkness, Soldier barks.

I'm on my feet in a flash. "Hey, be careful!"

"Damn dog tried to jump me." Lum is crouched in the grass, the gun in his hand. "Come on. He's got something."

Off to the left, Soldier bursts out of the grass, runs across the rocks, and dives back into cover before Lum can find the trigger or the range.

"He's just playing."

We don't find Soldier right away. He's buried himself deep in the grass, but we can hear the low rumbling noises he makes in his throat. We can hear him grunting, too, and gagging, as if he's trying to chew and swallow at the same time.

"Call him," says Lum. "Tell him I won't shoot him."

"Tell him yourself."

"He won't believe me."

When we finally find Soldier, he's lying on his belly. His ears are back and his mouth is locked around something large. Lum leans forward to get a better look. "That's disgusting."

"It's just a ball," I say.

Soldier stands up, growls, and drops the ball at his feet. As soon as it hits the ground, he snatches it up quickly, takes several steps back, glances at us, and drops it again.

"Look again, cousin," says Lum.

Soldier rolls it over in the moonlight, and I can see that it's not a ball at all.

"Is it human?"

"Not anymore." Lum coaxes the skull away from Soldier and cleans the slobber off on the grass. Someone has looped a long red ribbon through the eye sockets. "Nice colour," says Lum, and he wraps the ribbon around his finger.

"Where'd it come from?"

Most skulls you see in the movies are white and chalky. This one is soft yellow and shiny and smaller than I would have imagined. Lum lets the skull roll off his fingers. When it hits the end of the ribbon, he jerks his wrist and catches the skull on the bounce. "Maybe it's not a skull," he says. "Maybe it's a yo-yo."

Soldier stays low in the grass and watches the skull float above him.

"No dirt on it," says Lum, "so he didn't dig it up."

"So?"

Lum holds the skull out and lets Soldier jump for it. "Makes you wonder what else she threw away."

"The woman?"

"Who else?"

All the way back to the bridge, Soldier trots by Lum's side, his ears up, his eyes watching every movement Lum makes. The chain-link fence across the entrance to the bridge is beginning to sag and flatten out in places. The "No Trespassing" sign has disappeared.

"You know what?" Lum leans against the wire. It sways under his weight. "It could have been my mum. She was always doing crazy stuff like that."

Sometimes Lum remembers that his mother is dead, and sometimes he forgets. My mother says it's probably best to leave it alone, that in the end, Lum will work it out for himself.

"Yeah," says Lum, "it could have been her." And he turns and scales the fence, swinging over the top and dropping down the other side. "You should get your mum to move back to Bright Water."

"She likes it here."

"She only moved to Truth because your father did."

"They're thinking about getting back together."

"Your dad still messing around with Lucy Rabbit?" Lum tosses the skull into the air. Soldier barks and lurches forward, hitting the fence with his shoulder. Lum catches the skull and flips it back and forth between his hands.

"What about Indian Days?" I say. "Maybe your father could get the band to hire us."

"To do what?"

"I don't know. Help out at Indian Days. Do some work around the RV park."

Lum smiles and jams the skull on the barrel of the gun and holds it up like a wand or a flag and waits, as if he expects something to happen. "Bunch of trailers from Georgia showed up at Happy Trails yesterday."

"Okay," I say. "We could show them around."

"Cherokees. On their way to Oklahoma."

"They're going in the wrong direction."

"Maybe they're taking the scenic route." Lum tests one of the planks with his foot. The vibration rumbles out into the night. "There's this girl."

"At Happy Trails?"

"She's a little weird," says Lum. "You ought to meet her."

"Why?"

"Because you're weird." Lum moves onto the bridge. The plywood decking has already begun to weather, to twist and bubble up like pieces of thin meat in a hot pan.

"Better get back to the rez." Lum holds the gun high over his head. Below, the fog hangs low and velvet on the river, but on the bridge, everything is star bright and clear. In the light, the skull shines like stone. "Go a few rounds with the old man before I shoot him."

The planks turn and tremble as Lum shifts his weight, feeling for a rhythm in the wood. "It's powwow time," he shouts. "Old Agency drum, take it away!"

Soldier stands frozen by the fence, his ears arched as if at any moment he expects Lum and the skull to tilt and fall. But Lum moves gracefully, effortlessly along the girders, like a dancer, until the curve of the bridge begins its descent into Bright Water, and he vanishes over the edge.

CHAPTER TWO

═══

When I wake up the next morning, the record player is going and my mother is sitting at the kitchen table cutting an old shirt into pieces and stacking the pieces in piles. The shirt is blue with thin red stripes. It's not one of mine, so it must be a shirt my father left behind.

"You call that music?"

"It's the 'Parigi, o cara' from *La Traviata*," my mother says, and she rips an arm out of the shirt and drops it on the floor. "Violetta sings this as she tries to get into her dress."

"Sounds like Soldier when we leave him home."

"And then she dies in the arms of Alfredo."

Two or three mornings each week, before she opens the beauty shop, my mother goes out behind Santucci's grocery and picks up any flowers that Mrs. Santucci hasn't been able to sell. Most of the bunches are in pretty bad shape, but my mother trims the stems, cuts off the dead parts, and arranges them in a vase. Then she warms up the phonograph my father bought at a yard sale just before he left and loads a stack of records on the spindle.

Some of the songs are okay. I don't mind "Ol' Man River" and "Can't Help Lovin' Dat Man" from *Show Boat*, and parts of *The Desert Song* sound exciting. *Carmen* has a couple of good tunes and Soldier likes one of the pieces from *South Pacific* that sounds like a lullaby. But most of the songs are awful things, all about love and death and doomed painters and jealous bullfighters, in languages nobody understands.

The records belonged to my grandfather, who had gone to Italy for a war and had come home with a taste for operas and musicals, *The Student Prince*, *Tosca*, *Damn Yankees*, *La Bohème*. My mother knows all the songs by heart, and her voice blends in so well with the records that you can hardly tell them apart. She could have been an actress, she likes to tell me, and I believe that this is true, for she moves around the beauty shop as if she knows where to place each foot, when to turn, and how to hold her head so that her hair catches the light that comes in through the plate-glass window. Some mornings, when the shop is empty, she'll follow the music around until all the records have dropped. And then she'll turn the phonograph off. With a quick, hard gesture that reminds me of my grandmother wringing the heads off chickens.

"Now that school's out," my mother says, "I guess you'll be looking for something to do."

There are no pans on the stove and I don't smell anything tasty like sausages or bacon. The woman on the phonograph sounds as if she's on her last legs. "What's for breakfast?"

"The railroad might be hiring for the summer," says my mother.

"Sausage?"

"You should check with Wally Preston over at the job gate."

"Eggs would be okay."

My mother takes the quilt from the basket and spreads it out across her lap. "Cereal's in the cupboard," she says.

"French toast?"

"Spoon's in the drawer."

"Lum and me found a skull up on the Horns."

"I hope you left it there," she says.

"Lum says it's human."

"I hope you didn't let Soldier chew on it."

"We saw a woman, too," I say. "Guess what she did."

"I hope you weren't spying."

"She jumped off the Horns into the river."

My mother reaches into the quilt basket and takes out a tin box. Inside are all sorts of odds and ends. Paperclips, coloured stones, pieces of fur, candles, buttons, fish bones, sticks, glass, and bits of dry stuff that look as if they should have been thrown out long ago.

"I have to go over to Bright Water after work." My mother takes a coloured stone out of the box and tucks it into a piece of netting.

"Granny's?"

"You don't have to come." My mother loops the needle through the netting and draws the thread tight against the material. She doesn't look at me. She keeps her eyes on the quilt.

17

"What about supper?" I say.

"There's food in the refrigerator."

"How about we order a pizza?"

My mother shakes her head and sighs the way she does when Soldier runs off and doesn't come back for a couple of days or when I forget to wash my dishes or clean my room. I'm used to it, and it doesn't affect me the way it does other people who don't know her as well as I do.

"What would you think," she says, "if I went away for a day or so?"

"Where would you go?"

"I don't know."

"Why?"

"Oh, just to get away," she says. "The shop wears me out after a while."

"How about Edmonton?" I say. "We could go to the mall."

The bell on the front door jingles, and I hear someone step into the shop. My mother pushes the quilt to one side of the couch and stands up. "When you see your father," she says, "ask him about the car."

The phonograph clicks and a new record drops onto the turntable. I sit in the kitchen for a moment and listen to a guy whose name I can't remember start to sing about how tough knights are supposed to be and what good-looking women want and how much fun it is to live in Camelot.

When I get out to the shop, Lucy Rabbit is sitting in the chair, her head done up in yellow plastic wrap. She has her earphones on and you can hear some of the music leaking out the sides of her ears. Soldier is lying on the floor watching my mother pat Lucy's hair into a lump.

"Of course, there are safer ways to make a living," says Lucy over the music, "but you have to admit that smuggling's sort of romantic."

"He doesn't do that anymore," says my mother.

"I saw a movie about smuggling," says Lucy. "With Robert Mitchum."

"Who?"

"No, it's the Stones." Lucy rocks her head from from side to side. "Hey, hey, you, you," sings Lucy, "get off of my cloud."

Lucy Rabbit carries a picture of Marilyn Monroe around with her in her purse. She got it out of an old magazine and had it sealed in plastic at the Coast to Coast store so it wouldn't get bent or torn. It's a famous picture, I guess, because my father and Skee Gardipeau and even Miles Deardorf all know about it. In the photograph, Marilyn is standing with her dress blowing up around her legs. She's trying to push her dress down, but she has a smile on her face as if she's having a good time or is really annoyed with everything and just wants to go home.

Lucy has a theory that Marilyn Monroe was really Indian and that she was adopted out when she was a baby. Lucy likes to hold the picture up next to her face. "Take a good look," she says. "What do you see?"

I guess I can see a general resemblance, and I suppose if someone were to look at Lucy and the photograph long enough, they might mistake the two of them for sisters. Which is why Lucy wants blonde hair. So she can look exactly like Marilyn.

"Can't do much about the tan," Lucy tells my mother each time she comes to the shop, "so let's work on the hair."

Lucy has been coming to my mother for several years trying to get her hair to turn blonde, but the closest my mother has been able to get to the kind of baby-soft yellow-white dandelion hair that Marilyn has is flaming orange.

"She was probably Cree," says Lucy, "or maybe Ojibwa."

My mother tells Lucy that she doesn't think Lucy's hair will ever go blonde, that it's so black to begin with it probably hasn't got a clue what blonde looks like. And even after my mother has cut Lucy's hair so it has the right general shape and set, it looks more like a spool of copper wire or a rusty scrub pad.

"I've never heard that she's Indian," my mother says whenever Lucy brings up the subject.

"Well, you'd want to keep something like that a secret, now, wouldn't you."

Soldier comes over and puts his head in my lap. He's heard all Lucy's ideas about Marilyn Monroe before and would rather go out and play.

"What are you up to these days?" Lucy says to me.

"Not much."

"You got a girlfriend yet?"

"Lum and me saw a woman jump off the Horns last night."

Lucy slips her hands out from under the apron and fingers an imaginary guitar. "Jumping Jack Flash," she sings, "he's a gas, gas, gas!"

At first, the orange was a little weird, but because no one else in Truth or Bright Water had hair anywhere near that particular shade, it sort of made Lucy a celebrity. Lum took to calling her Bugs Bunny because, he said, she looked like a carrot.

"What's up, Doc?" he'd say whenever he saw her.

"Ah," Lucy would say whenever she saw him, "it's the wascally wabbit."

And she was easy to see. You could spot her all the way across the football field every morning on her way to work at the band health centre, and you could follow her as she roamed up and down the produce aisles at Safeway. Even in the Frontier, when the lights dropped way down for a night scene or a scary moment, you could see her hair flash in the dark as her head bobbed over a tub of popcorn and a medium soft drink.

"You hear about Carol?" Lucy is nodding her head to the music and tapping the arm of the chair.

"Carol Millerfeather?"

"The very same," says Lucy.

"She getting married?"

"Now wouldn't that be a shocker," says Lucy. "Nope, she got one of those grants. She's going to try to start a community theatre group right here in Truth."

"Theatre?" says my mother.

Lucy shakes her head. "As if Carol didn't have enough to worry about."

Once, my mother ordered a special peroxide all the way from Montreal. She worked it into the hair, wrapped the hair up in a rubber bag, and let everything sit for an hour. The bag was dark blue so you couldn't see what was happening inside. We all thought that Lucy was finally going to get the blonde hair she'd always wanted, so we were disappointed when my mother took the bag off.

On the positive side, her hair was a brighter and cleaner orange than before, as if someone had taken the time and effort to scrape off the tarnish and polish each strand. But it wasn't blonde, and in the end, that was all that counted.

Lucy slides the earphones off her ears and leans forward. "Saw your sister the other day," she says to my mother. "When did she get back?"

"You have to start taking better care of your hair," says my mother quickly, but the cat is already out of the bag.

"Auntie Cassie?"

My mother takes a bottle of conditioner off the shelf and sets it on the edge of the sink so Lucy can see it.

"Auntie Cassie's back?"

My mother doesn't hold with lying, but sometimes pulling the truth out of her is harder than dragging Soldier away from a telephone pole. Sometimes you can see the answer in her face. Other times you have to guess.

"Is that why you're going to granny's?"

"There'll be lots of time for visiting."

"I want to come," I say. "It's no big deal. I've seen you guys fight before."

"We don't fight." My mother pushes on Lucy's hair. It moves around in the wrap, sliding from side to side like cooking lard on a warm pan. "Sometimes we disagree."

"She's going to put on a play," says Lucy. "Guess which one."

"Carol?"

"What about auntie Cassie?"

"Of course, Carol," says Lucy. "Who've we been talking about?"

"Something by Shakespeare?" says my mother.

"God, no!" says Lucy.

"When do we go?"

"A Neil Simon comedy?"

Lucy smiles and gulps down a mouthful of air as if she's getting set to dive under water. "*Snow White and the Seven Dwarfs!*"

My father says that Lucy has a laugh that sounds like a herd of crows stampeding through a minefield. Lucy always catches me off guard with that laugh. "But she's going to change it," says Lucy. "Bring it up to date."

"I don't know," says my mother. "I think she should start off with something everyone knows."

"Indians," says Lucy. "Instead of dwarfs, Carol is going to use Indians."

Lum says Lucy wants to be Marilyn Monroe because no one gives a

21

damn about Indians but everybody likes blonds. Even Indians. "You ever see anybody famous who wasn't blond?"

I pointed out that Sylvester Stallone wasn't blond and neither was Jim Carrey, but Lum said that being white was the same as being blond.

"Franklin's got the powwow tent up," says Lucy. "Bright Water is starting to jump. A bunch of people from Georgia pulled into Happy Trails the other day and have already set up their trailers."

"Georgia's a long way to come," says my mother.

"Cherokees," says Lucy. "Can you beat that?"

"You going this year?"

"Always go," says Lucy. "Indian Days are the only time we make any money without having to fill in a form."

"Elvin said he did pretty good last year."

"Lucille and Teresa Rain are praying for Germans," says Lucy, and she raises her eyes to the ceiling. "Germans and Japanese."

My mother lifts the edges of the plastic wrap and the stink of peroxide floods the room. Soldier drops to the floor and tries to bury his nose in the wall. "Too bad the landfill project fell through."

"Now that was one of Franklin's dumber ideas," says Lucy. "Using Turtle Coulee as a garbage dump."

"Could have used the jobs," says my mother.

"All that junk was starting to slide into the river." Lucy makes a face and squeezes her lips together. "You got any idea what's buried out there?"

My mother finishes Lucy's hair and puts her under the dryer, but you can see the colour hasn't moved an inch. Lucy snugs the earphones into her ears and closes her eyes. My mother gathers up the towels and takes them back to the washing machine. I follow her and stand by the door and wait. "All right," she says, finally. "You can come if you want to." She leaves the towels in a pile on the floor and goes back to the kitchen. She sits down on the couch and pulls a corner of the quilt across her lap.

"You okay?"

"Fine," she says.

"You want a root beer?"

"That would be nice, honey."

"Can I have one?"

22

I get the root beer from the refrigerator. My mother goes to work on the quilt, stitching pieces of the shirt over part of the pattern that I thought she had finished.

One time, Miles Deardorf took a picture of Lucy with the Polaroid camera he uses for taking pictures of houses, and Lucy sent it in to a Marilyn Monroe look-alike contest that a fancy restaurant in Los Angeles was sponsoring. There were all sorts of prizes including an all-expenses-paid trip to Hollywood and a small part in a movie. Lucy told my mother she didn't care about the trip or the part in the movie, but that a big-screen television would be nice. "They're giving ten of them away," Lucy told me. "I like my chances." She didn't win the grand prize or the television, but she did get a free video of *Some Like It Hot*, which Lucy said was Marilyn at her best.

"You going to try out for a part in Carol's play?" I ask my mother.

"Maybe."

"You should," I say. "You'd make a good Snow White."

This is the right thing to say. My mother starts to smile. "Snow White's the lead."

"Snow White has dark hair," I say. "And you've got dark hair."

"Might be nice to have a Prince Charming."

"That's *Sleeping Beauty*," I say, "or *Cinderella*."

My mother smooths the quilt and runs her fingers over the buttons. She leans back, closes her eyes, and begins humming to herself. Out in the shop, Lucy sits under the dryer reading a magazine. She rocks back and forth in the chair mouthing the words to "Satisfaction," while the dryer whistles around her head like a spring storm.

CHAPTER THREE

A week after the Sacred Word Gospel people left Truth for Prairie View, Miles Deardorf put on his gold blazer, drove out to the bluff in his white Lincoln, and nailed a "For Sale" sign up on the side of the church. For the next few months or so after that, people from Missoula or Helena or Great Falls would show up and begin talking about turning the church into a pottery studio or a bed and breakfast or a weekend retreat for business people from Denver and Los Angeles.

But that wasn't what happened.

I was in Railman's with my father when Miles stopped in to announce the sale. "Sold the damn thing," Miles told Skee Gardipeau and everybody else who was at the counter.

"Didn't know you could sell a church," said Skee.

"Hell," said Miles, "I can sell anything."

"So, who's the lucky winner?" said my father.

Miles stood up and straightened his blazer. "Monroe Swimmer."

"Monroe Swimmer!"

"The very same."

"Thought he was dead," said Skee.

"Got a call," said Miles, "from his agent."

"His *what?*"

"In Toronto."

Everyone started smiling, and Skee asked Miles if he was putting something up his nose again, besides his finger.

"Evidently," said Miles, and he began to smile, too, "the big chief's got a wad of money and a fine eye for real estate."

"So, what's he going to do with a beat-to-shit church?" said Skee.

"Who knows," said Miles, looking at my father. "And who cares. Big-time Indian artist like him. Maybe he's going to tear the damn thing down and put up a tipi."

As soon as word that the church had been sold got around, everyone in Truth and Bright Water began talking about Monroe Swimmer. Lee Patterson at the *Truth Free Press* remembered Monroe as a series of minor offences: shoplifting batteries at the Coast to Coast store, sneaking into the Frontier without paying, painting graffiti on the sides of boxcars.

Lucille Rain, who ran a gift shop on the reserve with her sister Teresa, remembered Monroe as a bit of a joker. One time, she told us, he borrowed a tuba from the Mormon church over in Cardston and got his auntie to make him a pair of short pants out of elk hide with elk hide suspenders. And when Indian Days came around and the crowds of tourists were everywhere, he marched through the booths and the tipis, puffing on the tuba, pretending to be the Bright Water German Club.

"He said it was the least he could do," said Lucille, "seeing as how Germans were so keen on dressing up like Indians."

Gabriel Tucker, who owned Tucker's Sporting Goods, liked to tell the story about the time Monroe took a couple of barricades from a construction site and blocked off Division Street at the level crossing. It took everybody an hour or so to figure out it was a joke, and by then the traffic was backed up on both sides of town.

"It was pretty funny," Gabriel told us, "as long as you weren't in a hurry to get somewhere."

But there was also a darker side to Monroe. According to Skee, he liked doing dangerous things like hopping freight cars as they came out of the yards on the fly and riding them all the way to Prairie View and back, or running the rapids below the bridge on an inner tube during spring flood. One winter, Skee watched him slide all the way across the Shield on his belly before the river had completely iced over, just because Sherman Youngman had told him it couldn't be done.

"If the new bridge had been there back then," Skee told us, "he would've jumped off the damn thing just to see how long it took to get to the river."

Some of the stories were probably true and some of them were probably false, but everyone who knew Monroe agreed on one thing. He could draw. When he was in high school, he made extra money every Christmas painting reindeer and Santa Clauses on store windows, and each summer, during Indian Days, he sold pen-and-ink landscapes to the tourists who came through. He had even gotten a scholarship to the art program at Wild Rose Community College and would have graduated if he hadn't left in the middle of his second year and gone to Toronto.

Why Monroe left Truth and Bright Water was a mystery. Lucille Rain figured it had to have something to do with women or money, because almost everything else that happened in the world did. There was the story that Monroe had gotten someone pregnant, but Lucille said you shouldn't confuse rumours with gossip and that rumours shouldn't be repeated. What intrigued Lucille the most was what Monroe might have done once he got to the city. She was pretty sure that Toronto had more Indians than it wanted already.

"Edna says they've got Ojibwas coming out their ears and that they're up to their bellies in Mohawks and Crees."

Lucille was sure Monroe would do all right in the city because he had a sweet mouth. But she wasn't sure that there were many people, even in Toronto, who were interested in buying prairie landscapes or paintings of reindeer and snowmen.

Skee said he wasn't surprised when Monroe left. "Nothing much to keep him. Family's only good reason to stay in Truth and Bright Water." Skee figured Monroe had gone to Toronto because no one knew him there and because, in a city, there were lots more interesting ways to kill yourself than staring at the bottom of a beer can or breaking through thin ice.

Miles Deardorf had arrived in Truth long after Monroe left, so Miles never knew him. But when Monroe bought the church and everybody began talking, no one came up with more stories about Monroe than Miles. My father said that Miles had real estate friends in Toronto who knew Monroe, and that Miles probably made up the rest of the stories as he went along.

"Some people are like that," my father told me. "You can bet it comes in handy selling houses."

When Monroe first arrived in Toronto, Miles told us, he got a job at the Royal Ontario Museum. On weekends, he would go down to Queen Street and paint animals on brown butcher paper and try to sell them for a few dollars. But there was already an Indian artist in Toronto who had made a name for himself painting on butcher paper, and even though Monroe's stuff was pretty good, he couldn't give it away.

Then one day (if you believed everything Miles said), Monroe got really angry, walked down the block to a popular restaurant on Queen Street, and began painting a pack of wolves eating a moose on the front window. Some of the customers thought it was exciting, seeing a real artist at work while they were eating, but the owner was put off by all the blood and the crushed bones, and called the police. When they arrived to talk to Monroe, he began throwing paint at them and fending them off with his brushes. The police beat him up, confiscated his paintings, and tossed him in jail for creating a disturbance.

"Couldn't really paint worth a damn," Miles told us. "But, hey, did that stop Picasso?"

The next thing anyone heard, Monroe was in a warehouse on King Street, painting giant canvases filled with swollen, shadowy figures stuffed into distorted police cars and army tanks, chasing pastel animals and neon Indians at murderous angles across long, dark stretches of prairie landscape.

Miles figured Monroe got lucky, that he landed in Toronto just as being an Indian was becoming chic, and that if he hadn't been Indian, he would have been sucking up soup at the Salvation Army. And maybe that was true. But whatever the reason, Monroe's paintings began to sell, and in no time at all, according to Miles, Monroe was rich.

"At the very least," Miles told us over coffee at Railman's, "a person should have to work for the money they get."

"What about hockey players?" said my father.

"My point exactly," said Miles.

Miles's stories were pretty lively and full of energy, and when he got to telling them, everyone who was listening would nod and say yes, that sounded like Monroe all right.

Monroe bought the church in the fall. The following spring, two large moving vans pulled into the Big Sky Truck Stop and one of the drivers came to the counter, roused Beth Mooney out of her copy of the *Truth Free Press*, and asked her how he could get to the old Methodist church.

"Looks like you've got a load," Beth told him, and she folded the newspaper into fourths so she could talk and read at the same time.

"Almost didn't make the scales," said the driver.

"All that for Monroe Swimmer?"

27

"Who knows?" said the man. "We just drive the trucks."

Beth was on the phone before the driver got back in his truck, and by the next day, everybody began looking around for signs of Monroe. Miles drove out to the bluff a couple of times, just to check on the property, and came back to report that, so far as he could tell, there was no one at the church. Then one night, about two weeks after the moving trucks arrived, the lights in the church went on.

Nobody went up to the church right away to say hello to Monroe, and Monroe didn't come into town. By the end of the second week, when he hadn't made an appearance, people began to talk.

"Sure as hell no law says he has to be neighbourly," Miles told my father.

"That's right," said my father. "Some artists like to be hermits."

"Maybe he's one of your 'reserved' Indians," said Miles.

"For all anybody cares," said Skee, "he can stay up there until the second coming."

"Maybe he has some 'reservations,'" said Miles.

Skee told Miles that we all got the joke, that it was a dumb joke, the kind of dumb joke real estate agents and used-car salesmen told all the time, and to shut the hell up.

"Artists are like that," said my father. "That's what artists do."

After the first month, Miles drove out to the church with a bottle of wine to welcome Monroe to the community.

"If he's there," Miles told Skee, "he's not answering the door."

"You look in any of the windows?"

"It's private property," said Miles.

"What he means," said my father, "is that the windows are too high off the ground for him to see in."

"He's got to be there," said Skee. "You can see his lights at night."

"Could be an electric eye," said Miles. "Soon as night comes, the lights go on, so people think you're home. You can buy them anywhere. He's probably in Toronto right now having a great dinner at some fancy restaurant."

"You don't like the food around here," said Skee, "you can always go to Toronto, too."

Monroe Swimmer was the topic of conversation for the next couple of weeks, and then people turned back to more immediate issues such as dry land farming and the bridge. And in all that time, no one noticed that Monroe had got out his brushes and had begun to paint the outside walls of the church.

Monroe began with the east wall first, and because that wall faced over the prairies and because you couldn't see it from Truth or Bright Water, no one knew anything was happening until Joanne Virone and her sister Christine came back from a shopping trip in Prairie View and noticed what Monroe had done.

But by then it was too late.

CHAPTER FOUR

For the most part, Division Street runs east and west through Truth, but like the river, it doesn't run straight. It comes into town from the south, turns west, and follows the tracks to the level crossing. Then it heads north for half a mile, turns east, and runs straight until it dead-ends in front of the fire hall. All of which can be confusing for tourists and other people who come to town for the first time because, essentially, there are two Division Streets, one that is north of the tracks and one that is south of the tracks. For example, my father's shop is on Division Street South along with Safeway, Tucker's Sporting Goods, Deardorf's real estate office, and the Coast to Coast store, while my mother's shop, Railman's, Santucci's grocery, and the Frontier theatre are all on Division Street North.

Soldier and I duck in behind Railman's, cut across the train tracks, and head for my father's shop to see what he's doing and to tell him about the woman and the skull. The lights are on and the Karmann Ghia is still sitting at the side of the building and it's pretty easy to tell that it hasn't been moved. When my father first got the car, he threw a piece of yellow plastic over it and tied everything down with green rope. But over the months, the wind and the rain and the snow have forced the plastic down around the seats, leaving the remains of a dry lake under the dash.

My father is working at the band saw and is surprised to see me. "Something wrong?" His eyes are hard slits as if the light in the room is too bright.

"No, everything's fine," I tell him.

"Right." My father hits the switch on the band saw and brushes off his jeans. "Don't you have school?"

"It's summer now."

"That's right." My father waits for a moment. "Your mother send you?"

"No."

"Just bored, huh?"

My father is a great believer in coincidence and in fate. Good luck. Bad luck. Things coming in threes. Destiny. He has an old deck of playing cards, and every so often, he takes them out and tells fortunes. Sometimes he does a little smuggling. But most of the time he's a carpenter. There is nothing he can't make out of wood. He's famous for his animal mirrors but he makes other things, too. Benches, tables, birdhouses, doghouses, fancy signs.

"So, how you doing?" he says.

Bowls, music boxes, duck whistles, picture frames, walking sticks, cribbage boards, napkin rings. Rosewood toothpicks.

"Fine."

Russian olive golf tees.

"How's the dog?"

"He's fine."

Sometimes, if business is good, he gives me a couple of bucks for the matinee at the Frontier. Or we talk. "How's your mother?"

"She's fine, too."

Most of the stuff my father makes, he makes out of pine or oak or cedar or fir. Sometimes, when he has a little extra money, he buys pieces of special wood that come from places like South America or Africa.

"She ask about me?"

"All the time," I say. "She asked about the car, too."

"Now don't that beat all," says my father. "I was just thinking about that the other day."

"Still waiting for parts, right?"

"Takes a while," says my father. "You wouldn't believe how hard that foreign stuff is to get." He goes to his work table. "What do you think of these?" There are about a dozen wooden figures arranged in a circle on the workbench. I can't tell what they are supposed to be, but they sort of look like dogs.

"Neat."

"I saw an advertisement for the same sort of thing, only carved out of stone. You know how much the guy gets for them?"

"No."

"One hundred and fifty dollars. You believe that? One hundred and fifty dollars!"

"For a dog?"

My father picks up one of the figures and turns it over in his hand. "It's not a dog. It's a coyote. See, it's howling at the moon."

"Neat."

"Everybody's going crazy over traditional Indian stuff. I figure I can sell these for fifty bucks as fast as I can make them."

I pick up one of the coyotes. There isn't much to it. Just wood and two tiny black stones for the eyes. On the bottom of the coyote, my father has signed his name.

"You got to do that," he says, "so they know it's authentic."

"Hundred and fifty bucks for a stone coyote?"

"No. That guy makes turtles. But you know what he does?"

I shake my head.

"He gets these little cards printed up. On the front is an explanation about the turtle and what it symbolizes."

"So you know what you got."

"That's it. And on the back, there is a write-up about the artist. The guy with the turtles signs everything with his Indian name. Clever, huh?"

"Yeah."

"Figured I'd put my treaty number on the card so there's no question."

"About what?"

"A lot of this stuff comes out of Japan and Taiwan, so it's hard to tell unless you got a card." My father moves the coyotes so they all face out. "What do you think?"

"Great."

"Figure I'll make about two hundred or so, take out an ad in a couple of magazines, and sit back. With any luck, the money will pour in."

"Just like the guy with the turtles."

"Right."

"How'd you do with the squirrel feeders?"

"Not so good. Couldn't figure out a way to keep the screw from turning." My father smiles and grabs me in a headlock. "You hungry?" I can feel his knuckles on my head.

"Sure," I say, and I try to stomp on his foot. But he's too fast.

"Me, too," my father says and lets me go. "This about your mother?"

"No."

"I heard she has a boyfriend."

"She does?"

"You'd tell me if she did, right?"

"Sure."

My father brushes the coyotes off the table and into a shoebox. "You going to give me a hint?"

"It's sort of about a woman."

"Okay," my father says, and he fakes a jab at my stomach. "Well, you've come to the right place. You hungry?"

When we get to Railman's, Miles Deardorf and Gabriel Tucker are at the counter arguing about a hockey game. My father slides onto a stool near the end by the jukebox and I follow him. We sit there for a moment and wait. "Hey, Skee," my father shouts. "Where the hell are you?"

Skee Gardipeau sticks his head out the pass-through. He's a large man and his head just fits. He always frowns, and he's frowning now.

"What's the special?"

"Same as always, Elvin," says Skee.

"How about two specials then."

Skee wrinkles his nose as if he's going to sneeze. "You want that with potatoes and corn or with corn and potatoes?"

"Maybe with potatoes and corn." My father smiles and elbows me gently.

Skee lumbers out of the kitchen. He stops at the pass-through and shouts the order back into the kitchen. Then he comes over to where we are sitting. "That chair finished yet?"

"Almost done, Skee."

Three or four flies are twitching on the counter. Skee flicks them away with a rag. "Like to sit in it before the summer's out."

"You can count on me." My father takes three of the coyotes out of his pocket. "Hey, what do you think of these?"

Skee picks up a coyote, looks at it, and snorts. "What the hell is it?"

"It's a coyote. You ever see all that shit they advertise in the sports magazines?"

"Like fishing lures?"

"That's right."

"This ain't a fishing lure."

"No, it's a coyote."

"'Cause if it's a lure, it ain't going to work."

"There's this guy who sells stone turtles," says my father. "He gets a hundred and fifty bucks a pop."

Skee leans on the counter and sags onto his forearms. "This one of those Indian things?"

"There's good money in it," says my father. "Fifty bucks apiece. Easy."

Skee puts the coyote on the Formica and squints at it.

"Twenty-five?"

"I don't know, Elvin," Skee says. "You're beginning to remind me of Monroe."

"Hell, Skee, Monroe's an artist." My father turns to me and grins. "This is business."

"How come they lean to one side?"

"It's a coyote," says my father. "Did I tell you that?"

The specials arrive. The potatoes are thick and full of lumps. The corn is tough and shiny and mixed up with pimentos and bits of green pepper. My father presses the corn into the potatoes with his fork and looks at me.

"How's the chicken?"

"Pretty good."

"The secret to good fried chicken," says my father, "is in the salt."

Skee comes out of the kitchen with a pot of coffee and a magazine under his arm. "So, what's this kid of yours going to do when he grows up?"

"Beats me," says my father. "Better ask his mother."

"Deardorf figures his kid's going to be an accountant." Skee pours my father another cup of coffee and sets the pot down in front of me. "That's the way to do it, all right."

"What's that?"

"Aim low," says Skee. "Avoid disappointment."

Skee and my father have a good laugh, and I laugh along, too.

"How old's he now?" says Skee. "Thirteen?" He puts the magazine on

34

the counter. It's one of those men's magazines. I've seen them before and they're pretty neat.

"Fourteen," says my father.

"I'm fifteen," I say. "My birthday was last week."

"That's right," says my father.

"So, what'd your old man get you?"

My father smiles at Skee and puts his arm around my shoulders. He reaches over and flips the magazine to the centrefold. "Jesus," he whispers to me. "What do you think about that?"

We eat the rest of our lunch in silence. The coyotes sit on the counter. My father begins humming to himself. I push the chicken around my plate and try to think of ways to tell the story of the woman and the skull so that it won't sound stupid and made up.

My father wipes his plate with a biscuit, pushes back, and slides off the stool. "Stay put," he says. "I'll be right back." He's out the door before I can say anything.

Skee sees him leave and comes back over. "Your old man desert you again?"

"Nope," I say. "He'll be right back."

"Tell him to hurry up and build that chair, would you?" Skee picks up one of the coyotes by the head and looks at it.

"Pretty good, huh?"

Skee lays the coyote on its side and flicks it with his finger. It spins in a tight circle, bumps up against the coffee cup, and slides into the other coyotes. "You know how they kill dogs?"

"Who?"

"Coyotes." Skee wipes his hands on his apron. "They pretend that they're hurt or scared. So, the dog starts to chase them, thinks it's going to be easy."

"Coyotes are sort of traditional."

"Pretty soon the dog is tired." Skee looks at me and begins to laugh. "And that coyote turns around slick as spit and cuts the dog's throat."

I look at Skee, but I don't know if I'm supposed to laugh, too, so I just smile. Skee scoops my father's plate off the counter and dumps it into a plastic tub. "So," he says, sucking his lips in, "what you been up to?"

"Nothing much."

Skee puts the magazine on the counter and turns the page. There's a picture of a woman rubbing soap all over her body. "You got a girlfriend yet?"

"Nope."

"But you're looking, right?"

"I'm looking for a job. Lum's looking, too."

"Lots of girls in Bright Water." Skee leans against the ice cream freezer.

"We might try the railroad."

"Sure," says Skee. "Railroad always likes to hire a bunch of Indians in the summer."

"Cleaning boxcars, right?"

"You know why that is?"

"Nope."

"'Cause they can't find a bunch of whites dumb enough to do the work." Skee closes the magazine and rolls it into a club.

"I'm saving up for a car."

Skee lowers his eyes. I can see the rolled magazine twitching in his hand. "If those assholes hadn't screwed up the bridge, there'd be lots of work for everyone." His arm snaps forward and the magazine explodes on the counter. "You know what I mean?" He turns the magazine over and checks the bottom. There's nothing left of the flies but a few pieces and a bloody skid mark on the formica.

I sit at the counter and wait for my father, and I try to imagine who it was that fell into the river that evening, and what she had in mind. And where she went. My father bangs in through the door with a smile on his face and drops a twenty dollar bill on the counter. "Keep the change," he shouts at Skee.

I walk with him back to his truck. "I've got some cheques coming in," he says. "You know what that means?"

"Money for mom?"

"What the hell does she need money for?"

"I don't know."

"You ever been hungry?"

"Nope."

"And she's got the shop, right?" My father takes a box out of his pocket.

36

"Look, next time you come by, we'll make some time and have that talk." He smiles and ruffles my hair. "About women."

"Maybe we could practise my driving."

"Hell, yes," he says. "You're almost a man." My father looks up and down the street. "In the meantime," he says, "use these," and he presses the box into my hand. "Happy birthday, son." My father turns and leaves me standing in front of Railman's. "Don't worry," he shouts as he gets in his truck. "There're instructions in the box."

As he drives away, I remember the coyotes. They are still sitting on the counter. I look in the window just as Skee comes out of the kitchen and dumps my plate into the tub. He sees me and nods. Then he picks up the money and drags a rag across the counter, pulling the pieces of corn and the gravy and the chicken fat and the coyotes over the edge and into the garbage.

CHAPTER FIVE

Three years ago, the new highway from Pipestone was going to pass through Truth and cross into Canada at Bright Water. The foundations for the bridge that would connect the town with the reserve were poured, and everyone started talking about the steady stream of tourists who would stop at the border to catch their breath before pushing up to Waterton or Banff, or dropping down into Glacier or the Yellowstone.

The bridge was half completed when construction came to a halt. One day, the crews were working on the concrete forms for the decking. The next day, they stretched chain-link fencing across both ends of the bridge, packed up all their equipment, and disappeared.

The Sacred Word Gospel people were not far behind. Almost as soon as construction on the bridge stopped, they packed up and headed for Prairie View and were long gone before anyone realized that they hadn't taken the Cousins with them.

"No reason why they should," Skee told us. "Not their dogs anyway."

Which was true. The Cousins were hanging around the church long before the First Assembly of God moved in, and they had been there when the Baptists sold the church to the Nazarenes.

My father said that some of the old people told him that the dogs were there before the church had even been built. Lum figured the missionaries brought the dogs with them to keep the Indians in line.

"It's history," he said. "The Spanish did that with the Indians in Mexico."

The story I liked best was the one Lucy Rabbit's grandfather, Charlie Ron, liked to tell about how the dogs had originally been small and brown, and how hanging around the church and having to listen to all the lies that white people told every Sunday had turned them large and black. Except for the white ruff at their necks, which made them look a little like penguins. Or priests.

My grandmother didn't have any strong opinions about the Cousins. "In the old days," she told me, "dogs helped to guard the camp."

"Against soldiers?"

"Other things, too."

"Like what?"

"Ghosts," said my grandmother. "They watched out for ghosts."

I don't think my grandmother believed in ghosts, but I could see where the Cousins might worry a ghost if one ever came around. They had certainly worried Miles Deardorf when he went to the church to nail up the "For Sale" sign. According to Miles, the Cousins had growled at him, chased his car, and snapped at the tires.

"Dogs that don't get fed on a regular basis revert to being wild animals," said Miles. "The most humane thing to do is to go up there and shoot all three of them."

Skee said that so far as he knew, no one had ever fed the Cousins, not the Baptists, not the Nazarenes, and certainly not the First Assembly of God, and that he would just as soon shoot lawyers and real estate agents as shoot animals who were minding their own business.

Sunday mornings, when the church was up and going, you could always find the Cousins sitting on the porch of the church like crows on a wire, their bodies leaning into each other, their heads cocked at the same angle, their pink tongues hanging out of their mouths. They never barked, which made them seem friendly, but if you got up close and looked into their eyes, the only thing you would see was your own reflection.

Nobody paid much attention to the dogs, and when the Sacred Word Gospel left and the dogs disappeared, everyone assumed that they had either run off or been killed by coyotes.

CHAPTER SIX

It is not until after my father has driven off that I notice Soldier is missing. I look in the alley in case he is rummaging around among the garbage cans or having a nap in the shade. He could have gone back to the beauty shop, but I'm pretty sure that he's taken off on one of his adventures.

Soldier doesn't have many bad habits. He doesn't chew things. He doesn't bite. He doesn't bark much. And he doesn't stick his nose in your crotch the way a lot of dogs do. Generally, he comes when you call him, but once in a while he runs away.

Every morning, my mother lets Soldier out to do his business, and in five or ten minutes, he's back at the door looking to get in. But some days, the minute the door is open, he's down Division Street on the run, and you can tell he's not coming back. It doesn't matter how hard you yell at him or what you say. He doesn't turn around and he doesn't stop. Of course, he always comes home. Sometimes he's whining at the door the same evening. Sometimes he stays away for days. My mother thinks he runs away because he is upset or angry. I figure he does it because he's bored and just wants to have some fun.

I've watched him enough to know that, when he runs away, he always heads for the river, and you would think that I would be able to find him easily. But whenever he goes off on one of his escapades, he vanishes. No one sees him. No one hears him. It's as if he falls into a hole in the middle of the prairies and has to spend a day or two or three digging his way out.

I stand in front of Railman's and wait. I'm not anxious to go back to the shop. Whenever my mother sees that I have some free time, she finds jobs for me to do. I could go out to the job gate and talk to Wally Preston, but there are usually half a dozen men hanging around the gate looking for day work, and while Wally is nice enough, he always hires the white guys before he hires Indians. I think about going over to Bright Water, but there's no guarantee that Lum can get away. Sometimes he has to work for his father, and with Indian Days so close, this is probably the case. Besides, I'm not keen to walk the bridge.

Early in the spring, after most of the snow had disappeared, Lum's cousin, Emery Youngman, decided to come across the Shield and catch an old John Wayne western at the Frontier. He got more than halfway across the bridge when he stepped on the edge of a warped plank and was thrown off the bridge decking. Emery banged his head pretty good and he tore his shirt, but when he tried to get up and climb back onto the plywood, he discovered that his leg was jammed tight in the rebar and the wire.

Emery yelled for a while and then he spent that night under the stars. He might have been stuck there for days had it not been for Maria Topalovich and her daughter Nokia who were fishing the rapids below the bridge and happened to look up and see Emery laid out against the sky like a trout in a net. Emery's father, Sherman, and Eddie Baton and Wilfrid First Rider made their way out onto the bridge and tried to pull Emery free, but Emery's leg was stuck. In the end, they had to call the fire department in Truth for help.

The guys who showed up in their fire hats and heavy rubber jackets were none too happy. They had been called away from their supper, and as Gabriel Tucker pointed out, it wasn't the first time that they had had to pull some fool kid from Bright Water off the bridge. It took four of them most of an hour to get their equipment across the planking and cut Emery free.

"Next time," Gabriel told Sherman, "get your own damn fire department to help."

"Don't have one."

"Then keep your kids on their side of the river."

This led to about twenty minutes of name-calling, chest-pushing, and general threats, but no punches were thrown, and in the end, everyone went home angry.

Sherman yelled at Emery all the way back to Bright Water, but it really wasn't Emery's fault. Besides walking the bridge, there are only two other ways to get from Bright Water to Truth. If you have a car and the time, the most convenient way is to drive down to Prairie View, cross the river and the border there, and drive back up to Truth. All of which takes about forty minutes. The only other way is to pull yourself across on Charlie Ron's ferry, an old iron bucket suspended on a cable over the Shield. There's enough room in it for four people and it's safe enough, but after Charlie Ron died and they built the bridge at Prairie View, the ferry didn't get used much. A few of the elders still use it, and some of the guys take their girlfriends out on the ferry at night so they can neck in private. Tourists are always snagging the cable and getting stuck in the middle of the river, and once a guy from a movie crew took a look at the ferry to see if they could use it in a film. Lum and Jason Scout call it the Toilet, and most of the kids from the reserve would rather swim than be seen sitting in it.

Hardly anyone from Truth uses the ferry. Except for Indian Days, there's no particular reason to go from the town to the reserve. And except for my mother and me, everyone else in Truth has a car.

In the end, I decide to head out to the Horns and look around. If Soldier is hiding near the river, I might be able to spot him from the rocks. And if I don't find him, I can always search the area for clues. Maybe I can find out who the woman was or what she was doing there or where she went.

Behind the firehouse, the prairies begin in earnest, as if a line has been drawn between the town and the land. I can see the church from here and a solitary bird turning lazy circles in the dry air, but beyond that, there is nothing but grass and water and sky.

When the Methodists built the church, they built it on the highest point of land they could find, so no matter where you stood, on either side of the river, you could always see it. In those days, the church must have been fairly impressive, stuck as it was alone against the horizon. But now, with Truth being a modern town, the church has all but disappeared behind the Chinook Motel, the Farmer's Bank, and the Continental Oil tower.

Halfway up Rabbit Coulee, I can see there's no point in going to the Horns. Some of the kids from town are already there. Joel Deardorf is on the lower ledge trying to work up the courage to jump. Joe Richards, Peggy Richards, and Peggy's boyfriend Andy Layne are dog-paddling in

about the Cousins for the moment, because when I look back at the platform, they're gone.

It's tricky climbing steps you can't see, but when I step inside the church, I can't see anything in there either. I have to stop just inside the door and close my eyes so they can adjust to the darkness.

"Don't mind the mess," says a voice.

I open my eyes quickly.

"Renovation is a bitch."

I try to find the voice, but the church is still black and the voice sounds far away.

"This your dog?"

"I guess," I say, and I close my eyes again.

Soldier barks.

"Yeah, that's him." I can see a little now, and the first thing I notice about the inside of the church is that all the pews are gone. "I'm looking for Monroe Swimmer," I say to no one in particular.

There are boxes and paintings and rugs and couches everywhere. It all looks expensive and nothing like the dinette sets and the recliners you see for sale on television.

"You bring a portfolio?"

This time, I follow the voice to the front of the church. In the far corner, a man sits in a chair. Soldier is beside him. "You Monroe Swimmer?"

The man comes forward, and as he does, I can see that he's in a wheelchair. He's dressed in jeans and a bright yellow T-shirt that says "Monroe Shocks." My father put a pair of Monroes on his truck when the old shocks wore out, so I guess they're pretty good.

"Famous Indian artist," says the man, as if he's announcing someone important. His hair is long and black and tied back with a piece of red cloth.

"What?"

"You're supposed to say 'famous Indian artist' after you say 'Monroe Swimmer.'"

The man rolls into the light of one of the high windows. He's older than I imagined. And aside from the hair, which reminds me of Graham Greene's hair in *Dances With Wolves*, he looks ordinary.

45

"Everybody does." The man grabs the wheels and spins himself around. Soldier dances after him, anxious to help. "Monroe Swimmer," the man shouts as he spins around again. "Famous Indian artist!"

It all looks pretty weird, and I'm not sure what to do. "So, you're Monroe Swimmer?" I ask again.

The man stops and waits.

"Famous Indian artist?" I figure it's best to play along.

The man leans out of the chair, makes a low bow, and takes off his hair. "Until I come up with something better." Monroe hangs the wig on the back of the chair and wheels over to where I'm standing. "So," he says, rubbing his head, "let's see the portfolio."

The wig really throws me for a moment. Now Monroe's hair is short, and most of what you can see is grey. "I don't have one," I say, which is true seeing as I don't know what a portfolio is.

Monroe looks at me and smiles. "Confidence. I like that in an employee."

"Employee?"

"You came about the job, right?"

I can be fast when I want to be. "Right."

"'Blessed is he who has found his work; let him ask no other blessed-ness,'" says Monroe. "You're the first applicant, so you have the inside track."

The church doesn't remind me much of our place. It's larger, and it has windows. At the back of the church is a bed and a large oak dresser, both of which look old. Against one of the side walls is a piano. I don't play piano, but if I did, this would be the piano I would want. It's all sparkling wood with nickel-plated pedals and decorative plates. The front panel is open fretwork so you can see the hammers as they swing forward and strike the strings. Across the top is a low back panel of carved wood with a round little beaver in the centre. And just above the keyboard is a fancy gold decal that says "Bell Pianos, Guelph, Ontario."

"So," says Monroe, looking around the room, "what do you think?"

The windows are tall, and several are filled with stained and bevelled glass. One of the windows is a religious scene of some sort. There's an old man with a white beard who has a book in one hand that is nothing but clear glass because you can look through it and see the sky outside.

I figure they probably ran out of stained glass when they got to the book, or the window got broken and that piece had to be replaced.

Next to the old man is a small child, and next to the child is a skinny dog with skinny legs. I don't know the Bible well enough to know who these figures are supposed to be, but my guess is that the old guy is God and that the kid is Jesus. The dog is probably a pet or maybe one of the animals from the ark who escaped the flood.

"I'm just getting started in here," says Monroe. "Had to get the outside going before winter. You hungry?"

"Sure."

"Grilled cheese?"

"Sure."

Monroe heads back to the kitchen. "Look around," he shouts. "Make yourself at home."

There is no altar at the front of the church. I look around to see where Monroe has moved it and that's when I see the buffalo. It's not real, and I know that right away, but it's pretty good.

"Swiss or cheddar?"

The buffalo is taller than I am and lighter than I think. I go over and push on it, and it rocks back and forth.

"Processed?" I tap the buffalo a couple of times. It sounds dull and hollow, and I figure it's paper mâché or something like that. In the very centre of the church is a large wooden box. It is carved and painted, but I can't see any way to open it. There's no lid and there are no seams. My father would like a box like this.

"Beautiful, isn't it?" Monroe comes out of the kitchen with two plates on his lap. "It's a bentwood box," he says. "The Northwest Coast tribes make them."

"It's great."

"I bought it when I was in Vancouver." Monroe puts the plates on top of the box.

"What's it for?"

"Storing things."

The cheese isn't processed, but it's good.

"What'd you think of my buffalo?"

"Neat."

47

"It's the first one I did."

"Is it paper mâché?"

"The real ones are on their way." Monroe smiles at me and eats his sandwich. It's quiet in the church. You would think you could hear the sound of the wind outside, but you can't. We eat like that. In silence. "You want another one?"

I shake my head.

"So," says Monroe, "you want the job?"

I look around the room. "Doing what?"

"Helping me," he says.

"With what?"

Monroe puts on the wig and starts rolling around the room. He circles the buffalo a couple of times. "I'm planning to do some restoration work."

"Neat." I don't know if I like Monroe better with the wig or without it.

"And you can help me."

"Neat."

"And I'll pay you."

I think I like him better without the wig. "How much?"

"Plenty," says Monroe. "Did they tell you I'm crazy?"

"They said you were dead," I say.

"'It is better to be a fool than to be dead,'" says Monroe, and he leans towards me. "I've been waiting for you," he whispers. "Did you know that?"

I shake my head.

"It's true." Monroe shakes my hand. "Congratulations," he says. "When can you start?"

I don't know what to say.

"Day after tomorrow," he says. "That's when the truck arrives." Monroe grabs the wheels and rolls himself backwards towards the door so he can watch me all the way. "You ever been in a museum?"

"No."

"You ought to see the stuff they have in museums." Monroe waits at the door, the wheelchair leaning against the sill. "Pull me over," he says. "And don't dump me."

48

"The paint job's pretty neat," I say. "How'd you do it?"

"Don't tell anyone you saw me."

"Sure."

"It's a surprise," says Monroe. "I want the whole thing to be a surprise."

Outside the church, the wind is blowing. From the porch, I catch glimpses of the green square in the tumbling grass. The kite is so high in the sky that if the string broke, it might never come down.

"Is that yours?"

Monroe nods and shades his eyes. "'Teaching the Sky About Blue.'"

"It's a kite, right?"

"Thought I'd better start with the easy ones first."

"What about the green thing?"

"'Teaching the Night About Dark' is going to be a lot trickier."

The Cousins are nowhere to be seen. Soldier steps off the side of the porch as if he can see what he's doing and waits for me in the grass.

"So the green square is art?"

"Can you imagine all the grass in the world that colour?" Monroe straightens his wig and turns his face into the wind. "Exciting, isn't it?"

I feel my way off the porch, searching for the steps with my toes, and by the time I reach solid ground, Monroe has disappeared back inside. Soldier is waiting for me at the green square. I stand on the platform, close my eyes to a squint, and stare at the church from different angles to see if I can figure out how Monroe has managed the trick. It must have something to do with the paint and the way the colours of the land and the sky carry over into the wood.

In the distance, clouds are on the move, thick and white. But as they clear the bridge, they begin to separate and change, and by the time they reach the church, they look like long, slender bones. They settle for a moment in the afternoon sky before the current catches them, and they float over the horizon as if they were being carried along on a river.

CHAPTER SEVEN

When Soldier and I get back to the shop, my mother is waiting for us. She's sitting in front of the sink, her hands gripping the arms of the chair as if she expects it to try to bolt out the door. "You're late." She's wearing her good dress. "Get changed."

"It's auntie Cassie," I say. "Why do we have to get dressed up?"

I see my mother's hands squeeze down on the arms of the chair. Soldier leans against me with his head and tries to move both of us towards the back and cover.

"All I have are jeans and T-shirts."

My mother closes her eyes and relaxes her fingers. "Find something with a collar," she says.

My mother gets a little tense whenever auntie Cassie comes home. My father thinks it's because auntie Cassie travels all over the world while my mother is stuck in Truth and Bright Water. I figure it's because they're sisters and are excited to see each other and don't know where to start.

I look through my drawers, but in the end, the only thing I can find is the green knit shirt my father got me when he came back from Edmonton. I've never worn it because it is the same colour as the carpet they use at the miniature golf course behind Mel's Drive-In and because it has a red patch on the front that says "Four Square Farm Store."

My mother is standing by the front door, arguing with Soldier. The door is open just a crack and Soldier is trying to manoeuvre his way past my mother's leg. "Stay," she tells him.

Soldier feints left and goes right, which is what he always does, so my mother's ready for him. She shoves her knee into his side and pins him to the wall. "Go," she tells me, and I open the door quickly and slip out. I can hear Soldier and my mother jockey for position along the wall, but from the street, looking in through the window, all I can see are the flowers in the green vase.

"No!" my mother shouts, and the door opens and she backs her way out. Soldier drives a shoulder past her legs and has his head through the door. But just when it looks as if he's going to escape, my mother reaches down quickly and flicks his nose with her finger.

"Go back," she says, and she flicks him once more, harder this time.

I'm not sure that flicking is fair. Soldier whimpers and pulls his head back into the shop. My mother shuts the door and locks it.

"He's not as bad about the ferry as he used to be," I tell her.

"Don't have the time to fool around," says my mother.

"If we had a car," I say, "we could take him with us."

"Talk to your father."

Soldier is at the window with his face pressed hard against the glass. When he sees me, he does a little leap and wiggles around. I wait until his back is turned before I follow my mother down to the river.

"If we had a car, we wouldn't have to ride the Toilet."

My mother doesn't even glance back. She picks up the pace, and by the time I catch up with her, she's already standing on the platform. "You want to do it?" she says.

I wait for her to climb into the bucket before I release the cable. "If we had a car," I tell her, "I could practise my driving."

My mother opens the box at the side of the bucket, takes out the old leather gloves, and puts them on. She pulls hard on the line and the bucket swings out into space, creaking as it pitches and rolls like a log in a flood. "This is the way everybody used to cross the river," my mother tells me as she pulls us along.

"The good old days, right?"

"When Cassie and me were girls, nobody had a car, and this was the only way to get to Truth."

The sun is behind the mountains now. The light flattens out across the prairies and the air cools. As my mother hauls us across the river, the fog rises off the Shield, thick and low, and by the time we get to the middle, the river is gone and it feels as though we're floating above the clouds and that if we were to fall, we'd fall for years before we'd find the water.

"This ferry is a landmark," says my mother.

"Cars hadn't been invented yet, right?"

My mother stops pulling for a moment and looks over the edge of the bucket. "It's been here since the beginning of time," she says. "Did you know that?"

"The ferry?"

"No," she says. "The river."

My mother takes the gloves off and puts them on the box. Then she leans back against the side of the bucket and begins to hum. I can see that she's thinking about singing, which means we could be here all night. I put the gloves on and grab the cable. The bucket jerks and lurches forward.

"Not so hard," says my mother.

I pull hand over hand, trying to keep the pulls smooth and quick. The bucket settles into a rhythm and we slide across the river. My mother begins singing a piece from *The Desert Song* that is particularly awful. I put my back into it and pull faster.

My grandmother lives in Bright Water. She has a small house just up from the river, a chicken coop, and a large garden. Beyond the garden, under a row of cottonwoods, is an old silver trailer that my grandfather won in a poker game. My grandmother keeps it tidy in case someone comes visiting whom she doesn't want in the house.

The trailer is made out of the same stuff as aluminum foil, and when the sun hits it and sets the shell on fire, it looks like a roasting pan just come out of the oven. But inside it's dark and cool, and you feel as though you've just walked into a cave.

By the time we get to Bright Water, my grandmother and auntie Cassie have already moved to neutral corners. There's a pot of coffee and a plate of cookies on the table. The two of them sit patiently in the floral wingbacks, sipping coffee and munching gingersnaps, waiting for the bell to ring.

"Hi, auntie Cassie."

"Tecumseh!" Auntie Cassie slips out of the chair. "Last time I saw you," she says, "you were a baby."

"No, I wasn't."

Auntie Cassie grabs both of my hands and spins me around slowly. "Now you're as tall as me."

"Taller."

"And strong, too, I see." Auntie Cassie laughs and takes my head in her hands and kisses me, hard, on the cheek. "There," she says, "that's better."

"He's a little old to be running around with lipstick marks on his face," says my mother.

"How you going to know who I've kissed if you can't see the kisses?"

"Whole world knows who you've kissed," says my grandmother.

There is a ritual to auntie Cassie's returns. Auntie Cassie tells us all about the places she has been, the things she has done, and the people she has met, and my grandmother sits quietly, perched in her chair, her chin thrust out like a beak, her thin, leathery arms folded against her body like wings, waiting for something to move in the grass.

"So, we left Sydney," says auntie Cassie, "and drove up the coast in Terry's Volkswagen as far as Rockhampton. When we got there, Terry pulled off to the side of the road, turned off the engine, and said, 'Okay, which way do you want to go?'"

"I'd go east," I say, even though I haven't heard the first part of the story.

"You can't go east," says auntie Cassie. "That's the ocean."

"Okay," I say. "I'd go north."

"That's what Terry said," says auntie Cassie. "But you know what I said?"

"Who's Terry?" says my mother.

Most of the time, my grandmother sits with her eyes closed. But every so often she will raise her lids just a crack, lean out of her chair towards auntie Cassie or my mother, and work her jaw back and forth, as if she is chewing on something tough or nasty.

"Pat had a thirty-foot sloop that we sailed from Papeete to Mooréa."

"Who's Pat?"

"But the best place," says auntie Cassie, "was this beach just outside of Tofino on Vancouver Island. Chris has a house there and each morning we would go out and watch the surf break on the rocks. That's all we would do. We'd take a thermos of coffee and some bread and jam and watch the surf."

Once auntie Cassie came home with an older woman who was supposed to be really rich. The woman had one of those fancy German cars and she talked with a funny accent. I thought she was from Montreal or Newfoundland, but my mother said that she was from Sweden.

"I wanted to see the Red Indians," the woman told me.

"Here we are," I said.

The woman didn't wear any makeup. Her hair was cut short and her skin was the colour of winter ice. I was staying with my grandmother at the time because my mother was trying to get the beauty shop set up in Truth. I slept at the back of the house and could see the trailer from my window. That first night, I could hear them laughing and having a good time. It was hot and I couldn't sleep, so I climbed out the window and snuck over to the trailer. All of the windows were too high up for me to see anything, and after I had walked around the trailer looking for something I could stand on, I just walked up the steps and knocked on the door.

There are people in Truth and Bright Water who think my grandmother is a witch, that she can do things such as turn herself into a bear or a wolf or a mountain lion whenever she feels like it. It's not true, of course, but she can work words down deep in her throat so that they come out sounding like something an animal would make if it were angry or hungry, and when she puts on her bulky sweater and looks at you hard, she seems heavier and fiercer than she really is. It's all in her eyes. They grow large and darken into deep pools beyond light and sound, darken down to depths where black shapes float in black water.

"So, how have you been?" says my mother.

Auntie Cassie looks at my grandmother, and I can see the two of them are ready to start round two. "Fine," says auntie Cassie. "Just fine."

I grab a gingersnap. "How long you going to stay?"

"Long as it takes," says auntie Cassie, and she gives me a big smile.

"For what?"

"Now wouldn't you like to know," says auntie Cassie.

"I suppose this is about Mia," says my grandmother.

Things go quiet then as if somebody has done something rude and no one wants to admit that they did it. Auntie Cassie looks at the floor. My mother closes her eyes and rocks herself ever so slightly.

"Another life," says Cassie. "Another time."

"Who's Mia?"

"So, how have you been?" says my mother.

The woman from Sweden opened the door. Through the screen, I could see that all she was wearing was a bra and panties. She was smoking a cigar and holding a glass.

"It's the little Red Indian," she called back to auntie Cassie in her strange voice. "What shall we do with him?"

Auntie Cassie was sitting on the bed. On the table in front of her was a deck of cards.

"Do you want to play pokie?" said the woman from Sweden.

"Poker," said auntie Cassie, and she lay back on the bed and began laughing.

Auntie Cassie and my mother look a lot like each other. I haven't really noticed it before, but seeing them sitting there together, you can tell they're sisters without looking twice. Auntie Cassie is a little taller and her hair isn't quite as dark. And she smiles a little more than my mother. But that's about it.

Except for the tattoo on her hand.

"What's Elvin up to these days?" asks auntie Cassie.

My grandmother shifts in her chair and the legs cut into the hardwood.

I look at my mother. "He's making little wood coyotes," I say.

"Shit," says auntie Cassie, and she starts to laugh.

"Watch the mouth," says my grandmother. "There's a child in the house."

Auntie Cassie shakes her head and smiles. "Don't worry," she says to me, "she's not talking about you."

"You going to stay?" I ask.

Auntie Cassie straightens her skirt. "Now aren't you the Curious George."

"Mom wanted to know."

"Monroe Swimmer is back in town," says my grandmother casually, her lips yawning around her teeth.

Auntie Cassie sits back. She's smiling, but the hand with the tattoo is clenched and the letters on the knuckles are pulled tight and stand out against the skin. A I M. I don't know if auntie Cassie has really been a member of the American Indian Movement or if she just got the tattoo to be cool.

"You remember Monroe." My grandmother closes her eyes and holds her hands in her lap so you can't see the fingers.

"He's painting the old church," I say, and this must be the wrong thing to say because everyone stops talking.

"Honey," says my mother at last, "why don't you go out and check on the chickens."

"They're asleep."

"Check on them anyway."

"This adult stuff?"

"Go on."

"I won't listen."

"Go on."

Inside the trailer that night, in the light, you could see right through the Swedish woman's underwear. I tried looking at the deck of cards, but every time the woman spoke to me, I had to look at her.

"Do you know how to play poker?"

"Sure."

"All right," said the woman, and she sat down in the chair. "You can deal."

Auntie Cassie sat on the bed in a pair of pants and a bra. She was drinking but not so you could tell right away. I won the first hand, and before I could pick up the cards to deal again, the Swedish woman reached around and undid her bra and slid her breasts out of the cups. They were large and white and soft, and the nipples were dimpled with tiny creases and tucks, like golf balls.

"That's better," she said, scratching under each breast as if it really itched.

On the next hand, I wound up with three sevens. "I call," I said.

"Two pair," said the Swedish woman, and she laid her cards on the table. "Kings and nines." She looked at me and hooked a thumb in the waistband of her panties. I could see she was hoping to take them off.

"Beats me," I said quickly, and I threw my hand in.

"Maybe you should go back to the house," said auntie Cassie.

"Let him stay," said the Swedish woman. "I'll be great."

"Good," said auntie Cassie. "You'll be good. If my mother knew he was out here, she would kill me."

"Do you have your teeth yet, young Indian boy?"

"What?"

"Have you seen a woman naked before?"

"No."

"Refreshing," said the Swedish woman. "Deal the cards."

It's really dark out and I'm sorry we didn't bring Soldier because I'd have someone to talk to. I can hear the chickens behind the wire, and I think about shaking the coop just to see what they will do.

The chicken coop is a wooden lean-to with a larger open area that is penned off with wire. My grandmother told me she never knows exactly how many chickens she has because it always changes around supper-time. I counted them once and there were thirty-seven. According to my grandmother, there are only three kinds of chickens in the world: layers, fancies, and meat birds. "The layers aren't worth smoke," she'd say. "And the fancies are four feet short of a yard."

At the side of the coop there is a long hook that my grandmother uses for catching the birds. I'm always amazed at the ease with which she snakes the hook around the pen, catching a chicken and dragging it flapping through the dirt. Or the quickness with which she can snatch it up by its feet and break its neck.

I walk to the side of the coop, push my lips through the wire, and make soft coyote noises. Nothing. I growl a little. Nothing. I bark and rattle the wire and some of the chickens come alive, but they're too stupid to be much fun. So, I go back to the house and stand next to the window. My mother and auntie Cassie and my grandmother haven't moved from their chairs. I lean against the window frame so my ear is right at the opening just as round three begins.

"What about him?" auntie Cassie says. "Why is it always just me?"

My mother is trying to talk at the same time, but I can't hear what she is saying. Monroe's name gets mentioned once, and my grandmother says a few not-so-nice things about my father, but mostly there are long breaks when no one talks, and I wonder if my grandmother knows that I'm listening and is aiming her voice low so only her daughters can hear her.

My mother raises her voice to say that "not everyone gets what they want," but who the everyone is and what it is they don't get is not mentioned. I stay by the window and throw rocks at the eggplants in the garden, and then I throw a few at the trailer. When I hear the front door of the house open, I get up and head for the coop. I hang on the wire, my back to the house, as if I've been watching the chickens sleep the whole time.

I glance over my shoulder just in time to see my mother come into the garden. In the moonlight, she looks pale and thin, and she's limping as if she's been injured or has a cramp from sitting too long. And it is only when she turns and walks towards the trailer that I realize I've made a mistake.

"Don't blame me." Auntie Cassie smiles and opens the trailer door. "Everyone was alive when I left."

I played cards with the Swedish woman and auntie Cassie, but nobody took off any more clothes. Around one o'clock, auntie Cassie sent me back to the house, which was okay with me because I was tired. I was halfway through the garden when the lights in the trailer went out and I was stuck in the dark. It took me a while to work my way back to the house, and even after I was in bed and almost asleep, I could hear auntie Cassie and the Swedish woman in the trailer whispering to each other and laughing.

Early the next morning, auntie Cassie and the Swedish woman drove down to Prairie View to get some food. I wanted to go with them but they said no, that they had some looking around to do and weren't sure when they would be back. Which was just as well, I suppose, because they never came back.

I asked my grandmother what had happened, but she didn't say much. She sat at the table, wrapped up in her sweater, and practised growling into her coffee, sending shock waves all the way to the bottom of the cup.

I go into the house. My mother and my grandmother are sitting in the same chairs. "The chickens are fine," I say, before my mother can tell me to go back outside.

"It's okay," she says. "We should be heading home."

Most of the cookies are still on the plate. I take a couple while I stand there. "Where's auntie Cassie?" I ask, even though I already know.

"I'll be out for Indian Days," my mother tells my grandmother, and she puts her sweater on and goes to the door.

My grandmother's eyes are closed. "The box on the counter is yours," she says to me without moving. "And next time, don't tease the chickens."

When my mother and auntie Cassie were kids, the principal of the elementary school on the reserve, a young white man named Arthur Circle who had come from Ontario the year before, showed up at my grandmother's door to talk to her about her daughters. There were some problems, Mr. Circle told my grandmother, problems that he was sure she would want to know about. Then he took out a folder and began reading teachers' reports that complained about everything from inattentiveness to disruptive behaviour.

My grandmother listened to Mr. Circle for a while, and then she snuggled down in her sweater and began coughing. At first, they were just low chuffing coughs aimed at the floor, but as Mr. Circle turned each page in the folder, the coughs gathered force and took on weight and shape and began to fill the room.

My mother said you could see that Mr. Circle was getting nervous. His face was covered with sweat. He pulled his feet in under the chair and began looking around the room and losing his place. Then suddenly, in mid-sentence, he stood up, excused himself, and was out the door without even saying goodbye.

My mother and auntie Cassie watched him from the window as he walked and then ran to the band office, turning back every few steps, looking over his shoulder to see what was coming up behind him.

The box on the counter is full of vegetables and chickens. It's heavy and I have to carry it by myself. My mother walks all the way to the ridge before she stops and waits for me.

"What happened to auntie Cassie?"

"Nothing," says my mother. "Nothing ever happens to Cassie."

The fog has filled the river valley. I take a few steps forward until it is right at my feet. In the moonlight, the fog glows like steel, and it looks as if you could step out and walk across it all the way back to Truth.

"Look at that," I say. "You can see the Frontier from here."

My mother puts her arm around me. "It's pretty, isn't it?"

"Looks great from here."

"It always did," says my mother, and she turns and begins walking down the trail to the ferry, leaving me standing on the ridge alone.

CHAPTER EIGHT

My mother's quilt is not the easy kind of quilt you can get at the Mennonite colony near Blossom or one of the fancy machine-stitched quilts you could get in Prairie View at the Woodward's store before it went out of business, and that is probably why it's taken my mother so long to finish and why she is still working on it. Along with the squares and triangles and circles of cloth that have been sewn together, patterns with names like Harvest Star, and Sunshine and Shadow, and Sunburst, my mother has also fastened unexpected things to the quilt, such as the heavy metal washers that run along the outside edges and the clusters of needles that she has worked into the stitching just below the fish hooks and the chickens' feathers.

My father told me that my mother started the quilt just after I was born and that it had started off simple enough, but that even before he left us and went to Truth, the quilt had begun to be a problem.

"In the beginning," he told me, "everything was pretty much squares and triangles."

"What happened?"

"Who knows."

The geometric forms slowly softened and turned into freehand patterns that looked a lot like trees and mountains and people and animals, and before long, my father said you could see Truth in one corner of the quilt and Bright Water in the other with the Shield flowing through the fabrics in tiny diamonds and fancy stitching.

"It's one of those obsession things that women get," my father said. "Like wanting to be beautiful or wanting to have kids."

After a while, my father told me, my mother began coming up with a bunch of weird things to sew into the quilt. "Chicken feet," my father said. "And hair."

"The porcupine quills look nice."

"I bought her a really nice pair of earrings once, and they wound up on the quilt."

I wanted to know the story behind the needles and the fish hooks, but my father said that those came later, that I would have to ask my mother about them. My father figured that the quilt was a way my mother had of dealing with frustration and disappointment. "Finding all that weird stuff and wasting time sewing it on probably helps calm her down," he said.

"She's stuck a lot of new things on since you left."

"Did she ever take the razor blades off?"

"Nope, they're still there."

"Not sure I'd sleep too well knowing that," said my father. "What about you?"

"All the dangerous stuff is on top."

You could see people on the quilt but you couldn't tell who they were. My father decided that a tall figure with a yellow and blue face was him and that I was a piece of cloth that looked more like a purple jelly bean than a person. Towards one side, away from everything else, was a piece of rose terry cloth that reminded me of a sleeping child.

"You know the difference between a bull and a steer, don't you?" said my father.

"Sure."

"Then I'd stay away from that quilt."

My father was probably right, but it looked as if you'd be safe enough as long as you were under the quilt and weren't moving around on the outside, trying to get in. What I liked best were the needles. When you held the quilt up, they would tinkle like little bells and flash in the light like knives.

CHAPTER NINE

The next morning, when I get up, the shop is quiet, and I figure that my mother has gone over behind Santucci's to sort through any flowers that Mrs. Santucci has thrown out. This is fine with me because it means that she's not washing someone's hair and wasting all the hot water. Even at the best of times, the water is never really hot, and if I don't get to the shower first thing, all that's left is lukewarm. Or cold.

I stand in the tub and let the water run over my head and shoulders, smooth and warm, and as the bathroom turns to steam, I lean against the wall and close my eyes and try to imagine what the woman was doing on the Horns.

My first theory is that she's angry about something. Maybe her boyfriend or her husband has left her. Maybe she stuffs his favourite clothes into a suitcase, drives out to the river in a fury, and throws everything into the water. Maybe she's so angry she jumps in herself. Maybe she loses her balance. In any case, the water calms her down. She swims back to shore, climbs back up to the Horns, gets in her truck, and drives away.

This theory is simple and complete. The only problem is that there are better places to throw a suitcase into the river. And closer. You could go across the tracks on Division Street South to the overlook and toss a suitcase off there. The woman might have wanted privacy, but angry people generally don't care about things like that. When Ida Jerome caught her husband, Jerry, with Stella Watson, the whole town knew about it. The moment it happened.

But if the woman was angry, why was she dancing? I'm working on this when I hear the toilet flush and the water pressure drops to a trickle.

"Hey!"

"You in there, cousin?"

"Lum?"

"Quit playing with the soap." Lum tosses a towel against the shower curtain. Part of it loops over the bar and hangs there.

"I just got in," I say.

"You don't have that much to wash."

The water returns to normal and I put my head back under the spray in order to drown out Lum's voice. The tub drains slowly and the water is up to my ankles now. I'm just beginning to enjoy myself again when I feel something bump up against my butt. It makes me jump, and when I turn around, I see Lum's arm sticking through the shower curtain. In his hand is the skull.

"Have you seen a bone around here?" Lum says in that stupid tinny voice of his, and he moves the skull up and down as if it's talking.

"You been drinking again?"

"A teeny-weeny bonie." Lum balances the skull on the edge of the tub and then lets it slide down the porcelain. It hits the water, tumbles over, and floats up against my leg. It bobs around in the soap suds for a moment and then settles to the bottom of the tub. The skull looks funny sitting there, half-submerged, the soap slick floating in and out of the eye sockets.

"Your brother's drowning," I tell Lum.

"Just don't piss on him." Lum's hand dives into the shower and snatches the skull out of the water like a hawk hitting a fish. "Yuck!" shouts Lum. "What's this white shit all over him?"

"It's soap."

"Pervert!"

My second theory is that the woman's boyfriend or husband has died or been killed. She packs his favourite clothes in his favourite suitcase and drives out to the Horns. When she gets there, she discovers that she can't bear simply to throw the suitcase into the river, so she jumps in with it and, as a gesture of love, floats along with the suitcase for a ways before she sets it free in the current. She swims to shore, gets out, has a good cry on the bank, climbs back up to the Horns, gets in her car, and drives away.

That would explain why the woman didn't throw the suitcase off the overlook. She wanted to be alone. Sorrow is different from anger.

When my father left Bright Water and moved to Truth, my mother didn't yell and throw things the way you see women do in the movies. She stayed in the house and worked on the quilt. I was pretty sure she was angry, but maybe she was sad at the same time.

When I come out of the shower, Lum is sitting at the kitchen table, wrapped up in my mother's quilt, eating toast and drinking apple juice.

"Hey! Take it off. My mother sees you with that and I'll catch shit."

"I'm not going to hurt it." Lum stands up and spins around in a tight circle so that the feathers lift away from the quilt like tiny wings and the ribbons tremble like tongues. "There any more apple juice?"

"You drank all the juice?"

"Water's better for you anyway," says Lum. "This stuff's mostly sugar."

"Thought you were in training."

"Long-distance runners need sugar."

There's a pan on the stove. It's empty, but I can still smell the sausage. "What else did you eat?"

"A traditional Indian would never ask that question." Lum folds the quilt up and puts it back in the basket.

"My sausage, right?"

"Protein." Lum opens the oven and takes out a plate with three sausages on it and hands it to me. "How do you expect me to win the race without protein?"

"How many did you eat?"

Lum picks up the newspaper and settles in behind it. "It says here that Indians make up the largest percentage of Canada's prison population."

I put four pieces of toast in the toaster and look in the refrigerator to see if there is more juice.

"That suggest anything to you?" says Lum.

"Like what?"

"Maybe we shouldn't be wasting our time looking for jobs."

The toast pops up. I butter it, wrap it around the sausages, and squeeze the bread so that the butter pools up around the meat. "My father's not in jail," I say. "And neither is your father."

"There's a line." Lum closes the paper and puts it on the table. "You have to wait your turn." He leans over and comes back up with the skull. He bounces it on the table and rolls it over to me. It doesn't roll very well. It rocks from side to side like the drunks you see outside the Silver Spur on Friday night.

"Where you want to hide it?" Lum pushes his lips at the skull on the table.

"Why do we have to hide it?"

"Evidence," says Lum, as if that answers the question. He grabs the skull and starts towards my room. "How about your closet? We could bury it under all the junk."

"No good," I tell him. "Soldier'll just dig it out."

"How about the cupboard?"

"Mom's always in there."

"Under the sink?"

"Worse."

Lum stands in the middle of the kitchen, his hands on his hips. Soldier comes in from the shop, following the aroma of sausage. He glances at the stove and then comes over and leans against Lum's leg.

Lum reaches down and pulls at Soldier's ear. "How about we cram it up the mutt's ass."

The building my mother rents was once a hardware store and warehouse. It is a long narrow affair that smells vaguely of paint thinner and oil. At the front, where my mother has her shop, the ceiling has been lowered, so when we first moved into the building, it felt as though we were moving into a cave. But my mother borrowed a ladder from my father, even though they weren't talking to each other much, and painted the ceiling and the walls a bright yellow, so when the sun comes in through the plate-glass window and lights up the red enamel sink and the second-hand white and turquoise hair dryer, the place feels warm and cheery and seems larger than it really is.

The back area is cooler, and everything beyond the shop is dark grey. My mother was going to paint the kitchen and the bathroom and the bedroom off-white or sand, but she never got around to it. It's not so bad though, and if we had a couple of windows in the back area, the only other thing we'd really need is a second bedroom so my mother wouldn't have to sleep on the couch. But there aren't any windows in

this part of the building. And even with all the lights on and the television going, you feel as if you're sitting at the bottom of a well.

"What's up there?" Lum peers into the darkness.

"Nothing much," I tell him. "Rafters."

"Let's take a look."

There's a wooden ladder built into the wall. It takes you up to the first
set of rafters. I've forgotten how high off the floor the rafters are. Lum
is right behind, nudging me along with the skull.

"Where's that little bone?" he squeaks. "Yummy, yummy."

"Go chew on your own bone."

As I inch my way along, I plow up the dust with my crotch and push
it over the edge of the rafter. It drifts down like snow, twinkling into the
light.

"You ever fall?" says Lum, and he pokes me in the back with his fist.

"Knock it off."

I don't see the first set of braces until I run into them. They're set at
angles to the main joists. At the second brace, someone has pounded a
large nail halfway into the wood. "How about here?"

Lum hands me the skull. I loop the ribbon over the nail and lower the
skull until it hangs just below the rafters and above the light, as if it's
floating in space. Soldier walks around in a circle looking up at us, but
I'm pretty sure he can't see anything.

"Hear your crazy aunt is back," says Lum.

"She's not crazy."

"The one with the tattoo, right?" Lum blows on the back of my neck.
"The one who thinks you're a girl."

"She doesn't think I'm a girl."

"She sent you a doll."

"That was a mistake."

"She dying or something?"

"No."

"Nobody comes back to Truth and Bright Water," says Lum, "unless
they're crazy or dying."

"Monroe Swimmer came back," I say.

"Number one," says Lum, and he shoves me again, and this time I have
to grab onto the rafter with both hands.

The third theory is more melodramatic, and suicide sounds too much like a movie for me to like it much.

But maybe someone the woman loves has left her or has died, and she's depressed. Maybe the suitcase is full of her own clothes and all the precious things she has in the world. She finishes dinner that evening and cleans the house. Then she puts on her best dress and drives to the Horns. She waits on the cliff for the moon to rise, and just as it does, she clutches the suitcase to her chest and jumps off. Of course, she sinks immediately, and as the water's cold, even in the summer, the shock brings her back to her senses. The suitcase is lost, but she is able to stagger to shore, wet and freezing and embarrassed, find her truck, and drive home.

It's an okay theory, but there are better ways to kill yourself. Everybody knows that putting a hose in a car's exhaust, or taking a lot of sleeping pills with whisky or maybe even beer, or cutting your wrists with a razor blade in a bathtub full of warm water, or jumping out the window of a tall building — and there are several tall buildings in Truth — would be quicker and more effective. So, if she went to the river to commit suicide, she wasn't serious, and was probably just looking for attention.

When we get down, Soldier is waiting for us. His ears are up and his head is cocked to one side. I look up at the rafters to see if I can find the skull. Soldier sits back and stares into the darkness. His body quivers and he begins to drool again.

"You can't see anything," I tell him.

"Not to worry," says Lum. "Dog couldn't find a pole if you tied him to it."

The front doorbell rings, and Soldier forgets about the skull for the moment and hurries into the shop. When Lum and I get to the front, my mother is dumping an armload of flowers into the sink.

"You find the sausage?"

"Yeah," I say, "but Lum ate most of them."

My mother turns and smiles at Lum, but I can see she's looking at his eye. "How's your father?"

"He's fine," says Lum.

"Everything ready for Indian Days?"

"Just about."

My mother works on the flowers, dropping the dead ones into the garbage, stacking the live ones beside the sink. "Be sure you and your father stop by my mother's lodge."

Lum shrugs.

"We haven't talked to him in a long time." My mother holds a flower up to the light. Most of the blossoms are dead, and I figure she's going to dump it. But she snips at it here and there and she winds up with a single flower on a spindly stem. "Not since the accident."

I'm sorry my mother has brought this up. Lum nods and chews at one of his fingers. "He's been busy."

My mother lays the flower on top of the live ones and takes down the big blue vase. "You know you're always welcome."

"Sure." Lum is already moving towards the door. Soldier is right behind him.

"We got to get going," I say.

My mother shakes the water off the flowers and puts them in the vase. For a moment, I think she's going to say something else, but she doesn't. Instead, she runs her fingers gently through the flowers, fluffs them so they spread out like an umbrella, and sets them in the sun.

The skull is the problem. Any one of these theories works fine until I get to the skull. The easiest way to manage it is to forget it altogether. It probably has nothing to do with the woman. There are bones all over the coulees. Lum and I have found plenty. Cows, rabbits, skunks, coyotes, deer. Rib bones, leg bones, jaw bones with teeth, back bones. Skulls.

When we were living in Bright Water, Lum and I would take some of the more interesting bones we found to my grandmother, who knew her bones.

"Skunk," my grandmother would say. "This is skunk."

Neither Lum nor I could tell the difference, so all we could do was guess. "This one is a . . . deer? Right?"

My grandmother would bring the bone up to her ear, as if she were listening for something. Sometimes she'd smell it. And then she'd set to running her fingers all along the length and around the curves until she found what she was looking for.

"Cow," she'd say. "Right here. Cow."

The railroad tracks run east and west, and cut Truth in half. If you're in a car, you can only get from one side of town to the other at the level crossings, but if you're on foot, you can cross anywhere you can scale the fence or find a hole in the wire.

The main railroad yards are to the southeast behind a low swell. You can't see the yards or the round house or the repair sheds from town, and if it weren't for the smoke and the noise of the cars being shunted onto sidings and the main track, you might not even know the yards were there at all. Four sets of tracks run through Truth, but in the yards, the tracks lie beside each other twenty deep with lines of boxcars and engines stacked so close that when you pass between them, it feels as if you're walking down a narrow hallway or along the bottom of a ditch. Here everything is always in slow motion, cars swaying forward and back along the steel rails, trunk to tail, like a chorus line of elephants.

Somewhere behind the first string, a yard engine slams into a line of cars, and we can hear the brittle creak of metal as brake lines are released and cars are shunted and dropped and added. Several of the boxcars are open. Lum walks the line until he finds a straw car. "This one," he says, and he climbs in.

The straw cars are fruit cars, and at this time of the year, most of them are packed with melons. The cars are unloaded before they get to Truth, but if you catch them before they hit the wash line, sometimes you can find a melon that is mostly good, buried among the smashed and rotting pieces.

Lum lies down in the straw. "Check it out."

I don't figure I'm going to find anything, but I kick my way through the straw just in case. Soldier jumps on the straw and burrows into a corner until all you can see is his butt. It's cool inside, but already I can hear the heat swelling the sides of the steel car, and I can feel the heavy smell of rotting fruit rising out of the straw.

"Find anything?"

"Just pieces." I go over and stand by the door, just in case someone comes along the tracks and catches us in the car. "We could always wash boxcars," I say. "It isn't a great job, but it's a job."

"Washing boxcars isn't a job." Lum stands up, sets his feet, and pretends he's holding one of the high-pressure hoses the washers use to clean the cars. "It's an adventure."

"There are worse things than washing boxcars."

"Whoooosh!" Lum yells, and pulls the valve open.

In the cool dark of the car, I watch Lum play the hose into the corners and along the floor, and I imagine the water exploding under the straw and breaking against the metal walls like waves trying to come ashore.

I figure the skull is prehistoric. The whole area around Truth and Bright Water is full of dinosaur bones, and it makes sense that you might find a prehistoric human skull mixed in with prehistoric animals. Maybe that's why the skull is small. Maybe it's not a child's skull after all. Maybe humans who lived back then didn't have very big heads.

Or maybe the bluff was once a burial ground. Maybe at one time we buried our dead there and then forgot about it. Maybe if you dug down a little in the grass and the clay, you'd find entire tribes scattered across the prairies. Such things probably happen all the time. A little rain, a little wind, and a skull just pops out of the ground.

Lum comes over and sits down in the doorway and dangles his feet off the side of the boxcar. The sun bends in from the south, rushes past us, and pours into the car. Lum reaches out and taps a round dance rhythm on the metal door.

"If we don't get jobs," I tell him, "we won't have any money."

"So, what else is new?"

Lum picks up the rhythm and the power, using his knuckles to drum the door. "I know guys who make their living on the powwow circuit."

"Like who?"

"Nobody from around here," says Lum. "But we could."

"Drumming?"

"Drumming, singing, dancing." Lum switches to an intertribal. "You spend the winter learning to sing and dance, and as soon as spring comes, you pack everything into a pickup or a van and you head out on the circuit."

"We don't have a car."

"We'd have to get one."

"What do you make?"

"Gas money, food, if you're just average. Prize money if you're good."

"Sounds okay."

"You know how to sing?" says Lum.

"Nope."

"Drum?"

"Nope."

The whole time he's talking, Lum is hammering the door with his fist. It's as if he's forgotten what his hand is doing. The fist is moving pretty fast, but you can see that the skin around the knuckles is beginning to redden and crack.

"That's what I want to do."

"Go to powwows?" I say.

"No," says Lum, "get out of Bright Water."

One time, when I took some bones over to my grandmother, I asked her why everything came in threes.

"Who told you that?"

"Dad mentioned it."

"Ah," she said. "That explains it."

"So, he's right?"

"Wouldn't know. My mother said everything came in fours."

"Fours, huh?"

"Deer," she said, "have four legs."

"What about birds?"

"And turtles have four legs."

"Yeah, but people only have two legs."

"In the olden days, when we were smarter," my grandmother said, looking straight out the kitchen window, "we had four."

Lum stops drumming the side of the car and wipes his hand on his jeans. "Did I tell you we got skins at Happy Trails?"

"Cherokees, right?"

"They pulled up in a bunch of beat-up trailers, like the one your grandmother has."

"They're here for Indian Days, right?"

"Why else would they come?"

"Lucille and Teresa are praying for Germans."

Lum jumps down onto the gravel between the long strings of boxcars and flatbeds and tankers, and unzips his fly. "My father's hoping for a bunch of Americans. He's got this new scheme."

"What is it?"

"You'll have to see it to believe it." Lum rocks his hips back and forth as if he's trying to write his name in the gravel.

"Give me a hint."

Lum zips his pants up and starts jogging along the line of cars. Soldier and I jog with him. As long as he doesn't go any faster, I can keep up. Our shoes crunch on the stones as we go, and the echoes carry off the railway cars, strange and dangerous, as if we are stepping on eggs. Or running on bones.

Lum takes the stopwatch from around his neck and hands it to me. Up ahead, I can see where the boxcars end. Lum presses the pace, and we leave the shelter of the cars and angle out across the corner of the yard to where an old wooden trestle bridges an open oil pit. In the distance, a locomotive comes towards us, dragging a string of cars.

"What about jobs?"

"Time me!"

Lum breaks ahead of me, and I can see that he's not going to wait, that he's decided to race the train to the trestle. Soldier goes with him. I'm already slowing down when the train roars past me. The noise and the wind throw me off my stride, but it doesn't matter because I'm not trying to prove anything.

"Soldier!"

Lum is flying across the yard at a dead run. He takes the angle and catches the engine at the swing of the curve, runs alongside it until the embankment rises to meet the trestle and the gravel shoulder begins to narrow and falls away. Soldier goes as far as the gravel shoulder before he calls it quits, but he's not happy about being left behind. He stands by the side of the tracks and barks as Lum runs alongside the engine.

You can see that Lum's going to run out of room, that he'll be forced to give it up, to peel off and come back down the embankment. But instead of slowing down, Lum drops his head and kicks hard, and as the slope disappears, he sidesteps onto the tracks just ahead of the engine and leads the train across the bridge.

I can't imagine that the train people are too happy about Lum's being on the tracks in front of them. But they don't blow their whistle and they don't slow down, so maybe they're busy with something else and haven't noticed him. Or maybe they don't care.

One thing is for sure. If he slips on the gravel or stumbles on a tie, he's dead.

But he doesn't. He stays just out of reach of the train, and all the way across the bridge he holds it off, until the tracks begin the climb out of Truth, and the train loses speed and begins to fade.

The idea that the skull is prehistoric or has come from an old burial ground is fine until you get to the dirt. Once, when Lum and I were out on the coulees, we found a ground squirrel skeleton just below the prairie grass. The skull was a tiny thing, but when I dug it out, it was heavier than I would have guessed.

"Look at this." I tossed the skull to Lum, and he held it up to the light and shook it.

"Ground squirrels," said Lum, and he stuck a stick into an eye hole. "They got dirt for brains."

The skull was filled with dirt, as if it had been poured in hot and left to set and cool. Both of us worked on it with sticks, but the dirt was like the bone itself, and after a while we gave up. Lum put the skull on a rock and crushed it with his foot. Even then, after you peeled the pieces of bone away, the dirt remained intact, hard as stone.

But the skull we found on the Horns was clean. Inside and out, it was clean. Almost spotless. As if someone had taken the time to wash and polish it before setting it in the grass for us to find.

Soldier and I wait in the shade of the boxcars to see if Lum is going to stop and circle back to check the time, but he has already made the top of the grade and is moving fast out across the long flat that follows the river to Prairie View.

Against the arch of a cloudless sky, he looks like a dark bird gliding low across the land.

CHAPTER TEN

One year, when we were still all living together in Bright Water, my mother decided we should take a vacation. I voted for the West Edmonton Mall. I had seen brochures of the place, and Lucy Rabbit had even been there and said it was neat. But my mother wanted to go camping, to get into nature and see stuff like animals and scenery. I told her we saw that all the time, but she said the mountains were different. She wanted to go to Waterton Lake, hike around a little, and maybe rent a cabin on the water for a week or so.

My father didn't want to go anywhere. He had too much work to do, he said, and needed to get it done.

"Doesn't stop you from going to Prairie View when you want to go."

"That's business."

"So is this," my mother told him. "Family business."

In the end, my mother got her way, and we borrowed a tent and some sleeping bags from Lucy Rabbit's brother Gorman and a cookstove from Franklin, and we packed the truck up and headed for the Rockies.

"What am I going to do?" I asked my mother.

"You can fish."

"That's the second-to-last thing I want to do."

Waterton Lake looked like one of those postcards that Gabriel Tucker had in his sporting goods store for the tourists who stopped in for hunting licences and bullets. There was an old hotel on a hill overlooking the lake, and, of course, my mother had to stop just to see the place. It was old, and it smelled old, and the people who were sitting around in the lobby looked old. There were a couple of tour buses parked out front and everyone on the buses was over fifty at least. I saw a couple of kids, but they were dressed like their parents and moved around as if they had never been outdoors in their entire lives.

My father stayed outside and smoked a cigarette. "I'm going to watch the view," he told my mother. "And think about the money I'm losing."

The inside of the hotel was mostly logs and planks and big branches, and my mother dragged me back and forth, reading a bunch of boring junk out of one of the colour brochures that someone had left lying about on a table.

"Take a guess at how old this hotel is."

"Who cares?"

My mother went to the front desk to see how much a room would cost. She came back smiling and said that they had a few vacancies left, and that we could get a nice room for one hundred and fifty dollars.

"Is there a pool?"

"The lake's right there."

"That much for just a room?"

"It's a world-heritage resort."

My father stayed outside, smoking and looking at the lake, so he didn't get to hear about the price of the room until we were setting up our tent at the campsite. "How much?"

"That's what they said."

"Must be why this sorry-ass campsite is costing us twenty bucks."

"Why?"

"Because we get a view of the hotel."

My mother cooked up some rice and hot dogs and we got some soft drinks out of the cooler. After we had eaten, we sat on stumps and watched the sun settle into the lake. "What do you think now?" she asked me.

I should have told her that I was beginning to like Waterton Lake, just to make her happy, but I didn't. "Don't worry," she told me, "tomorrow's going to be a lot more fun."

It rained all the next day. We sat in the tent and played rummy and fish. The tent leaked a little at one side, and we had to keep shifting around because our legs would get cramped. Every so often, my father would unzip the flap and go out into the rain. We'd wait for him, look at our cards, and plan our strategies. After a while, he would come back in, wet, and we would begin again. I did most of the talking.

"They should put in a miniature golf course. I bet they could make a lot of money off that."

My mother didn't mind the rain. It was an adventure, she said. After each hand, she would carefully add up the scores and write them on the back of one of the brochures she had picked up at the Prince of Wales Hotel.

My mother was right, of course. The mountains were different from Truth and Bright Water. In the mountains, everything was bowed in and close. On the prairies, you could see forever. In the mountains, the air felt heavy and dark. On the prairies, the air was light and gold.

The next morning, the rain stopped and we went for a walk along the lakeshore. My father and I had a contest skipping stones across the lake. "So, what do you think?" he said.

"About what?"

"Your mother's vacation."

"It's okay."

"Pretty exciting playing rummy in a wet tent," he says. "And the mosquitoes are a lot of fun, too."

"Rain's stopped now."

"Your mother wants to hike to Crypt Lake." My father picked up a large, flat rock and threw it sidearm so hard I was sure it was going to bounce up and rattle off across the surface all the way to the far shore. Instead, it buried its nose in the water and sank immediately. "And she wants to take a boat ride up the lake and back."

"Great."

My father stood on the shore and watched the spot where the rock had disappeared, as if he expected it to come floating to the surface. "And that," he said, spitting into the lake, "is your lesson for today."

My mother walked behind us. Every so often, she would stop, bend over and pick up a small stone, and put it in her pocket. Sometimes my father would wander off ahead, looking for larger rocks to throw in the lake, and I would be left alone between them. Most of that day, we walked along the shore tossing rocks in the water until my shoulder started to ache, and then my mother got out the map she had picked up at the ranger's station and said we should climb a small hill called Bear Hump.

"It'll give us a view of the lake and the mountains and the prairies all at once."

"Got that already," said my father.

"If it's clear," my mother said, "we'll be able to see all the way into the United States."

Going up Bear Hump wasn't too hard, and I got to lead. We stopped twice on the climb so my father could have a cigarette. My mother was right. The view was great. And it kept changing. The sun would go in and out of the clouds, and when it went in, the lake turned deep green and grey, and when it came out, the lake flashed silver and black. My mother stood on the edge of the cliff with her arms wrapped around her. My father sat on the edge of a rock and swatted deer flies.

That evening, after we got back, my father told us that he had to go into town. "Forgot something," he said.

My mother was not happy about this. "Can't it wait?"

"It's business."

"What about our vacation?" said my mother.

"You mean your vacation."

"All right," my mother said, "what about my vacation?"

"I'll be back before you know it."

After my father left, the rain returned, gently this time, and my mother and I sat in the tent with the flap open and watched the clouds pour in over the lake.

I figured my father would show up the next morning, but he didn't, and by noon my mother gave up.

"Let's go for that boat ride," she said.

"What about dad?"

"He can catch up."

The cruise around the lake was interesting, and if I hadn't gone, I would never have known that the Canadian/United States border ran right through the middle of the lake. When the guy driving the boat told us that, I expected to see a floating fence or inner tubes with barbed wire and lights, something to keep people from straying from one country into the other. There was a cutline in the trees along with border posts on opposite sides of the shore, and a small border station to mark the line. We floated over to the station and the boat driver rang his bell and we all waved.

When we got back to camp, there was still no sign of my father. We had plenty of food, and we had the tent, and the townsite was right there, so we were in good shape.

"So, what do we do now?"

"Tomorrow," said my mother, "we go to Crypt Lake."

We didn't go to Crypt Lake. My mother slept in the next morning. I waited to see what was going to happen, but I finally gave up and walked over to the lake and practised skipping stones. I practised until I got hungry, and then I went back to the tent. The flap was open. The food was waiting for me in the cooler, but my mother had disappeared. I figured she had gone to the bathroom or something like that, but when she didn't come back, I went looking for her. I found her sitting in a chair in the lobby of the hotel. She was in a corner by herself in front of the windows that overlooked the lake.

"You okay?"

"This is what vacations are all about, you know."

"Sitting?"

"Relaxing," said my mother.

There were sailboats on the lake with bright white sails, and in the bay around the corner from the lake itself, a tour boat was just pulling away from the docks. "We could still go to Crypt Lake."

"No point in doing everything the first trip," she said. Her eyes were heavy and her hair was pulled straight back away from her face and tied with a rubber band.

"So, what do you want to do?"

"Sit," she said. "I think I'd like to sit."

My mother sat in the hotel all day. In the evening, she came back to the tent and we had dinner. "There's a bus at seven," she told me, after we had cleaned up.

"What about dad?"

We packed everything up and carried the tent and the stove and the sleeping bags and the cooler into the townsite, and waited for the bus at the Petro-Can station.

"Maybe his truck broke down."

"Maybe it did."

As soon as we got settled in our seats, my mother closed her eyes. I don't think she was asleep, but she didn't talk and she didn't move the whole trip. I leaned against the glass and watched the road, just in case I spotted my father coming back to bring us home.

CHAPTER ELEVEN

━━━

I don't figure I'm going to see Lum for the rest of the day, so I head to my father's shop to see if he was serious about showing me how to drive. If I'm lucky, he's found the parts for the Karmann Ghia and I'll get to practise with a sports car, but I can see right away that nothing has happened. The tarp still sags over the seats and the tires are still flat.

My father is bent over his workbench. Wisps of smoke are rising over his shoulder.

"What're you making?"

"Hey," he says. "You're just in time."

"More coyotes?"

My father holds up a thin piece of wood that has been bent into an oval. "What do you think?" I look at it, but I have no idea what it is. "It's great."

"I use a heated awl to make the holes," he says. "Any fool can drill them."

Sometimes my father tells me what he's making, and sometimes I have to guess. "Maybe mom would like one."

My father stops what he's doing and looks at me. "A fishing net?"

I look at the oval again. I still don't see a fishing net. "You just stick it . . . in the water?"

My father picks up a short piece of wood. "The handle goes on like this." Now it looks more like a fishing net. My father takes a finished net off the wall. "This is what they look like when they're done."

The mouth of the net is a thin wooden hoop that has been twisted once and bent into an oval. The handle is a piece of oak with an inlay of darker wood. The net is woven through the holes in the hoop and held in place with fishing line. My father hands me the net. It's as light as air. "The fat cats from the city will eat these up. If I put them in an oak case and sign and number each one, I can get a hundred and fifty apiece." My father bends over and waves the net around a couple of times, as if he were landing a fish. "With any luck," he says, "I'm going to be a rich man."

"Then you can come home," I say, for no particular reason.

"Don't worry," he says. "I won't forget you." He stands there for a moment without moving, as if he's thinking about telling me something else, but has forgotten what it was. "How's it hanging?" he says at last.

"Lum and me are still looking for jobs."

"How is that nephew of mine?"

"He's going to win the Indian Days race."

"He pretty fast?" My father turns the fishing net around in his hands.

"You bet."

"Living with Franklin, you'd need to be fast." My father stands up and dusts off his jeans. "You want to make some money?"

"Sure," I say. "How much?"

"Depends."

"Smuggling?"

"I've got to take some stuff over to Bright Water." My father holds the net up to the light. "Could use an extra set of hands."

"What sort of stuff?"

My father reaches over and ruffles my hair. "You're beginning to sound like your mother."

I should probably ask my mother if I can go, but since we go to Bright Water all the time, I figure it's okay.

"You old enough to make decisions for yourself?"

"You bet!"

"All right," my father says, and he hangs the net back up on the wall. "Let's get going."

"Can I drive?"

My father laughs. "My truck?"

"Sure."

"My truck would whip your ass."

"Lum drives his father's car."

"Franklin wouldn't let Jesus Christ drive his car."

When my father moved to Truth, he bought an old U-Haul truck from Gabriel Tucker, who had bought it from the U-Haul dealership just before it moved to Prairie View. Most of the writing on the sides of the truck has worn away, but you can still see where it says "Adventures in Moving." My father goes to the back and unlocks the door. "Come on," he tells me. "Give me a hand with this stuff."

Inside are large barrels set on their ends and stacked two high. My father puts on a pair of gloves and hops into the back. "You're a smart boy," he says. "What do you think sells across the line?"

There's a smell in the back of the truck that isn't very pleasant. Soldier backs up and waits by the Karmann Ghia.

"Gold?"

"Shit." My father leans against a barrel and smiles. "Gold sells anywhere."

"Car tires?"

"Too bulky. Not enough profit."

"Stereos? Televisions?"

"They do okay."

"Cigarettes?"

My father rolls a barrel onto the lift. "Not anymore. Those asshole politicians in Canada dropped their taxes and ruined the business."

"That's too bad."

"What's your mum's new boyfriend like?" My father rolls another barrel onto the lift, so I can't see his eyes right away.

"Doesn't have one."

"You'd tell me if she did, right?"

"Sure."

"We're still married, you know," he says. "So that gives me some rights." The lift jerks a bit at first and then lowers the barrels to the ground. "Take a guess," says my father. Each of the barrels is made out of yellow plastic, and each has a red and white sticker on the side that says "Bio-Hazardous Waste."

"Radiation?"

"Nope."

"Killer viruses?"

"It's the junk hospitals can't toss down the sink," says my father.

"Like body parts."

"Who knows. They just pay me to make it disappear." My father runs a hand through his hair. "It's enough to make you want to give the whole thing up."

"Smuggling?"

"No, marriage." My father reaches into his pocket and takes out a deck of cards. "Pick a card," he says.

I pick the ten of diamonds.

"The money card," says my father.

"We going to be rich?"

My father looks at the rest of the barrels in the truck. "No danger of that," he says.

We stack the barrels at the side of the shop. In addition to smelling bad, they're also covered with an oily slick that sticks to my hands and pants. Soldier watches us for a while, but by the time we've finished, he's disappeared again.

"Soldier."

"Dog's a hell of a lot smarter than either of us."

"Soldier!"

"Let him go," says my father. "Can't take him with us anyway."

"Sure we can."

"They won't let dogs across," says my father. "Used to be the same for Indians." He holds up his hands. The gloves are covered with a reddish-black stain. "Better wash up. No telling where those barrels have been."

I use the soap with the pieces of pumice in it, and I scrub my hands and arms all the way to the elbows until they hurt, but the smell doesn't go away and my hands still feel sticky. My father brings the truck around, and I get in on the passenger's side. "You got a clue how to drive a stick?" he says.

"Sure."

"If you expect to drive this truck," says my father, "you're going to have to learn to lie better than that." He lights up a cigarette and looks at me. "Bet you don't drink either."

"Beer."

"That right?"

The smoke fills the cab. I start coughing.

"If this bothers you," says my father, "just tell me."

"It kind of stinks."

My father cracks the side window, sucks on the cigarette, and blows a stream of smoke out the side of his mouth. "You know, your mother's not right about everything."

You'd think that the air conditioner would pull some of the smoke out, but it doesn't.

"Started smoking when I was twelve. How old are you now?"

"Fifteen."

"Fifteen." My father pushes back from the wheel and looks at the side mirror. "Lots of things in life will kill you faster than cigarettes."

Just outside Truth, the road climbs out of the river bottom and runs across the plateau in a straight line to Prairie View and the Canadian border. My father has to shift gears as we start up the grade. "Watch this," he says.

I sit there and wait, but nothing happens. Suddenly, there's a car passing us as if we're parked. It's dark green and has a long, narrow front end. The car streaks up the hill. We chug along behind it, losing ground all the way.

"Now, that's a car," says my father.

"Auntie Cassie's friend had one like that."

"One of these days, you'll see me driving one. A red one."

"Me, too."

The truck slows and the engine whines, as if someone has stepped on its tail. My father curses and shifts down. "Up ahead," he says.

Near the top of the grade, I see two figures by the side of the road, and for a moment, I imagine that it might be Lum on his way to Prairie View and Soldier heading out on another of his great escapes.

"Skins," says my father, and he pushes the accelerator all the way to the floor.

It's a man and a woman. I don't recognize them at first. The woman's thumb is out, and as we pass, I can see that she is trying to smile. The man looks straight ahead as if he doesn't see us at all.

"Jimmy and Crystal Sweet." My father shifts down. "Out of money and out of luck." I look at my father, but he shakes his head. "Drunker than skunks and twice as mean."

I watch them in the side mirror until we hit the crest of the hill.

"So, what can I tell you about the world?" My father lights up another cigarette. "Ask me anything you want."

I shrug my shoulders.

"You know all about drinking?"

"Sure."

"How about . . . sex?"

"How many times you been in jail?"

My father smiles and blows smoke against the windshield. "Sounds like your mother's been telling you stories."

"Lum told me."

"It's no secret," he says. "What else do you want to know?"

What I really want to ask my father is why he and my mother broke up. But I don't. "Why we going to Bright Water?"

"Business," says my father. "Only reason to go to Bright Water is business."

The sun is hot, and even with the air conditioning, I start to get sleepy. I lean up against the side of the cab. Ahead, by the side of the road, I see a dead ground squirrel on its back with one of its paws sticking up in the air, as if it started across and then had second thoughts or came out of cover to try to flag down a ride.

By the time we get to Prairie View, the truck is so full of smoke I don't know how my father can see the road. "Border's coming up," he says. "Time to get rid of it."

"What?"

"The grass."

"Marijuana?"

"Canadian border guards find even a little bit of seed, and they go apeshit," says my father. "Better lose the booze, too."

"You're kidding, right?"

"Canadian jails are worse than the Mexican ones."

"But you're kidding, right?"

"You know why?" My father gears down. We slide through the American border and roll to a stop at a log office with a Canadian flag on a pole. "Mexican jails are full of Mexicans," says my father, "but Canadian jails are full of Indians."

A couple of guards come out to the truck and ask us all about liquor and cigarettes, and my father shakes his head and smiles and talks like the Indians you see in the westerns on television. We have to stop by the side of the building so the guards can look in the back of the truck, but there's nothing there, so it's okay.

"Welcome to Canada," the guard tells us. "Have a nice day."

As we clear the border, my father looks at me. "They love that dumb Indian routine. You see how friendly those assholes were." He finds a radio station, and we listen to country and western music as we drive north. He stops smoking for a while, and that is a relief. "You ever been to Blossom?"

"Nope."

"Haven't missed much," says my father. "Province only has two cities and Blossom isn't one of them."

"I haven't been to Calgary either."

"The rest are piss stops and doughnut shops."

At first, I thought the answer to the dead animals along the side of the road was that some were faster than others. The faster the animal, the less likely it was to get hit by a car. But there were more ground squirrels on the side of the road than porcupines and more deer than skunks. So, speed wasn't it.

For a while, I thought it might be colour, that some animals were easier to see than others. Ground squirrels were tan and blended in with the landscape. Skunks were mostly black and would be hard to see at night, and around dusk, a deer might look like a pile of dirt. And that would explain the magpies.

I am almost asleep, and at first, I don't know if my father is talking to me or if it's someone on the radio running for office. "You know what's wrong with the world?" My father reaches under the seat and comes up with a bottle. The label says "Wiser's."

"Is that whisky?" I say.

"Whites," he says. "It's as simple as that." My father passes me the bottle. I take a sniff. It's iced tea, and it's pretty good.

"That's because they took our land, right?"

"Nope."

"Because they broke the treaties?"

"Double nope."

"Because they're prejudiced . . . ?"

"That what they teach you in school?" My father takes the bottle and has another drink. "Listen up. It's because they got no sense of humour."

"Skee tells some pretty good jokes."

"Telling a joke and having a sense of humour," says my father, "are two different things."

We get to Blossom just before noon and pull into a parking lot. There's a big red sign on a long, low building that says "Lionel's Home Entertainment Barn."

"Indian guy owns this," says my father. "White guy went bankrupt a few years back and had to sell it. Now that's funny." We get out and open the back of the truck. "Not many times you see that happen."

Inside the store, there are rows and rows of stereos and VCRs and disc players. One wall is nothing but televisions all stacked up on each other. If you look hard and use your imagination, it looks like a map of North America. My father talks to an Indian guy who looks sort of like John Wayne, only not as heavy. He shakes hands with the man and heads for the back of the store. I follow him.

"Grab a dolly," he says. "These boxes are ours."

I can see why he needs me now. The boxes are large, and they're heavy. It takes both of us to wrestle them into the truck, and by the time we're done, I'm really hot and sweaty.

My father pulls the door down and locks it. "Time for lunch," he says. "You hungry?"

"You bet," I say.

"Got just the spot."

We eat lunch at a café owned by a woman from the Blood reserve near Fort Macleod. "I went to school with her," my father tells me. "Probably the only town in America where two Indians own anything."

"We're in Canada."

"Hell," he says. "I guess that explains it, all right."

Lunch is pretty good. I have a Houndburger, which is really a cheeseburger, and some fries with gravy. My father has a bowl of Dog du Jour, which turns out to be chicken noodle.

"Where do we go next?"

"You having fun yet?"

"You bet."

"How old you say you are?"

"Going on sixteen."

"And you know everything there is to know about sex."

"They showed us a film."

"At school?"

"Right."

"The old in and out, huh?"

"What?"

My father pays the bill and we get back in the truck. As he starts the truck, he begins to laugh. "Little more to it than that, son." He is still laughing when we turn the truck around and head west.

Whenever you see a dead animal on the road, you generally see magpies. They hop about on the body, pecking and squawking, fighting with each other over the soft parts. Cars don't spook them. They wait until you're right on top of them before they give up their dance and head for the sky. Some of them fly right at the car, veering off only at the last moment. They're easy to see. Even at a distance, you can't miss them. They don't blend into anything and they aren't particularly fast. And you never see a dead magpie by the side of the road.

"Did that sex film have real people in it?"

"Nope," I say. "Just drawings and stuff."

"Okay," says my father, "listen up." My father has only been married once, so far as I know, but I figure he knows something about sex, so I listen. "And that's what women want. You understand?"

Some of the stuff is interesting, and some of it is gross.

"Come on," he says. "Ask me anything."

I figure that now is as good a time as any. "Why did you and mom break up?"

My father looks at me, and then he looks at the road. "You better ask your mother about that."

"I did."

"What'd she say?"

"She said to ask you."

We stop at a warehouse just outside Blossom and pick up four more boxes. These boxes are larger and have to be loaded on the truck with a forklift. The only marking is a sign at one end of each box that says "This End Up".

"What's in the boxes?"

"What do you figure?"

"Giant wood coyotes?" I say, hoping I can joke my father into telling me.

"Hell," says my father, "nothing that useful."

The only other thing I can figure is that some animals are smart and some are stupid. From the number of ground squirrel bodies along the side of the road, I'd guess that ground squirrels are close to brain-dead. Deer must be pretty dense, and skunks aren't much better. Porcupines may be slow, but they've got enough sense not to try to cross the road when there's a car coming. And magpies. Magpies look witless, but in the animal world, they could be geniuses.

When we get to Bright Water, we drive through without stopping. At the top of the hill, my father pulls the truck onto the shoulder. "What do you see?"

"Mountains."

"Look again." In the distance, a small herd of buffalo appears out of nowhere and begins wandering in our direction. "One of Franklin's great ideas."

"The buffalo?"

"The very same," says my father.

"They're kinda neat."

"Tourists," says my father. "Franklin figured that a herd of buffalo would bring in the tourists and help fill up Happy Trails."

"I remember."

"That was another of his great ideas."

"The tourists?"

"No, the RV park."

The buffalo arrive at the fence. They slide along sideways, watching us out of the corners of their eyes. When they stop moving and stand still, they look like rocks. "Vision Quest Tours was last year's idea," says my father. "And the junk in the back is part of this year's disaster."

One of the bulls puts his head against a fence post and leans into it.

89

Every so often, he looks up and shakes his head. I figure he's thinking about having a go at the truck.

"Skee's got a couple of buffalo skulls at the restaurant."

My father grins at me and hits the horn. The bull flinches, but he doesn't move. "You know how to tell an old-time buffalo skull?"

"Something about the colour?"

"A hole," says my father. "All the old-time buffalo skulls have a nice round hole in their heads."

"Bullet holes, right?"

"Naw," says my father, "they're air-conditioning ducts. You still want to drive?" He hops out and comes to my side. As soon as he opens the door and gets out, the buffalo skitter back from the fence. "Only way to learn a thing," says my father, "is to do it."

I slide across and behind the wheel. My father climbs in and shuts the door.

"Put your seat belt on," he says, and he fastens his. "You got a clue how this thing works?"

My father shows me the ignition and the brake and the clutch, and tells me about RPMs and gear ratios and compression. He doesn't spend a lot of time on any one item, and the more things he tells me, the more nervous I get.

"You're not going to drive us off a cliff, are you?"

I grab the wheel and shove down on the clutch. As I reach for the ignition, I feel the truck start to roll backwards.

"Wrong way."

I forget the clutch and hit the brakes. My father jerks forward in his seat. "You got about six hours before the sun goes down."

I put the truck in neutral and start the engine. My foot's on the brakes and my leg is beginning to cramp. I put the clutch in, pull the stick into first, and let up on the clutch. The truck lurches forward a few feet and dies. I try it again. Same thing. The buffalo come back to the fence. All of them face the truck this time.

"Those history books you get in school say that railroad sharpshooters killed off all the buffalo, but that's not true." My father leans up against the door and closes his eyes. "Most of them just took off and never came back."

I start the truck again.

"Your audience is waiting," says my father. "Try letting up on the clutch slowly and get it rolling before you give it any gas."

I start it again, and it lurches forward and dies. I do this for fifteen, maybe twenty minutes.

"This is fun," says my father.

I finally get the truck moving. It jerks along in first gear, and I'm doing okay until I have to look down at the knob to see where to go next.

"Second gear!" yells my father, over the whine of the engine.

When I try to shift from first to second, the sound is so sudden and frightening, I forget about the clutch and the gas, and the truck dies and drifts off onto the shoulder of the road. I take a deep breath and look around. The buffalo are gone.

"Just like that." My father looks out the window at the empty prairies. "Soon as the smart ones got a good look at Whites, they took off."

"So, where'd they go?"

"That's the mistake we made." My father settles into his seat, pulls his cap down, and closes his eyes. "We should have gone with them."

I try again, and this time I get from first gear into second gear. I see my father smile, so I go for third.

Or maybe ground squirrels and skunks and deer and porcupines and magpies are just like people. Some are lucky, and some aren't. Some get to drive nice cars, and some wind up by the side of the road.

Each time I start the truck, it gets a little easier. Pretty soon, I'm in third gear most of the time, and all I have to worry about is steering. The road climbs a little and then changes to gravel and begins to narrow. My father signals for me to stop. Below us the prairies open up, and the land curves down into a deep bowl. "That's where we want to go." In the distance, set in the high grass, a large tent stands by itself. "Try not to hit it," says my father.

The afternoon sun glistens off the canvas, and against the summer grass, the tent looks like white ice floating in a gold sea.

CHAPTER TWELVE

My mother became a beautician through no fault of her own. One time, I asked her how it happened, and she said it was just one of those things that you did when you were young. My grandmother said it was auntie Cassie's fault. What I had to understand first, my grandmother told me, was that auntie Cassie was older than my mother by a year, which I already knew. The second thing I needed to know was that my mother always wanted to be exactly like auntie Cassie.

"If Cassie did a thing," my grandmother said, "your mother would want to do it, too."

"What kind of things?"

"Just like you and your cousin."

"Like what?"

After auntie Cassie graduated from high school, she enrolled in a beautician program at Wild Rose Community College in Blossom. The next year, when my mother graduated, she signed up for the same program.

"Couldn't separate the two of them," my grandmother told me.

From there on out, my grandmother and the story wandered off in different directions, and all I knew for sure was that somewhere in the middle of her second year, auntie Cassie dropped out of school.

"Why'd she leave?"

"They even used to dress the same."

"Where'd she go?"

"People began thinking they were twins," said my grandmother. "If Cassie had decided to jump off a cliff, your mother would have been right behind her."

"But she came back."

"Who?" said my grandmother.

"Cassie."

My grandmother would pull her neck down into her sweater and clear her throat. "Cassie always comes back."

Where auntie Cassie went and what she did was a mystery. I figured that since my mother was there and since they are sisters, she would know. "You remember when you and auntie Cassie went to beauty school?"

"It was a community college."

"How come she dropped out?"

"A two-year certificate program."

"Where'd she go?"

"Today," said my mother, "anybody with a bottle of shampoo and a pair of scissors can call themselves a beautician."

"Is that when she joined the American Indian Movement?"

"Cassie?"

"You know, the tattoo."

"Oh, that," said my mother.

In the end, all I knew for sure was that after auntie Cassie left, my mother stayed on and graduated and came back to Bright Water with a certificate that said she knew what to do with hair.

One time, when auntie Cassie came home for a visit, I asked her about Wild Rose Community College, and she said she couldn't remember but that she had probably gotten bored with school and everything, and just left.

"Where'd you go?"

"Could have gone anywhere."

"What about the American Indian Movement?"

"What about it?"

"Did you go to Calgary?"

"Ask your mother," auntie Cassie told me. "Maybe she'll remember."

What auntie Cassie did remember was the good times that she and my mother had at the college. "We'd have hairdressing parties and invite all the good-looking guys over."

"Is that where mum met dad?"

"He was in wood shop."

"I'll bet you and mum had a lot of boyfriends."

Auntie Cassie laughed and rolled her eyes. "All the boys wanted to be our friends."

While neither my mother nor auntie Cassie could remember why auntie Cassie left Wild Rose Community College or where she went, they could remember other things. And over the years, each time auntie Cassie came home and they stopped being angry with each other, the two of them would stay up and tell stories about the good times they had had at school.

They'd always send me to bed before they started, but their voices carried so well that I could lie under the blankets and listen. There were a number of stories I liked hearing, but the one auntie Cassie liked telling was about the night she and my mother went to dinner at a fancy restaurant.

"The night at The Lodge," auntie Cassie would begin. "You wore that white dress."

"Long time ago," said my mother. "Not much point in digging up the past."

"I wore that red dress," said auntie Cassie, and she would begin to laugh. "You had your hair up, and I had mine down."

"Let it go."

"Remember what he said to me?" said auntie Cassie.

"Not really."

"Baby," said auntie Cassie, lowering her voice until it was almost a grunt. "You look good enough to eat."

"They were both drunk," said my mother. "You have to remember that."

"Yeah, but they wore suits."

The Lodge, according to auntie Cassie, was the fanciest restaurant in Blossom, with real cloth napkins and a waiter who put the wine in a bucket of ice and said he was from Montreal.

"All that yummy food," said auntie Cassie. "And what do they order? Steak and potatoes."

"At least the potatoes were baked," said my mother.

"Yeah," said auntie Cassie. "But if we hadn't been there, they would have ordered fries."

Halfway through dinner, my mother and auntie Cassie went to the bathroom. That's where they came up with the idea.

"Changing dresses wasn't as easy as it looked."

"It was a dumb idea."

"We were lucky no one came in."

"What do you mean?" said my mother. "Everyone came in!"

I tried to imagine my mother and auntie Cassie standing on the toilets in their slips, flinging dresses back and forth over the top of the stall, and I have to admit it sounded pretty funny. There were chairs and couches in the bathroom, and after my mother and auntie Cassie got the dresses straight, they sat down in front of the mirrors and fixed their hair. I tried to imagine a couch in a bathroom, but I couldn't.

"Yours went up," said auntie Cassie. "And mine went down."

When they got back to the table, my mother sat where auntie Cassie had been sitting, and auntie Cassie sat in my mother's seat.

"They didn't even notice," said auntie Cassie. "They just sat there and talked about hockey and what kind of trucks they were going to buy when they graduated."

"They *did* look at our tits."

"Oh, they did that all right."

Sometimes auntie Cassie and my mother laughed a lot when they told the story and sometimes they didn't, but auntie Cassie always did most of the telling.

"We met at nine."

"We met at eight."

"They were on time."

"No, they were late."

I knew the song was from one of my grandfather's musicals, but it wasn't one that I liked all that well. I couldn't remember the name, but everybody in it talked with a funny accent.

"Ah, yes," auntie Cassie sang, "they remember it well."

I figured that the other guy was Franklin, and that after the switch, auntie Cassie wound up with my father and my mother wound up with Franklin. The best part was while they were waiting for dessert. Franklin took my mother's hand and announced that this was the woman he was going to marry.

"That should have been our clue," said auntie Cassie.

"As if we had a clue," said my mother.

I thought the part where my father and Franklin got my mother and auntie Cassie mixed up was pretty funny, and I wondered how long it took them to figure out the switch and what they said when they discovered that they were with the wrong women.

CHAPTER THIRTEEN

━━

Coming off the hill is easy. I don't have to worry about the gears or the clutch or the gas pedal, and I can concentrate on keeping the wheels on the gravel. The truck picks up speed as we come down the slope, but I'm not worried because I know it'll slow down by itself when we hit the flat.

I can see Franklin's truck by the side of the tent, and I want to make a good impression. But we get going a little faster than I expect, and halfway down the hill, the truck slips off the gravel and buries the right side tires in the soft ruts on the shoulder. My father is thrown against the door, and instead of hitting the gas and horsing the truck back onto the road, I hit the brake. Hard. Which is the wrong thing to do.

"Gas!" yells my father.

But it's too late. The tires dig in, the springs bottom out, and the truck pitches forward on its nose. There is a terrible screeching sound as the boxes slide the length of the bed and slam into the back of the cab. This really ruins my concentration, and I stand on the brakes and ride them all the way down. I hold onto the wheel as hard as I can, but the rear end begins to come around, and by the time we hit the flat, the truck is starting to slide sideways.

"Shift," yells my father. The truck lurches forward, crowhops into the grass, and dies. My father waits for the truck to stop moving. "Clutch," he says softly.

I don't let go of the wheel.

"Maybe you should get out and strangle it," my father says. "Just in case it's still alive."

My hands are a little sweaty. So is my face. "It didn't whip my ass."

My father opens the door of the cab and steps onto the running board. "I'm going to clean out my pants," he says. "How about you?"

Franklin Heavy Runner comes out of the tent and waves at my father, and my father waves back. Franklin looks as if he's laughing, but I know this is just an illusion. "You figure you're a real truck driver now?" my father says to me.

"You bet."

My father drops to the ground. "Okay, then how about parking the truck up by the tent?"

"Sure."

"Close as you can get."

"Nothing to it."

My father turns and walks towards Franklin and leaves me alone with the truck. I've made a mistake and I know it, but there's nothing I can do about it. I set the brake. I find the clutch and step on it. I turn the ignition key, and the engine kicks over. So far, so good. I push down on the gas and let up on the clutch. The truck leans forward but doesn't move.

I try it again. This time, I release the brake, and the truck creaks and groans and rolls ahead. The engine starts to whine, but since the distance is short, I figure I'll just stay in first gear all the way. I'm feeling pretty good as I roll by my father. He's standing with Franklin and doesn't seem concerned, though I see him glance at the truck as I pass.

The tent is just ahead, and I begin to circle in so I'll wind up right beside it. I watch the tent stakes in the side mirror and am pleased at how close I've come to them without hitting any.

In the side mirror, I also see my father and Franklin stop what they're doing and begin to run after me, waving their hands. I'm sure they're shouting, but I can't hear anything. I look around, but everything is okay. I stop the truck next to the tent, set the brake, and open the door to the cab.

My father gets to me first. He's out of breath and has to wait before he can begin laughing. "Damn, son," he says. "You are one hell of a driver all right."

Franklin is hard on his heels and isn't smiling. "Where the hell you think you're going!"

My father motions for me to jump down. He puts his arm around my shoulders and walks me to the back of the truck. "I couldn't have put it any closer myself," he says. He unlocks the padlock and throws the door up. "I'm going to start moving the speakers," he says, and he hands me his knife. "Why don't you start cutting it loose."

"What?"

"The tent," says Franklin, and he grabs my arm and drags me around to the side of the truck.

It really isn't my fault. The tent has an overhang and my father didn't call that to my attention. The top of the trailer has hooked the overhang and torn away part of the tent, opening the canvas along one seam. A large flap of the tent is still stuck on the truck.

"You got any ideas about fixing it?"

I'm not sure what I'm supposed to say, so I hold up the knife to see if that's the answer.

"Good idea," says Franklin, and he takes the knife and points it at me. "But it's against the law."

I watch my father back the truck up so that Franklin can cut the flap free.

"Come on," my father shouts to me. "Let's see what else we can break." The speaker boxes are heavy. We get them off the truck and then have to drag them into the tent.

"Leave 'em," says Franklin. "Sherman has to wire them up and pour the concrete for the pads."

We walk back to the truck. Franklin and my father climb into the back and push on the boxes. The two smaller ones move okay, but the two larger boxes don't budge.

"Could have brought a forklift," says Franklin.

"No big deal," says my father. "We open the boxes here and roll them down the ramp."

Inside the first box is a motorcycle. A bright red motorcycle with black flames on the tank. It's not a car, but it's close enough. "I can help," I say.

"He wants to try for the daily double," says my father.

"No way he's getting near them," says Franklin.

"The tent wasn't my fault."

There's another motorcycle in the second box. This one is yellow with red flames.

"What do you think?" says Franklin.

"I think it's a dumb idea," says my father.

"That's why you're not chief."

"Damn straight."

The two smaller boxes are sidecars. They're painted the same as the motorcycles.

"This look like fun?" Franklin shouts at me.

"Neat!"

"It's going to be a real money-maker," says Franklin, and when he says it, he reminds me of my father.

"Yeah," says my father. "Just like the landfill."

My father and Franklin sit down on the grass and settle in with the instructions and the tools. My father gets a large wrench from the toolbox and begins working on the yellow sidecar. I stand around and try to be helpful.

"Indians Days start this weekend," Franklin says, and I guess he's talking to my father because he's not looking at me. "You see my kid around?"

"Nope," says my father.

"That's right," says Franklin. "You know why?"

"'Cause he's smarter than you."

"'Cause he's a lazy shit."

"He's practising for the big race," I tell Franklin. "He's really fast."

"Yeah, well, if you see him again, tell him that the only people in this world who eat are the ones who work for it." Franklin reaches out and whacks my father on the shoulder, hard. "Ain't that right?" My father snaps the wrench at Franklin's head. It comes pretty close, but Franklin doesn't flinch. "Ain't that right?" Franklin says again.

"Unless they can steal it," says my father. "Or get elected chief."

"Fuck you," says Franklin.

"Fuck you," says my father.

Franklin runs his hand over the chrome exhaust pipes. "You think that kid of mine can outrun one of these?" he says to me.

"No."

"Then he's wasting his time, right?" Franklin nods in the general direction of Happy Trails. "Bunch in from Georgia. Maybe they need a smart boy to show them around."

I can see that Franklin's not going to let me forget about the tent right away, so I wander up to the RV park, just in case there's something to do. The park is deserted except for the small group of trailers huddled in one corner. Most of them are a lot older than the one in my grandmother's yard, and a couple of them are pretty beat-up, as if they've been on the road forever. From a distance, they look a little like the covered wagons you see in old westerns.

The band built Happy Trails with the idea that tourists who came west would line up for the opportunity to camp on a Native reserve. It was Franklin's idea, and even my father said it should have worked and that it was a hell of a lot better idea than buying the buffalo or getting into the landfill business. But the year the band opened the RV park, the septic tank stopped working, and the mushy stuff that was supposed to flow in one end of the system and out the other began bubbling up in the washrooms and the showers and gurgling around the Winnebagos and the kingcab pickups and the Volkswagen campers, until most of the parking pads were covered with a soft mustard-coloured slick.

The band tried to get it fixed, but nothing worked. Some of the elders said that there were animals and other creatures in the earth who were tired of having shit dumped on them and that they had finally done something about it. Marvin Simon, who had taken a couple of Native culture courses at the University of Lethbridge, stood up in council and reminded everyone that, in the past, Indians were known to dump their refuse in holes in the ground, and that putting shit into the earth was more or less traditional. Carleton Coombs agreed with Marvin, but pointed out that there was a difference between shit and sewage.

"There's good shit," said Carleton. "And there's bad shit."

Mary Hicks waved Marvin and Carleton off and told the council that all this talk about "you know what" was making her angry, and that if they knew what was good for them, they would close the park, dig up the tank, and apologize. Franklin and the council thanked Marvin and Carleton and Mary for their concerns. Then they voted to add twenty new parking pads to Happy Trails, leave the old tank where it was, buy a new and larger tank, and bury it on the north side of the park.

The second tank worked fine, but the odour from the first backup never quite went away. Families would pull in and start to set up before they noticed the smell. Some stayed the one night, but most left before it got dark. The smell wasn't a particularly bad smell like the stench of rotting meat or an angry skunk. And it wasn't overpowering. It sort of crept up on you, foul and musty like bad breath or a lingering fart. Most days you could hardly notice it, but it was always there.

On the other hand, the view from Happy Trails was spectacular, especially when the late light flattened against the mountains, coral and gold. On those evenings, if you walked out to the point just beyond the park and looked west, you could watch the land swell and stretch, as if there were something large and heavy buried deep in the earth, and if you turned your back to Truth and Bright Water, you could imagine that you were the only person in the entire world.

And the smell didn't keep anyone away from Indian Days. By the weekend, the place would be packed solid with tourists, roaming through the camp and the booths with their cameras, taking pictures of the tipis and the buffalo and the dancers. People from Germany and France and Japan would wander around, smiling, asking the kinds of questions that made you feel embarrassed and important all at the same time.

"That your tent?"

I don't see the girl right away. She's standing in the shadows of one of the trailers.

"Nope," I say. "It belongs to the band."

The girl is younger than me and thin, with dark eyes and long thick hair tied back with a red ribbon. She reminds me of the Tailfeather twins over at Siksika. Or a bird.

"Where you from?"

"Georgia," says the girl.

"Vacation?"

The girl is wearing a long dress that is torn and frayed at the hem and at the sleeves, as if the material has been ripped rather than cut. It looks a little old-fashioned, but is probably a new style that hasn't gotten this far north yet. It's okay, but I don't think it's going to be a hit in Truth or Bright Water.

"I'm looking for my duck," says the girl. "Have you seen her?"

Down at the tent, my father and Franklin are still working on the motorcycles. "This is kind of a dangerous place for a duck," I say.

"Some people think a duck is a silly thing," says the girl. "But it was a duck who helped to create the world."

"Ducks are cool," I tell her. "I have a dog and he's pretty silly."

"When the world was new and the woman fell out of the sky, it was a duck who dove down to the bottom of the ocean and brought up the mud for the dry land."

"Great."

"Some people think it was a muskrat or an otter." The girl steps out of the shadows. In the shade she looks fine, but in the light, she looks strange, pale and transparent. "But it wasn't."

"You met my cousin the other day."

"The boy with the bad eye?"

"That's him."

"Rebecca Neugin," says the girl. "I'm pleased to meet you."

Below the RV park, in the deep grass, someone has built a large log corral with a long orange-plastic mesh chute that runs for half a mile or more across the prairies. There are about six buffalo wandering around in the corral and a couple of men sitting on the fence watching them.

"That your father?"

"No," says the girl. "That's Mr. John Ross. He's got the big red trailer."

"So, your father's the other guy?"

"No, that's Mr. George Guess. He reads books." The girl steps back into the shadows as if there is a line drawn in the ground past which she is not willing to go.

"Indian Days are this weekend. Maybe you'd like me to show you around."

"Watch out for my duck," says the girl, and she turns and disappears among the trailers.

It's almost evening before Franklin and my father match the instructions with the parts. Franklin fills both bikes with gas and oil, and my father gets them started. Franklin hops on the yellow motorcycle. My father gets on the red one.

The two of them ride around in circles for a while, and then Franklin runs his motorcycle up to the tent and shuts it down. He waves to my father, but you can see my father has other ideas. He guns his motor-cycle and takes off across the prairies in a looping run that sends him out to the river and back again. When he gets back to where I'm stand-ing, he has a big grin on his face. "Hop in."

The sidecar is deep, and it feels as though I'm sitting in a bucket. We start off gently, cruising through the grass, my father leaning the bike to the left and then to the right. When we get to Happy Trails, he stops and lets the motorcycle idle. "Hell of an idea," he says, looking over the fence at the asphalt pads and the electrical boxes set on short poles.

"What?"

"Building a graveyard all the way out here."

"It's not a graveyard."

"You smell that?" My father raises his head. "That's the smell of money rotting in the ground." He revs the motorcycle and turns it around. "You want to see what this thing can do?"

"Sure."

"Hold on," he shouts, and we explode out of the grass as though we're on a rocket. I try to see where we're going, but the wind comes so hard I have to close my eyes.

"Yahoo!"

When you're standing on the prairies looking out towards the river, the land looks flat and smooth. On the motorcycle, it feels as if we're jumping canyons and plunging off cliffs. The sidecar pitches and snaps, and I have to hold on with both hands.

I don't open my eyes until my father pulls up beside the tent and turns off the engine.

"Christ," yells Franklin. "It sure as hell isn't for your private amuse-ment."

"Piss off, Franklin."

"You blow the engine," says Franklin, "you own it."

"Blow me!"

Franklin turns away from my father and looks at me. "Your father's an asshole. Did you know that?"

"Nobody calls my son an asshole," yells my father. He is still sitting on the motorcycle, but I can see he's ready to get off.

"I'm calling *you* an asshole!" says Franklin.

"That's better," says my father, and he winks at me. "I am an asshole."

The two of them stay like that for a minute, like runners at the start of a race, and then Franklin turns away and spits on the ground.

"It's fun," says my father, and he gives the motorcycle a pat, "but it's never going to work."

"The guns come tomorrow," says Franklin. "It'll work."

"Sure," says my father, and he turns around and looks over at Happy Trails. "You're full of good ideas."

My father and Franklin drive the motorcycles up to the tent. I close the truck up and wait.

"You won't need the truck for the guns," Franklin says as they walk back. "The boxes should fit in a car."

"What's your point?"

"Shouldn't cost as much," says Franklin.

My father shrugs. "It costs what it costs."

"Tribe's not one of your welfare whores."

"I don't know," says my father. "Herd of scrawny buffalo, a beat-to-shit tent, and a mostly empty RV park. Looks like somebody's screwing it real good."

Franklin measures the distance to my father. "You can't see shit, Elvin."

"Got no trouble smelling it," says my father, and he climbs in the cab and starts the engine.

I climb in quickly, but he's already pulling away before I can get the door closed. I hear Franklin yell something over the roar of the truck, but I can't tell what it is. My father doesn't look at Franklin at all. He looks straight out the window. As the truck rolls through the prairie grass, my father turns to me. "You want to see how close I can come to those motorcycles?"

"Not particularly."

"You got a favourite?"

"What?"

"Motorcycle. You got a favourite motorcycle?"

"I don't know," I say. "Maybe the red one."

"Yeah," says my father, and he shifts into second and presses the accelerator to the floor. "That's my favourite one, too."

I think he's just kidding. But as the truck picks up speed, I look at his face, and I can see that he's serious. "It's okay," I say.

"UUUUUWHHEEEEE!"

I look in the side mirror. Franklin is standing in the grass, watching the truck bear down on the motorcycles. He doesn't move, and he doesn't wave his hands.

"I won't mind if we don't hit it."

Just as the motorcycles vanish under the hood of the truck, my father whips the wheel hard to one side. The truck slowly leans over, picks up its feet like a dancing elephant, lumbers past the motorcycles and the tent, and makes its way back up to the road. At the top of the rise over-looking Bright Water, he pulls the truck onto the shoulder and stops. I look around, but I don't see the buffalo anywhere.

"You know what's wrong with this world?" he asks me.

I figure he's testing to see if I've been listening. "Sure," I say. "Whites."

My father lights a cigarette. "Who told you that?"

"You did."

"Indians," says my father. "What's wrong with this world is Indians."

"Indians?"

"'Cause they got no sense of humour." He sucks on the cigarette and lets the smoke drift out of his mouth. "You know why Indians smoke?"

"This a joke?"

"'Cause we like getting burned."

"Lum smokes, but I don't."

"Franklin's a son of a bitch," says my father. "You know how he got elected chief?"

"He won the election?"

"He bought votes." I don't say anything. I can't tell if my father is angry or sad. And I don't want to ask. "Ten bucks," he says. "That's what a vote was worth."

"Lum and him don't get along too well."

"A lousy ten bucks."

The buffalo appear out of nowhere and begin moving towards the truck. Maybe they recognize it. Maybe they're just curious. They come slowly. And then they stop and turn back into rocks.

"Come on," says my father, and he gets out of the truck.

He walks over to the fence, takes off his hat, and throws in a handful of pebbles. "Watch this," he says. My father shakes his hat at the buffalo. They don't move. He shakes his hat again. "You see that?"

"Yeah," I say. "They're too smart for that trick."

"You know all about tricks, do you?"

"Cows will come running," I say. "Horses, too. But buffalo are smart."

My father shakes the hat some more. Nothing. "Buffalo are stupid," says my father. "The ones who stayed behind are stupid." He dumps the pebbles out of his hat. "Just like Indians." He sits down in the grass, leans against a fence post, and pulls his hat down over his eyes. The sun is still above the mountains, but it's getting late and I want to head home.

"Auntie Cassie's back," I say, hoping he's not planning on taking a nap.

The buffalo stay where they are. A large calf takes a few steps towards us and then thinks better of it and backs up.

"She travels all over the world," I say. "She's got some great stories."

At first, I think my father has gone to sleep. I don't hear him the first time because of the wind and because his voice is too low. "Are they still there?" he whispers.

"Who?"

"The buffalo."

"Yeah," I say.

My father nods his head, but if I hadn't been looking right at him, I wouldn't have seen it.

"Ready?" he says.

"Sure," I say.

Suddenly, my father leaps to his feet and shouts and waves his arms back and forth. "Bang," he yells. "Bangbangbangbangbangbang!" The buffalo back up a few steps and stop. My father raises his arm and works it like a rifle. "Bone-hard stupid," he says. "That's why it won't work."

"What?"

My father brushes the dirt off his jeans. "Franklin's new idea."

"The motorcycles?"

"When Franklin bought that herd two years ago, there were over one hundred and fifty head. You see one hundred and fifty buffalo now?"

"What happened to the rest of them?"

"Disappeared," says my father. "They just disappeared."

"I guess that's not too good for the tourist business."

My father picks up a rock and sidearms it at one of the fence posts. "You know why tourists come out here?" he says.

"Indians?"

"Nope."

"Buffalo?"

"Hell, roadkill is more exciting."

"The mountains?"

"The space," says my father. "They travel around the world to Bright Water because they've never seen space like this."

"I wouldn't mind a job where I had to travel," I say.

"And it scares the shit out of them." My father walks back to the truck and unzips his pants. He stands by the rear wheels, and as he pees, he waves his cock from side to side, splashing the tires and the side of the truck. "This is the way we should have signed those treaties." My father shakes himself and zips his pants. "You want to drive?"

"We're off the reserve," I say.

"So?"

"I don't have a licence."

My father smiles and throws me the keys. "It's okay," he says. "Neither do I."

I slide into the driver's seat and glance at the shifting pattern on the knob. My father leans forward on the dash and looks out the window.

"You know her?"

I don't see her at first. And then I do. The girl from Happy Trails. She stands perfectly still in the high grass, facing into the wind. "She's from Georgia," I say. "She's looking for a duck."

"Well, that's a start," says my father, and he reaches over and turns the key in the ignition. I don't have the clutch in and the truck lurches forward. "Take your time," he says. "Show her the buffalo."

I let the clutch out slowly and get the truck rolling before I try to give it any gas, and this works pretty well. I don't stall it, and it doesn't jump around too much. And once I'm safely in second gear, there's nothing to do but watch the road and steer. Up ahead, there's a dead porcupine by the side of the road. But I'm in third gear already, and we pass it by without even slowing down.

CHAPTER FOURTEEN

━━━

It's late by the time we get back to Truth. As we make the turn at the level crossing and come back along Division South, I tell my father he can just drop me off at Santucci's.

"You worried or something?"

"Nope," I say. "It's easier for you to turn around there."

My father swings the truck in tight against the curb. I open the door and start to get out. "You forgetting something?" he says.

I look at him for a clue.

"Don't look at me," he says. "I'm not going to tell you."

"This about the tent?"

"Man's got to look out for himself."

"I told Franklin I was sorry," I say.

My father sighs and reaches into his pocket. He takes out a wad of money and pulls a ten off the top. "What's this look like?"

"Ten dollars."

"Son," says my father, "you're an aboriginal genius." He sticks the ten in my shirt pocket and lights a cigarette. "So, what you going to do with all that money?"

I take the ten out of my pocket and fold it up nice and neat. "Maybe I'll buy a vote," I say.

"You got a smart mouth." My father smiles. "I'll buy three."

"You can't vote three times."

My father takes two more tens out of his pocket and drops them in my lap. "The hell I can't."

I don't know if he's fooling or not, so I let the tens stay in my lap.

"Don't spend it all in one place." My father blows a jet of smoke against the windshield. It hits the glass and curls back into the cab. "You have a good time today?"

"Yeah," I say. "The motorcycles were fun."

"Yeah, they were."

I open the door and jump down. "Maybe I could help you tomorrow."

"I can hardly afford me."

"I could drive."

My father smiles and revs the engine. "Today was fun," he says. "Tomorrow is business."

"You going to get Franklin's guns?"

"Franklin can get his own damn guns," says my father. "Got to take the work that pays."

The sun is behind the mountains now. The sky darkens down, the shadows stretch out, and for that moment, just before evening finds its way into night, the air freshens, the colours swell, and the prairies burn with light.

"Tell your mother I said it was okay." My father gives me a wink and shuts the door.

If I'm really lucky, my mother will be working late, fixing someone's hair, and I'll be able to waltz through the door, say my hellos, and slip into the back before she notices that the light has disappeared, but when I get there, I can see that the lights in the shop are out, and this is bad news. It means my mother is done for the day and is in the back waiting for me. I can tell her that Lum and I were down by the river, and we just lost track of time. I use this a lot and am not sure if it works anymore. Or I could tell her the truth, that I went to Bright Water with my father to help him deliver four speakers and two motorcycles with sidecars.

Telling the truth is always chancy. My mother might not be upset at all, but this is not a sure thing. I have seen her get upset over nothing, and other times, she lets serious matters go by without so much as giving them a glance.

When we were living in Bright Water, my father had a trick of coming home late or drunk or both. He would walk up on the front porch and sit down on the bench. Sometimes he would sit there silently. Sometimes he would sit there and sing to himself.

"Dad's home."

"Eat your food."

Some evenings, my mother would open the door for him, and he would wander in as if he had been lost all that time in the dark. Some evenings, she would tell me to open the door. But most of the time, she would sit on the couch and watch television and leave him to himself on the porch.

"What about dad?"

"He can come in whenever he wants."

I don't know why my father stayed on the porch. Maybe he was embarrassed because he had been drinking. Maybe he was angry that my mother wouldn't come out of the house and help him in.

"How about I go out and see if he's okay?"

"How about you finish your food."

My mother would sit in the house and my father would sit on the porch until it got dark and the air cooled. Then he would get up and walk to the garage.

As I open the door, I reach up and hold the bell. I slide through the door and close it behind me as quietly as I can and stand in the shop and wait. Nothing. I listen for the television, but I don't hear it.

The place is spooky. No sound. No lights. I make my way to the back, and when I get there, everything is dead black. I feel for the wall and the light switch, and as I do, I hear a movement in front of me, and before I can say or do anything, something large and heavy strikes me in the chest and I go down. I probably yell, but the first thing I hear is Soldier.

"Rrrruuuufff!"

"Hey!"

"Grrrrr!"

"Knock it off."

I get up and find the light. Soldier pulls his ears down and does his little doggie dance.

"So, you got home okay." Soldier wiggles to the couch and settles in against the coffee table. "And I suppose you think I'm happy to see you."

There's no note, and the only thing in the refrigerator that I can heat, without having to cook it, is a small bowl of brown beans. I look in the oven just to be sure, and then I butter up a couple of pieces of bread and make myself a bean sandwich. With ketchup.

I flip through the channels. There's an old western, a hockey game, and Bugs Bunny. "How about it?" I ask Soldier. "Indians or cartoons?"

It's not a very good western. It's all about some white guy who wants to be an Indian. The regular Indians put him through a ceremony where they force sticks through his chest and make him run around this pole dragging a couple of buffalo skulls behind him. I look, but I can't see if the skulls have any holes in them. The guy staggers through the ceremony without passing out or throwing up and gets to marry the chief's daughter. There's some nice scenery and some okay music.

There was a pattern to those evenings. My father would sit on the porch until it got dark. Then he would go to the garage, open all the doors and windows, turn on the saw, and crank up the radio as far as it would go. Even with the windows in my bedroom closed, the noise went through the house like a hard wind. I knew my mother could hear it, and I guess my father knew she could hear it, too.

I always thought that she would get tired of the noise and would go out and tell him to keep it down. That's what she told me whenever I played my radio too loud or had the television set too high. Some nights, the noise was worse than others, and Soldier would sneak into my room, climb on the bed, and lie across my feet.

"Don't be such a wuss," I'd tell him. "He's not mad at you."

I don't know what my father did in the garage, but he would run the saw for hours. I wouldn't be able to sleep, so I would lie in bed and listen to the pitch of the motor. Every so often you would hear the blade slow down and dig in, and I would imagine him standing in sawdust and wood chips, slowly cutting things into pieces.

It's a little boring being in the shop alone. Soldier is asleep, so there's no one to talk with. The movie is boring, too, but the buffalo skulls that the guy drags around behind him remind me of what my father said, and that gets me thinking about the skull that Lum and I found.

"What do you figure?" I ask Soldier. "You remember a bullet hole?"

Soldier grunts and his sides quiver, but he's just dreaming.

"You stay here," I say. "I'll check it out."

Climbing up is easy, but when I get out on the rafter, I can't see the skull. I crawl along the rafter all the way to the middle, but the skull isn't there. I go back and try another rafter. Same thing.

I find the skull on the third rafter, but by then, I'm feeling uneasy and I'm thinking that the skull may have been moving around in the dark, playing a game.

I check the ribbon. One end is hooked to the nail and the other end is still tied to the skull, so there's no way it can get loose. I can't see very well, but as I run my hands around it, I find a hole in the side of the skull. The hole is not exactly round. It's more jagged and uneven. I am sitting on the rafter running my finger around the hole when I hear the front doorbell. Soldier hears it, too, and he wakes up and begins barking.

"It's just us," my mother shouts.

I start back along the rafter as fast as I can. I'm hoping that my mother stops in the shop and cleans the sink or checks the hair dryer or something, but she keeps coming. Just as I get to the end of the rafter and put my foot on the ladder, she passes beneath me, and I have to pull back into the shadows. Auntie Cassie is with her.

"What a good dog," says my mother, and Soldier goes all happy and snorty.

Auntie Cassie walks around the room with her hands on her hips. "Jesus, Helen," she says. "Where are the windows?"

My mother scratches Soldier's ears and rubs his chest. "You want some coffee?"

"Elvin help out at all?"

I'm stuck, and there isn't much I can do about it. I try to get comfortable, but sitting on the rafter is hard. The board is skinny, and it cuts into my butt. I can feel parts of me going to sleep.

"There's tea, too," my mother says.

Auntie Cassie sits down in the chair. Soldier gets up and goes over to her and begins sniffing.

"So," says my mother, "you going to say anything to him?"

"Like what?" says auntie Cassie.

"Maybe he'll want to help."

Soldier starts licking auntie Cassie's hands. He does it to everybody, and I figure licking's one of his favourite things. The bean sandwich in my stomach begins to move around. I shift my butt and try to get comfortable, but each time I move, dust floats off the rafters and tumbles into the light.

"There's always someone who wants to tell you how to run your life."

"No danger of that," says my mother. "Don't know anyone who can tell you a thing."

"Sure as hell no point making the same mistake twice," says auntie Cassie.

Some nights, especially when it was warm, my father would sleep in the garage and only come into the house in the morning for breakfast.

"Hi, dad."

"Yeah."

"What were you doing?"

"What?"

"In the garage. What were you making?"

"Breakfast ready yet?"

"Maybe next time I could help you."

"There any coffee?"

You would expect that they would fight, that whatever sent my father to the garage and kept my mother in the house would be too much for either of them to contain. But they didn't. At least, not that I ever saw. My father would come in, sit at the table, and wait to be fed. And my mother would feed him.

The conversation is just getting interesting when Soldier stops licking auntie Cassie's hands and goes back to the couch. He sniffs at the couch and then looks around the room, as if he's lost something.

"If it were me," says my mother, "I'd say something."

"That's because you're a romantic," says auntie Cassie.

"Nothing wrong with a little romance," says my mother.

"Lasts about as long as cut flowers," says auntie Cassie.

Soldier drags his nose across the floor, looking like a bloodhound from a cartoon. When he gets directly below me, he sits down and looks up. His ears arch, and he begins making low whining sounds in his throat.

My mother stands up and goes to the closet. "What are you going to do now?"

"What I always do," says auntie Cassie.

My mother is in the closet for a moment, and when she comes out, she has a suitcase in her hand. "Then you might as well take this," she says.

When Soldier sees the suitcase, he stands up and trots over to my mother. He sniffs at the case and tries to reach it with his tongue. It's no big deal. I've seen the case before, and I know what's in it.

"Here you go," says my mother, and she holds the suitcase out to auntie Cassie.

Baby clothes.

I've opened the case lots of times, and inside are my old baby clothes. I found it one year at the back of the closet when I was looking for Christmas presents. I thought that my mother had put the baby clothes in the suitcase just to throw me off from finding something more inter-esting, so I checked to see if there was a false bottom or something hidden in the lining or the pockets.

Some of the clothes are really stupid, and some of them are cute in a goofy sort of way, but I can't remember ever wearing any of them. A few are still in cellophane wrapping as if they have never been used.

"I know it wasn't your fault," says my mother.

Auntie Cassie doesn't move. She stays in the chair. I can't see exactly what she is doing, but I can feel that the two of them are thinking about fighting. "Then what have you got to be angry about?" says auntie Cassie. She says it casually, as if she's checking on the time.

"Nothing," says my mother. "It's your life."

"Absolutely," says auntie Cassie.

My mother walks to the chair and puts the suitcase on auntie Cassie's lap. "So, here it is," she says.

"You know what you need?"

"Keep it down," says my mother, and she looks back at my bedroom.

"What you need," whispers auntie Cassie, "is a man."

My mother sits down and leans against the back of the couch and closes her eyes. "Had one."

"I didn't mean Elvin," says auntie Cassie.

"Neither did I," says my mother.

What I can't figure out is why my mother is giving auntie Cassie my baby clothes. Or why auntie Cassie would want them.

"Don't you think fifteen years is a long time to carry a grudge?"

"Sixteen," says my mother. "And nobody's carrying anything."

"This has nothing to do with him, you know," says auntie Cassie.

"So, why'd you come back?"

I can't see my mother's face, but I can hear her voice just fine, and I know I won't be coming down any time soon.

"Well, saying 'I'm sorry' isn't going to change things, is it?" says auntie Cassie.

"A little late for that now," says my mother.

"Don't worry," says auntie Cassie. "I'm not going to stay."

Every so often, when I get home from school and am bored, I watch soap operas, and this is the kind of conversation you hear a lot.

"You giving up?"

"Why not?" says auntie Cassie.

"What about Mia?"

"Gave up the first time." Auntie Cassie stretches her legs out and leans back. She sounds tired and ready to call a truce. "Second time should be a snap."

"I'm sorry about High Prairie," says my mother.

"No news is good news," says auntie Cassie. "You know what I want?"

"Yeah." My mother yawns and settles into the couch. She slips off her shoes and puts her feet under one of the cushions. "Dark chocolate truffles."

"My hair washed," says auntie Cassie. "I want my hair washed."

My mother yawns again. "Wash your own hair."

"Not the same," says auntie Cassie. "Tell you what. You wash mine and I'll wash yours. Like the old days."

"Forget it." My mother pulls her feet out from under the cushion and sits up. "So, what are you really going to do now?"

"Keep looking." Auntie Cassie stands up. "Come on," she says. "Let's play in the sink."

"It's eleven," says my mother. "Nobody likes to sleep on a wet head."

"So," says auntie Cassie, "who wants to go to bed?"

"I do," says my mother.

"Nothing there but cold sheets and a lumpy pillow," says auntie Cassie.

"Yeah," says my mother, "but look at the alternative."

One morning, my father came in from the garage and sat down at the table and waited for my mother to get up and feed him, as she always did.

"I'm hungry," said my father.

"Cereal's in the cupboard," said my mother.

"You still mad at me?"

"Spoons are in the drawer."

My father sat at the table and looked at my mother, and my mother sat on the couch with her back to my father. Neither one of them said a thing.

Finally, my father stood up and got his coat. "Nothing like a good breakfast," he said, "to start the day."

The next week, he packed his stuff in his truck and moved across the river to Truth.

I don't come down until I hear the water running in the sink. Soldier is sitting next to the suitcase, his head cocked so far to one side, it looks as if it's broken and ready to fall off.

"Baby clothes," I tell him, and I shake the suitcase just to be sure. Soldier sniffs at it and begins to lick one edge. "Leave it alone."

Soldier follows me to the bedroom and works his way under the bed. I put on my pajamas and mess up my hair just in case my mother comes in to check on me. I push the pillows around until I'm comfortable, and just as I'm falling asleep, I hear auntie Cassie start to sing. She sounds a lot like my mother. And over the sound of the water hitting the sides of the sink and the rise and fall of auntie Cassie's voice, I can hear Soldier snoring. It reminds me of those nights in Bright Water, lying in bed, listening to my father's saw trying to tear its way through hard wood.

CHAPTER FIFTEEN

———

Auntie Cassie has travelled all over the world, and whenever she gets to a new place, she sends us a postcard. We have postcards from places like New Zealand and Mexico, France and Japan. And once a year, sometime in July, she sends me a present. A boomerang from Australia. A box of seashells from Hawaii. A sweatshirt from Los Angeles.

The summer that I turned nine, she sent me a doll with dark hair and a dark blue velvet dress. The box was from Germany and it had a label on it that said it was insured for one hundred dollars, so I knew that the doll was expensive, but I wasn't sure what I was supposed to do with it.

"What am I supposed to do with this?"

"Play with it," said my mother.

"Girls play with dolls."

"Nothing that says boys can't play with dolls, too."

I made the mistake of telling Lum what auntie Cassie had sent me.

"Maybe she'll send you a skirt next time."

"She probably bought presents for a bunch of people and got them mixed up."

"Next time we play house," said Lum, "you can be the mum."

The following year, she sent me a box with a mirror in the lid and little drawers that pulled out. I showed it to my mother.

"You can put your stuff in it."

"Like what?"

"Anything that will fit."

"It's pink."

I didn't say anything about the box to Lum, but I told my mother to talk to auntie Cassie and get the problem straightened out. Before it got worse. The next year, I got a Swiss Army pocket knife that my mother said I couldn't use until I was older, and the year after that, auntie Cassie sent me a book.

"Did you talk to auntie Cassie?"

"When we were girls, this was one of our favourite books."

"Well, guess what?"

"What?"

"I'm not a girl."

"You'll like it," my mother said. "*Anne of Green Gables* is a classic."

Besides the knife, the present I liked best was a black bamboo flute from Japan. I got pretty good at it, but it hurt Soldier's ears, and one day, when I wasn't looking, he dragged it under the bed and chewed the ends off.

"How come she always sends me presents in July?"

"What's wrong with that?"

"Most people send presents at Christmas or for birthdays."

"You mean like your father?"

"But my birthday is in April." All in all, I didn't mind getting presents in July. They were always interesting. And they were always a surprise.

CHAPTER SIXTEEN

The first thing I do when I wake up is go to the kitchen and call Lum. The place is a mess, and I have to step over blankets and pillows and magazines. There are photographs all over the floor and on the kitchen table. My mother's quilt is piled up on the couch. The suitcase is open, and the baby clothes are arranged in little stacks next to a couple of wine glasses.

I let the phone ring eight times, and then I get Franklin. "Hi . . ." I say. "Is Lum there?"

"Shit!"

"I'm really sorry about the tent."

Franklin makes a hard sound with his lips, but he doesn't hang up the phone the way he sometimes does.

"Hey, cousin," says Lum. "Hear you're a driving genius."

"Wasn't my fault."

"Yeah, that's what the old man said," and Lum laughs. "Those were his exact words."

In the background, I can hear Franklin shouting about something. Lum's voice drops, and I have trouble hearing him.

"Tomorrow," says Lum, and when he says it, he sounds mysterious like a character in a detective movie. "Meet me at Happy Trails."

"This about a job?"

"Just be there," he says. "And bring *it* with you."

I wait for Lum to finish, but before either of us can say anything else, the phone clicks, and the line goes dead.

Some of the photographs on the table are ones I haven't seen before. A bunch of them are of auntie Cassie standing next to things like castles or a boat or a river or a large rock. There are a couple of older black and white photographs of auntie Cassie and my mother with two men. One of the guys is my father.

There is also a picture of a newborn baby. Its eyes are closed and its face is squished in. I figure it's me, only the hair doesn't look quite right. In all my other baby pictures, I have a head of black hair that sticks up in all directions, but in this picture, I don't have much hair at all, and it all lies down neatly against my head. On the back of the photograph, someone has tried to write something but the paper is slick and most of what was there has disappeared. All I can make out is a "J" and an "L" and the number one.

Soldier comes out of the bedroom, wanders over to the couch, and shoves his nose into the quilt.

"Watch out for the fish hooks," I tell him.

"What fish hooks?"

I don't startle easily, but I wasn't expecting anyone to be hiding under the quilt.

"Mom?"

"Close enough." Auntie Cassie sits up. Her hair is all pushed off to one side and her eyes look puffy.

"You guys have a party last night?"

Auntie Cassie wraps the quilt around her and closes her eyes. "I'd like some fresh-squeezed orange juice and some dry toast, please."

"If I made a mess like this, mom would really be upset."

Auntie Cassie keeps her eyes shut, but she's smiling now. Soldier puts his head on her lap in case she feels like petting something. I go to the cupboard and hold up the two boxes of cereal we have so auntie Cassie can see them. "You want the bear or the tiger?"

Auntie Cassie opens one eye. "Oh, God," she says.

"It's all we have."

"The bear."

I get the milk and a bowl and a spoon. "Where's mom?"

"Captured by Indians."

By the time I bring her the bowl of cereal, both of auntie Cassie's eyes are more or less open. "Is this me?" I ask, and I hand her the photograph.

Auntie Cassie looks at the photograph for a long time as if she's trying to remember something. She is still looking at it when the front doorbell jingles. "Wake up," my mother shouts from the shop.

Auntie Cassie pulls the quilt over her head. "Tell her I left," she says.

But it's too late. My mother swoops into the kitchen with an armload of gladiolas and carnations. Most of them are dead or dying. She drops the flowers in the sink and looks at auntie Cassie.

"Dawn of the Dead," she says. "I saw the movie."

Auntie Cassie closes her eyes and flops against the cushions. "He's making me eat bear cereal," she says.

"How about some nice runny eggs," says my mother, who is happier than I've seen her in a long time.

Auntie Cassie pushes the quilt out of the way and stands up. She's looking worse rather than better.

"Bathroom," says my mother, and she points in the general direction with one hand and begins sorting through the flowers with the other.

"You and auntie Cassie get drunk last night?"

"Nope," says my mother, as she plucks dead blossoms off the stems. "Just Cassie."

"She okay?"

My mother looks towards the bathroom and nods. "But she's going to be a while."

I go and get dressed, and by the time I get my cereal, my mother has arranged all the flowers in a vase.

"What do you think?"

"Great."

"There's nothing like flowers."

"How about money?"

"Have you found a job yet?"

I pick up the photograph and hold it out so my mother can see it. "Is that me?"

My mother leaves the flowers for a moment. She looks at the photograph, and now, she's not as happy as she was before. "Who knows," she says.

"Is it Lum?"

"No."

My mother turns back to her flowers. Auntie Cassie doesn't come out of the bathroom, so I have to forget about brushing my teeth and rinse my mouth in the kitchen sink. I put the photograph in my pocket. I don't think auntie Cassie or my mother will notice that it's missing, especially with the mess, but if they do, I can always give it back. I can hear auntie Cassie in the bathroom and what I hear doesn't sound good. My mother is sweeping the floor now and humming to herself. She has her back to me, but I can see her face in the mirror.

"Did you and auntie Cassie have a good time?"

"If you see your father," my mother says, "tell him to give me a call."

"Is it about the car?"

My mother puts the broom down and begins folding towels. "Just tell him to call."

Today is one of those rare days in Truth and Bright Water when the wind is not blowing. In the west, the chinook arch is beginning to form, so it won't last. But for now, the air is absolutely still.

Soldier stays right by my side all the way past the tracks and only breaks away for a run when we're deep in the prairie grass. The church doesn't look much different. A little more of it is missing now. Soldier climbs up the side of the coulee and heads for the east side. The kite is gone, and I don't see the green platform anywhere.

"Find the door," I tell Soldier, but he has other things on his mind. So, I do it myself. I put out my hand and walk straight forward. Then I back up and move a little to my right. Then I do the same thing to my left. I figure if I look hard enough and get just the right angle, I'll be able to spot it.

Soldier's ears come up suddenly, and he begins to growl.

"What is it?" Soldier takes two steps forward, backs up, and then heads out through the grass, snorting and sniffing. "Soldier!"

If it's a rabbit, he could be gone all day.

"Soldier!"

I can't see him now, and I can only guess what he's found. I hope it's not another skunk. I look back at the church and am thinking of ways to get Monroe's attention, when I hear Soldier bark. It's not a worried bark. It's an excited bark, and it sounds as if he's found something interesting. "If it's black, leave it alone!"

Soldier keeps barking. I give up on the church for the moment and go looking for him. "Nobody loves a stinky dog!"

Suddenly, the barking stops. I wait, expecting that Soldier is just catching his breath, but he doesn't bark again. "Soldier!" All you can see is the grass in all directions. "Where the hell are you!"

"Right here," says a voice behind me, and out of the grass pops Monroe Swimmer. "Where's your suit?" Monroe adjusts his goggles and takes the snorkel out of his mouth.

I guess I just stand there and stare.

"Come on in," he says. "It's really warm, once you get used to it." And he turns and disappears in the grass.

I move forward cautiously, and what I see is a little weird. The grass has been matted down in a large semicircle. Monroe is lying in the centre on his stomach. All he has on is a swimming suit. Soldier is lying next to him.

"You can be the shark," says Monroe.

I take one step back.

Monroe rolls over on his side and begins moving his arms above his head. "Help, help," he yells. "A shark!"

Soldier whines and digs at the ground.

"You said to come back today," I say.

"Aha," says Monroe, "a talking shark."

"You said there might be a job."

Monroe's suit is bright red with palm trees and white clouds. There's no one around to see me, so I squat down in the grass.

"Nothing like a swim before breakfast." Monroe is on his feet. He brushes himself off, pushes the goggles onto his forehead, and kicks off his fins. "'Wynken, Blynken, and Nod one night / Sailed off in a wooden shoe.' Do you know that one?"

"Sort of."

"Eugene Field," says Monroe. "'Sailed on a river of crystal light / Into a sea of dew.'"

"Neat."

"'And the children of Israel went into the midst of the sea upon the dry ground.'" Monroe takes off the goggles and the snorkel, picks up the beach towel, and wraps it around his shoulders. "You have a Bible?"

"I think my mother does."

"'Like little wanton boys that swim on bladders, / This many summers in a sea of glory.'" Monroe looks at the church. "God, I love Shakespeare. Don't you?"

"He wrote a bunch of plays."

"Absolutely," says Monroe. "Look at that." He stretches out his arms. The towel falls off his shoulders as he turns in a circle. "The sea," he says in a whisper.

Soldier is still lying in the grass. He watches Monroe as Monroe turns round and round.

"'A sea of grass.'"

"What happened to the wheelchair?"

"'Home is the sailor'" — Monroe gathers up the snorkel and the mask and the fins and the towel, and heads for the church — "'home from sea.'"

Soldier is out of the grass, hard on Monroe's heels. Monroe walks to the east side of the church, reaches into the prairie and the sky, opens the door, and both of them disappear inside.

I have to admit that Monroe is beginning to worry me, and I'm starting to think that cleaning boxcars or working for Franklin might be okay. I've just about decided to head back to town and check in at the job gate with Wally Preston when I hear a noise behind me. It sounds a little like my grandmother when she decides to be a bear.

But it's not her.

It's the Cousins.

They stand in the grass at the edge of the coulee with just their head and shoulders showing. They don't look particularly friendly, and since no one feeds them, I have to figure that they're hungry.

"Good dogs," I say as softly and as sweetly as I can, in case they can't see all that well and have me confused with Miles Deardorf. I glance over my shoulder. I think about calling Soldier, but I don't want to startle the dogs and get them upset.

"Good dogs."

I measure the distance to the church, and it's pretty clear that even if I got a good jump on them, and even if I knew where the door was, I would never reach it before they caught me. What I need is a stick. If they're not feeling friendly, I could use it to keep them away. If they were just looking for someone to play with, I could toss it over the side of a cliff.

"Good dogs."

I have to settle for a clump of grass pulled out by the roots, and when

I look up, the Cousins have vanished. They could be lying down, taking a nap, but I'm pretty sure I can hear them moving through the deep grass on their bellies.

"Come on," I say, and I shake the clump of grass. "Let's get the stick." And I toss the clump away from the church.

Nothing.

I pull up another clump of grass, just in case, and starting walking backwards slowly towards the church. I'm about halfway there when one of the dogs appears off to my left. How it got there so fast, I have no idea, but I can see it isn't interested in chasing sticks. Its ears are pulled in tight to its head, and its tail is dragging on the ground.

"Soldier!"

A second dog comes out of the grass to my right. Neither dog makes a sound, and they don't take their eyes off me for a second.

"Soldier!"

I don't even notice the third dog until it rises out of the grass in front of me. I back up a little faster, hoping to reach the side of the church before the dogs completely surround me.

"Hey, Monroe!"

The Cousins stop for a moment and wait.

"Open the door!"

And then they come at me in a rush, whistling through the grass. I throw the clump at the dog in front of me. I don't even come close, and I can see that running is the only thing left to do. I manage a couple of steps before I bang my shin on something hard and go down in a heap, and before I can turn around, the dogs are on me. And past me.

"Is this what you're waiting for?" Monroe is standing on the porch of the church with a string of hot dogs in one hand. Soldier is standing beside him.

The Cousins leap up onto the porch and begin wiggling around Monroe's legs.

"Take it easy," says Monroe. "There's plenty for everybody." And he begins dancing around the porch, waving the hot dogs about like sparklers, while the dogs jump and snap at them.

It's the platform. Or at least it feels like the platform. Only it's no longer bright green. Now it's the same colour as the grass and almost impossible to see. My leg is really throbbing, and I plan to tell Monroe that he can't leave things like this lying around.

By the time I limp to the church, Monroe has handed out all the hot dogs, and Soldier and the Cousins are busy wolfing them down. "You got to watch them," Monroe says. "If their blood sugar drops down too far, they get cranky."

Suddenly, the Cousins bolt off the porch and begin racing around in circles in the grass. Soldier stays by me for a moment and watches. Then he chases after them. The dogs flow back and forth across the prairies, trailing behind one another like the ties on a kite tail.

"Boy," says Monroe, "look at all those smiles."

"Remember that platform you built in the grass and painted green?"

Monroe shakes his head and looks sad. "It was more difficult than I thought."

"Why'd you paint it yellow? It's really hard to see."

"I didn't. I keep painting it green." Monroe goes to the porch railing. The kite string is still tied to the post. It heads off into the sky, vibrating as if the kite is still attached. I look, but there's nothing to see. Monroe tugs on the string a couple of times and then lets it snap back. "Peer pressure. There's not much you can do about it."

"You mean the kite's still there?"

"'He is the greatest artist who has embodied, in the sum of his works, the greatest number of the greatest ideas.'"

"So, what about the platform?"

Monroe shrugs. "Some of the ideas work, and some of them don't."

The dogs are on the run. They swing past the porch, take a hard left, and head towards the river. Monroe watches the dogs as they race through the grass, tussling and barking. Soldier is barking the loudest, and I can tell he's having a great time. At the edge of the coulee, the Cousins suddenly change direction and plunge into a stand of chokecherries. Soldier is right behind them.

"Stop him." Monroe puts his hand on my shoulder. "Call him back."

"What?"

"Quick. Call him back!"

I'm too late. Before I can do anything, Soldier has disappeared into the bushes.

"Soldier!"

For a moment, you can hear the faint sound of barking, and then there is nothing. Monroe is off the porch in a flash. I'm right behind when I hear a sharp cry, and Soldier bursts out of the chokecherries.

"Soldier!"

He turns to the sound of my voice and loses his footing. He goes down in a heap, bounces up, and scrambles over to me.

"Okay, okay," I say, and I squat down next to him and begin to pet him. He's shaking so bad I think he's going to rattle himself apart. And then he begins to pee. "Hey, watch it!"

Monroe kneels next to Soldier and runs his fingers through his fur. One side of Soldier's neck is covered with blood. Monroe looks at me and shakes his head. "Bring him inside."

Monroe heads for the church. I watch the bushes for the Cousins, but all I see is a large jackrabbit standing in the grass. It's the kind that Soldier loves to chase. He never catches them, but that's part of the game.

"Look at that," I say, trying to take Soldier's mind off his neck. I give him a pat to tell him it's okay if he wants to chase it a little, but he doesn't move. He lies next to me, pulls his ears back, and begins to growl. The rabbit is too far away to hear anything, but it turns to us anyway. Soldier jumps to his feet and begins barking. But it's too late.

I don't even see the dogs. They simply appear in the grass, three black streaks. The rabbit leaps and turns once, right into the jaws of the first dog and is crushed and torn in half. Soldier and I watch as the dogs drag the rabbit away. Just as they get to the edge of the coulee, Soldier growls and barks once. The Cousins stop and look at us for a moment. And then they slide into the bushes and disappear.

Monroe is in the kitchen, heating something on the stove. "Wash his neck with this." The cut is long but not too deep. Soldier waits patiently while I clean the wound.

Monroe has been busy decorating the place. The rugs have been arranged on the floor, and the walls have been hung with paintings and photographs and pieces of woven cloth, some of which remind me a little of my mother's quilt.

"Put some of this on it." Monroe hands me a small jar. "Boy," he says, "you got to watch those dogs." Soldier is calmer now, and he's stopped peeing. He puts his head in my lap and begins to whimper and cry.

"They're tricksters, those ones," says Monroe. "I'll bet they didn't mention the barbed wire." He puts his face next to Soldier's. "I'll bet they didn't tell you about the barbed wire at all."

I rub the salve into the wound. Soldier doesn't protest or flinch. He lies on the floor quietly. I rub his ears and scratch his chin. Every so often, he rolls his tongue around his muzzle and catches my fingers.

"Have you had breakfast?" says Monroe.

"A little."

"You hungry?"

"Sure."

"Can you cook?"

I've watched my mother cook, and I've warmed things up in a pan before, so I have an idea of what to do.

"Eggs Benedict," shouts Monroe. "Home fries with onions and some very thin, crispy whole wheat toast."

The refrigerator is mostly empty. There's a quart of skim milk and half a bottle of prune juice. I look under the cupboards for the potatoes. Then I go back to the refrigerator. "You don't have any eggs."

"'It is the nature of extreme self-lovers'" — Monroe's voice echoes off the walls and it sounds as if he's shouting down a well — "'as they will set an house on fire . . .'"

"And you don't have any potatoes."

"'. . . and it were but to roast their eggs.'"

"No onions either."

"Bacon!"

"I don't see any."

Monroe comes through the kitchen in his wheelchair. Soldier trots along behind him. "No," he shouts as he flashes past me, cutting a wide arc around the church. "Sir Francis!"

In the door of the refrigerator is a box of cereal. I shake the milk, and whatever is in the carton rattles. I put it back without looking. Monroe goes around the church a couple more times and then parks the chair under the stained glass window. "So," he says, "what's for breakfast?"

The cereal tastes a little weird at first, but the prune juice is sweet, and in the end, it's not too bad. Monroe sighs, and leans back in the chair. "I was the best, you know."

I look at the paintings on the wall. "Are all these yours?"

"These?" says Monroe. "None of these is mine."

"So, what do you paint?"

"I don't paint."

I can see where trying to have a conversation with Monroe could be tricky. "But you're a famous Indian artist."

"Absolutely," says Monroe, and he's out of his chair and pacing around the church. "I went everywhere. Paris, Berlin, New York, London, Moscow, Madrid, Rome."

"But you're not a painter?"

"Oh, I did that for a while." Monroe goes to the wall and straightens a small painting of a child holding a bird. "Made a bunch of money. Problem was, I was lousy. Stinko. Reactionary. Predictable."

Monroe is on the move again, and I figure it'll be safer if I stop asking questions and just let him talk. "What I was really good at was restoration."

"Cool."

"Nineteenth-century landscapes were my specialty." Monroe comes back to the table and pours himself some more cereal. "Have you ever seen a nineteenth-century landscape?"

"Maybe on television."

"They all look alike. Craggy mountains, foreboding trees, sublime valleys with wild rivers running through them."

"My mother has a quilt with some of that stuff on it."

"A primeval paradise. Peaceful. Quiet. Snow on the mountains. Luminous clouds in the sky. The rivers tumbling over dark rocks. Blah, blah, blah."

Monroe pours some prune juice into the bowl and waits for the cereal to turn purple.

"I went around the world fixing paintings. They said my brushes were magic. You believe that?"

"Sure."

"One day, the Smithsonian called me in to handle a particularly difficult painting. It was a painting of a lake at dawn, and everything was fine except that the paint along the shore had begun to fade, and images that weren't in the original painting were beginning to bleed through."

"And they pay you to fix things like that?"

"So I worked on the painting until it looked as good as new," says Monroe. "But something went wrong."

"You messed up?"

"The new paint wouldn't hold. Almost as soon as I finished, the images began to bleed through again."

"So, you had to paint it over."

"You know what they were?" says Monroe.

"What?"

"Indians," says Monroe. "There was an Indian village on the lake, slowly coming up through the layers of paint. Clear as day." He goes to the kitchen, opens a drawer near the stove, and takes out the wig. "Now, where were we?"

"You were crazy."

"I'm not crazy," says Monroe. "But I am rich. Have we decided what I'm going to pay you?"

"Not yet."

"No rush, I guess," he says. "You see that tarp?" Monroe walks towards the back corner. I follow him. It's dark there, and at first I don't see a thing. "Take it off."

The tarp is almost the same colour as the shadows. And it's heavy. Lifting one edge is easy enough, but pulling it off is real work. Underneath is a long line of iron figures stacked against each other like folding chairs. Even up close, I can't tell what they are supposed to be.

"Bring one out here," says Monroe. "Let's take a look at it."

The figure is heavier than the tarp. I'm afraid of scratching the wood floor and I'm hoping that Monroe will take the wig off and help. But he doesn't.

"What do you think?"

It's a buffalo. Or at least, it's the outline of a buffalo. Flat iron wire bent into the shape of a buffalo. I look back at the stack. There must be at least two hundred pieces.

"Three hundred and sixty," says Monroe, reading my mind. "I had them made up before I left Toronto. It's my new restoration project."

"Neat."

"I'm going to save the world."

"They must be worth a lot of money."

Monroe runs his hands along the curve of the iron, as if he is petting it. "We haven't much time," he whispers, and he looks around the church as if he expects to find someone hiding in the shadows. "We better get started."

For the next hour, Monroe and I drag a dozen iron buffalo out of the church and hoist them into the back of his pickup. At first, I think all the buffalo are the same, but as we move them from the church to the truck, I can see that they are all different shapes and sizes. For the first couple of trips, Soldier follows us out to the truck and back again, barking the whole time. I figure he can smell the Cousins because he doesn't wander off into the grass the way he normally does.

"Now for the fun part," says Monroe. "Come on." And he gets into the pickup and starts the engine. I have just enough time to jump in the cab before he pulls it into first and takes off across the prairies. In the side mirror, I see Soldier bolt out of the grass and chase after us. I'm just getting settled into the seat when Monroe hits the brakes and we slide to a stop at the edge of the coulee. "Here we are."

I get out and look back. We've only come about two hundred yards from the church. Soldier has been trotting along behind us, but when he sees that we have stopped, he picks up speed.

"You got any sweetgrass?"

"No."

"Tobacco?"

"No."

Monroe walks to the lip of the coulee and looks out across the river. "There's Canada," he says. Then he turns and spreads his arms. "And this is the United States." He spins around in a full circle, stumbles, and goes down in a heap. "Ridiculous, isn't it?"

I'm hot now, and I'm sweating, and I'm thinking that cleaning boxcars for the railroad wouldn't be a bad job after all.

"We should have a ceremony," says Monroe, dusting himself off. "Do you know any songs?"

"I know some musicals."

"A traditional song would be better."

"I know part of an honour song."

"Perfect."

Monroe beats his hand on the hood of the truck, and we stand on the prairies and sing the part of the honour song I know, and then Monroe insists that we sing the title song from *Oklahoma!* Monroe leaves his wig on for the honour song, but takes it off for "Oklahoma!" Soldier joins in, and when we finish, Monroe turns away and wipes his eyes.

"That was moving," he says, "wasn't it?"

"What do we do with the buffalo?"

What we do with the buffalo is drag four of them out of the truck and dump them on the ground. Monroe grabs a canvas sack out of the back, reaches in, and comes up with a long spike, the kind they use for laying track.

"Ever work on the railroad?"

"My grandfather did."

"Okay," says Monroe, and he throws his wig into the truck. "I'll hold them and you drive them."

Each of the buffalo has places on the feet for the spikes to go. Monroe steadies the buffalo with one hand and holds the spike with the other. "Don't hit me."

It's a little tricky hitting the spike with the hammer and missing the buffalo and Monroe's hand, but by the third buffalo, I get the hang of it. After we nail the fourth buffalo into the prairies, Monroe walks up a small rise and looks at the grouping. Then he runs down and we move one of the buffalo so it's facing east.

"Beautiful."

"Is this sort of . . . art?"

"'My trade and my art is living,'" says Monroe. "You want some lunch?"

"We don't have any lunch."

"*Au contraire,*" says Monroe, and he pulls a zip-lock bag out of his pocket. Inside, I can see long strips of jerky. "There's water in the truck, and you're standing on dessert."

We find some shade by the side of the pickup and settle in with the jerky and water. The wind is back now, and there are heavy clouds in the sky. But they are the thick, white kind that the wind kicks loose from the mountains and blows across the prairies in tall piles, and not the kind that bring rain.

"My auntie has a picture of you."

"She does?"

"When you were young." I'm not sure what to say next, so I eat the jerky and drink the water.

Monroe begins smiling and then he begins laughing. "Did I tell you I used to work for museums all over the world?"

"You restored paintings."

"Little Turtle. The name of the painting was *Sunrise on Little Turtle Lake*." Monroe turns and looks at the river. "Have you ever been in a museum?"

"No."

"You know what they keep in museums?"

"Old stuff from the past?"

"That's what they want you to think." Monroe wipes his mouth with his shirt, bends over, picks off a couple of cactus berries, and pops them in his mouth. "So, you know what I did?"

This is a bad habit that Monroe has. Making hard turns when I'm not looking. I figure this is what happens when you go crazy. "I painted the village and the Indians back into the painting." Monroe closes his eyes and settles in the grass. "Watch them in case they try to run away again."

"The Indians?"

"No," says Monroe, "the buffalo."

Soldier lies down next to him. The buffalo aren't going anywhere, so I close my eyes and curl up in the shade of the truck. The wind picks up speed, and as it does, I hear a low moaning hum. At first, I think it's Soldier having a bad dream, but when I look, I see that it's just the buffalo leaning into the wind like rocks in a river.

When I wake up, Monroe is gone. So is the truck. The buffalo are still standing on the prairies, and for a moment, they look just like the buffalo on the reserve. I walk to the edge of the coulee and look along the river. I look back to the church. No Monroe. I get Soldier up. He's dopey and silly and just wants to lie on his back and lick my hands.

"Come on," I tell him, and I clap my hands so he knows it's a game. "Let's find Monroe."

Soldier runs out in a long circle, rushes back past me, and heads up the hill. I walk slowly behind him. Halfway up the hill, I see faint tire marks in the soft earth. "Good dog!" It's hot, so I don't run. I figure I'll go as far as the top, and if I don't see Monroe or the truck, I'll just go home. Soldier trots on ahead and disappears in the grass.

I'm not expecting more buffalo, and for a moment, when I get to the top of the hill and they pop out of the grass, they startle me. There are three of them, all facing in my direction. Soldier is nowhere to be seen, but the tracks are easy to see now, and I figure that he has gone on ahead.

"Soldier!"

The tracks go down the hill and up the next. And then there's another hill, and another and another. I start to turn back, but I figure if Monroe is setting the buffalo up in groups of three and four as he goes, he'll run out of buffalo before long and can't be very far in front of me.

Of course, I'm wrong about that. By the time I get to the top of the fourth or fifth hill, I've already passed fourteen buffalo, which means Monroe's been back to the church at least once to pick up a new load. I try walking faster.

I find the truck and Monroe and Soldier at the bottom of a cut. Soldier is chewing on a piece of jerky. As soon as Monroe sees me, he gets up and pulls a buffalo off the back of the truck. "Just in time."

"Why'd you leave me?"

"You were sleeping."

"You could have woken me up."

"What do you think, two or four?"

"I almost went home."

"Or we could do three." Monroe drags the buffalo over to a thick bush. "Grab one of the skinny ones," he shouts. "This is the perfect place for a teenager."

We make three trips back to the church, and it's early evening before we've hammered in the last spike. Monroe sits on the tailgate of the truck and looks back the way we've come. You can't see the church, and you can't see the bridge, and you can't see Truth or Bright Water.

"Look at that," says Monroe. "Just like the old days."

I look, but I don't see much of anything. Besides the river, there is only the land and the sky.

"As far as the eye can see." Monroe looks at me and I smile. "Wait a minute," he says, and he runs around to the cab and comes back with the wig. "Here," he says, pulling the wig over my head, "now you try it."

I can see even less now. The hair falls in front of my eyes, and the wig itself smells funny. Soldier looks at me and cocks his head. There are times when he looks stupid, and this is one of them.

"Over there," says Monroe, and I try to follow his finger. "It's only a matter of time."

My mother is always telling me to use my imagination, and I guess this is one of those times to try. "Oh, yeah," I say.

"Each day, the herd will grow larger and larger." Monroe pushes off the truck and walks up the hill. "Before we're done, the buffalo will return."

I take off the wig and put it on the tailgate. Monroe wanders off, talking to himself. I don't follow him, and he's too far away to hear. I wonder just how crazy he really is, but I stand on the running board of the truck anyway and try to see what he sees.

All the way back to the church, Monroe tells me what a great job I've done and how much he loves my company, and asks if I will come back. "How many buffalo did we set up today?"

"Sixty."

"That's a start," says Monroe.

The light is low now, and from the church, I can see the first four buffalo. "Actually," I tell Monroe, "it's sort of fun."

"Fun!" Monroe spins on me. "Not fun," he says, low and hard. "Serious. This is serious."

He takes me by surprise. "I didn't mean a lot of fun."

"These buffalo aren't really real, you know." Monroe puts his arm around my shoulders and draws me close.

I don't want to make the same mistake again. "I don't know," I say. "They sort of look real."

Monroe's face explodes in smiles and tears. "Yes," he says. "Yes, that's exactly right."

We stand in front of the church. Monroe keeps his arm around me, squeezes me from time to time as the light turns and slants into the grass. "What do you see?"

"The church."

"I'm working on that," says Monroe. "What else?"

"The prairies?"

"How about the sky?"

"Sure."

"Anything else?" Monroe turns me so I'm facing the iron buffalo.

I don't want to say that I see the buffalo just in case I'm not supposed to see them. But I've run out of options. "Buffalo?"

Monroe smiles and shakes his head. "It would fool me, too," he says. "But you can't tell anyone."

"About what?"

"If they hear about it, it won't work." Monroe dips his head and puts his mouth to my ear. "Real buffalo," he whispers, "can spot a decoy a mile away."

CHAPTER SEVENTEEN

When Soldier and I get back to the shop, my mother is at the back, sitting on the floor surrounded by postcards and photographs. The place is still a mess. Nothing has been picked up from the night before. I look around to see if auntie Cassie is buried in the couch. Soldier picks his way through the pillows and the wine glasses and bangs his tongue into his water dish until all the water is on the floor. Then he turns himself around and falls down in a twist.

"You remember this?" My mother holds up a postcard with a picture of an old hotel with a lake in the background.

"Waterton, right?"

"Here's one of you when you were small."

I've seen the photographs and the postcards before. There are a bunch of me when I was a baby and some really old pictures of my grand-mother and some goofy-looking shots of my mother and auntie Cassie when they were about my age.

"This is when Cassie and me were at Wild Rose Community College."

"And that's dad, right?"

"That's him."

"Is that Franklin?"

My mother looks at the photograph for a moment and then puts it back in the box. "No," she says. "Has Soldier done his business?"

"He's okay."

"You should take him for a walk, just to be sure."

"It's dark out. We've been walking all day."

"Walk" is one of the words that Soldier knows, and as soon as he hears it, he's on his feet. He wiggles his way over to my mother and puts his head on her lap.

"You don't play with this dog enough." My mother rubs Soldier's ears. "He needs love, you know."

137

"Lum and me take him everywhere."

"It's not the same," says my mother, and she scratches Soldier's rib cage until his back leg begins jerking up and down. "It's not the same."

A couple of months after my father left Bright Water and moved to Truth, my mother began writing letters to cities all over Canada — Vancouver, Victoria, Calgary, Edmonton, Saskatoon, Winnipeg, Regina, Toronto, Montreal — and in no time at all, we began getting packages in the mail stuffed with brochures and magazines and maps and posters. As soon as each new package showed up, we'd open it, spread the brochures out on the kitchen table, and compare the new brochures with the old ones. I asked my mother what she was doing and she said she was just looking. I liked the pictures of Vancouver a lot and the ones of Halifax weren't bad either. I especially liked the cities that were near an ocean with sandy beaches and waves breaking over the rocks.

"What are you looking for?"

"If you could live anywhere in the world," said my mother, "where would you want to be?"

The Blue Jays were in Toronto, and even though I didn't follow baseball and even though they hadn't won a World Series in a while, it was still exciting to think about living in the same city where they were playing. Of course, you could get the same thing in Montreal, and if you liked hockey, you could go almost anywhere.

"How about Vancouver?" my mother said. "How about if we moved to Vancouver?"

"I guess."

"There's a good theatre community in Vancouver."

"Then you could be an actress."

My mother would smile when I said this, and no matter what city we settled on, you could see that moving out of Bright Water, away from the reserve, and becoming a real actress was one of her dreams.

I don't want Soldier to run off on me this late at night, so I get the leash out of the drawer. "You want to go for a walk?" I jingle the chain, and Soldier gets even more excited. "You want to go for a walk?" I do this until he gets cranky and begins to bark and jump on me. Then I fasten the leash and let him drag me to the door.

"When you get back, we need to talk."

"About what?"

"Things," says my mother, and she begins to pick up the wine glasses and the pillows.

By the time we hit the sidewalk, Soldier has worked up a full head of steam. He arches his neck and makes loud snorting sounds through his nose as he drags me along. I figure he smells something interesting or tasty and is determined to find it. When we get to the fire station, Soldier stops and curls his ears up into knots. Then he sits back, looks into the night, and begins to whimper.

There isn't much to see, but I look anyway. It would be easier if there were a moon. I flip the leash around like a whip, but it has no effect. I jerk on Soldier's collar, but all he does is drop to the ground and pull his neck into his shoulders.

"Come on," I say again, and I tighten the leash and slide the fur around Soldier's neck up against his head.

"Kick him in the ass."

The voice scares the hell out of me. I spin around, but all I can see are shadows.

"Man or beast . . . always works for me."

"Dad?"

"Scared the piss out of you, didn't I?"

"Nope."

My father walks out of the shadows, squats down beside Soldier, and scratches him behind the ears. "How's your mom?"

"You coming to see her?"

"Why? She busy?"

"Nope," I say, and now that I can see my father clearly, I can see that he's had something to drink.

"She with her new boyfriend?"

"What new boyfriend?"

"That why she sent you out to walk the dog?"

"Why don't you stop in," I say. "I'll bet she'd be happy to see you."

My father shakes his head and wipes his mouth with his sleeve. "I've got business." In the alley, I can see the back end of the old U-Haul truck.

"You going across the line?"

"Got to make a living."

Soldier whimpers once and throws his shoulders into the leash. My father turns and looks out into the night. "Dog sees something."

At first, all I can see are the stars and the tops of the coulees against the night sky. Then I see the lights, dim and vague, moving along the ridge.

"Parking lights," says my father. "Someone doesn't want to be seen."

"Smugglers?"

"Nope," says my father. "Hardly enough business for me."

"Looks like they're heading for the church."

"Run across that ground blind and you'll wind up in a hole. Six feet deep."

"Maybe it's Monroe."

My father blows on Soldier's ear. "Couple of years back, we heard he was dead."

"Monroe?"

"And then the sonofabitch turns up here."

"So?"

"So, he's not dead." My father turns and heads for the truck. "Tell your mother I said hello."

Soldier liked looking at the brochures and he had his favourites. You could tell because his ears would go up and he'd begin to drool. Winnipeg was his favourite. I think he liked Winnipeg best because, in one of the brochures, there was a picture of a large lake, and Soldier enjoyed swimming. He also liked Edmonton and Victoria. Victoria was easy to figure out because most of the pictures showed the ocean, but Edmonton looked dry and didn't seem to have any water at all, except for a river.

"How about if we moved to Toronto?"

"I guess."

"Native Earth Performing Arts is in Toronto."

I wasn't sure I wanted to move. I was angry with my father for taking off, but if we left and moved away, I might never see him again. And Lum probably couldn't come with us. I asked my mother about Soldier. She said that cities could be hard on dogs, and I told her I wasn't going anywhere without Soldier. My mother looked sad then, as if I had hurt her feelings, and she carefully folded the brochures and put them back in their envelopes.

I walk with my father to the truck, and even before we get there, I know what's in the back. Soldier wrinkles his nose and starts to slow down so that I have to drag him along.

"How you going to get across?"

"Lots of places to cross," says my father. "Hell, it's not fucking Russia."

"Why don't you just take it to the big dump in Prairie View?"

My father unlocks the back door and throws it open. Inside are the yellow barrels stacked nice and neat. "They don't want it. That's a real joke, isn't it?"

"What?"

"They don't mind making the mess, but they don't want the job of cleaning it up."

"So, where are you taking it?"

"Bright Water," says my father. "Always try to give my own people the business."

"Thought the landfill was closed."

"There's closed, and there's closed." My father shuts the door and sets the lock. "Franklin's still pissed off about his tent, you know."

"Franklin's pretty mean."

My father's eyes narrow. "He's your uncle."

"Yeah," I say, "but he beats up on Lum."

"Hell," says my father. "Nothing wrong with a spanking from time to time."

"Maybe you could say something to him."

"Franklin doesn't tell me how to raise my kid. I don't tell him how to raise his." My father fishes a cigarette out of his pack and lights it. He holds the pack out for me. "Just be glad I'm not like Franklin."

"I am."

"Only hit you when you deserve it, right?"

"Right."

My father smiles at me and taps me in the chest with his fist. "I love you, son," he says. "You know that, right?"

"Right."

My father climbs into the cab, the smoke from the cigarette floating around his head like fog. "Tell your mother I love her, too."

When my father heard that my mother was thinking of leaving Bright Water and moving to Toronto or Vancouver, he got concerned, and the very next day, he showed up on the reserve towing a car. I was playing ball with Lum and Martin and Joseph Fox in the field next to the band office when my father pulled up.

"What do you think?"

"What is it?"

My father put his arm around my shoulder and led me over to the car so I could get a closer look. "This," he said, "is a Karmann Ghia."

"Bummer," said Martin, whose father had a new Dodge pickup and a Chrysler van.

"It's a convertible," said my father. "You don't see many of them."

"Is it for me?"

My father smiled. "No," he said. "It's for your mother."

"She'll like that."

"You bet she will," said my father. "Got it off a guy in Blossom. Almost stole it."

The car was small and white. There was only room in it for two people and the interior was spare. I guess it was supposed to look sporty, but I would have preferred something like Teresa Rain's Firebird. My father went around to the back and opened the trunk. "How about this?"

I had heard of cars with their engines in the trunk, but the only one I had ever seen in Truth or Bright Water was Eugena Hunt's Volkswagen.

"Sort of like a Volkswagen," I told my father.

"It is a Volkswagen," said Lum.

"That's right," said my father. "This is their sports model."

I climbed in behind the wheel and pushed on the pedals. The carpet was all matted down and there was a long tear in the passenger's seat. "How come it smells wet?"

"It's a classic," my father told me. "A car like this will only go up in value."

My mother has cleaned up the pillows and the wine glasses and most of the photographs and postcards. She sits at the table with her quilt and a pair of scissors.

"We saw dad," I say.

My mother has cut a picture of her and auntie Cassie in a circle and is sewing it on the quilt just above the needles. "Did Soldier do his business?"

"We also saw a car up by the church."

"Because if he didn't, you need to take him out again."

The picture of my mother and auntie Cassie is when they were young. My mother has an apple, and auntie is trying to get it.

"Is that going to hold?"

"I guess we'll see," says my mother. She brings the needle up through the cloth and very gently pushes it into the paper. "I won't be here tomorrow."

"You going somewhere?"

"Maybe Waterton Lake for a day or two."

"With auntie Cassie?"

"I'll leave you twenty dollars in case of an emergency," she says. "And there's food in the refrigerator."

"With dad?"

"Do you think you can do that?"

"Sure."

"I'll be back for Indian Days." My mother ties off the photograph and cuts the thread. "Make time tomorrow and go to your grandmother's to see if she needs help with the tipi."

"She always puts it up herself."

"She's not as young as she used to be."

I'm sorry my mother has put the photographs away. "Do we have a picture of Lum and his mother?"

My mother lays the quilt down and looks at me. "Is Lum in trouble?"

"Nope. Just thought he might like a photograph of her if we had one."

"Is it Franklin?"

"Dad's going to talk to him."

My mother shakes her head. "It's Franklin's own fault."

"The accident?"

My mother carries the quilt to the basket. "I'll see what I can find," she says.

My father went to get my mother while Lum and I walked around the car and kicked the tires. Then Lum climbed into the driver's seat and began turning the wheel and making engine noises. "These things are gutless," he said. "Eugena's Beetle used to crap out if it even smelled a hill."

"It has a stick," I said. "That's better than an automatic."

"If it had an automatic," Lum said, "it wouldn't be able to move at all."

"And it's a convertible."

Lum looked at the car and shook his head. "Somebody saw somebody coming."

When my mother came out, she was surprised. But it wasn't the kind of surprise that made you feel good or made you want to laugh. The last time I had seen her look surprised like that was when Soldier was a puppy and had done his business next to the couch in the living room.

But my father didn't see it. He was all smiles and wiggle, as if he expected my mother had forgotten that he had left us and gone off to Truth. As if he expected that she would take him in her arms and tell him that this was the most thoughtful thing anyone had ever done for her. He stood there smiling and waiting as my mother looked the car over.

"What about the child you-know-what?" she said.

"I'm going to put in a new set of points and get all the belts changed."

"I don't need a car."

"As soon as I get it fixed up, you can drive over to Truth or Blossom or Prairie View, whenever you like."

"What I need is help with the bills."

"And I'm keeping an eye out for some good tires."

My father was still smiling when he got in his truck and dragged the

Karmann Ghia out of Bright Water and headed for Truth. My mother went home as soon as my father left, but Lum and I stood at the corner of the band office and watched the road that ran to Prairie View and the border long after my father and his truck and our new car had disappeared.

My mother and I sit on the couch and watch television. The picture of her and auntie Cassie looks as though it is sewed on the quilt to stay. Towards one of the corners, near the feathers and the squares of woven quills, I can see where my mother has begun work on a purple and red Flying Bird. I'm guessing that this is probably auntie Cassie come home, but I know it's too soon to tell.

CHAPTER EIGHTEEN

═══

Soldier is a brave dog, and he likes to go places, but he does not like crossing the Shield on the ferry. The next morning, when we get to the river and he sees what's up, he begins to cry, and he slows down until all he's doing is shaking.

"Don't be a baby." It's the same every time. I have to pick him up and put him in the bucket. "And no peeing."

As soon as Soldier is in the bucket, he goes all stiff and stops drooling. He stands there with his legs braced and watches me as I take out the gloves and rock us off the platform. When Charlie Ron was alive, he used to come down to the river every night and lock the bucket up in case somebody got drunk and did something stupid. But people kept breaking the lock. Lum said some of the guys liked to pull the bucket to the middle of the Shield just to make out with their girlfriends. I thought it was a pretty dumb idea, but Lum told me it was a great place to fool around.

"The Toilet?"

"Kirby Scout took Celeste Plume to the middle of the river and told her to put out or get out and walk."

"What'd she do?"

"You know the Plumes."

"She kill him?"

"Naw, just cut all the buttons off his shirt."

The view from the ferry is great, and as I pull the bucket across the river, I'm thinking that my father is probably wrong about the tourists who come west to take in the sights. There's nothing scary out here, just the land and the river and the mountains. Out here, space is just the distance between towns, and the only thing you have to worry about is the weather or the next gas station being open.

"What about it?" I ask Soldier. "You see anything scary?" Which is the wrong thing to say. Soldier looks through the slats in the bucket, and he begins to whimper, and then he begins to pee.

"Jeez!"

I stop the bucket in the middle of the river and let the wind swing us back and forth. Soldier is trembling now, and he begins to whine and make his eyes droop so that they look as if they're going to fall out of his head.

"Yeah, well, what about my shoes?"

Soldier doesn't like me to stop, and he doesn't like the bucket to swing. He starts growling, and then he begins to bark. He keeps this up until I grab the line and pull us across the rest of the way.

Lum isn't at the tent, and he isn't at Happy Trails. I walk around the park and look at the licence plates on the trailers. Besides the Cherokees from Georgia, there are folks from California and Utah and New Jersey. Three of the trailers are from Minnesota. Soldier circles each trailer, sniffing as he goes.

"Smells okay," I say. Which isn't exactly true. Soldier snorts and heads off across the prairies, loping slowly through the grass. I watch him until he disappears, and then I walk back to the tent and wait. Franklin has fixed the tear and you can hardly see it now. The concrete pads for the speakers have been poured, and the speakers have been set in place and wired. They stand at the corners of the tent, tall and black, facing out over the prairies, east, south, west, and north, looking for all the world like sentries guarding the camp against surprise attack.

I don't see Rebecca right away. She's sitting quietly inside the tent on one of the benches, looking at the ground.

"Hi," I say. "You find your duck yet?"

"Not yet," she says. "Was that your dog?"

"That was Soldier."

"Dogs don't like me."

"Soldier likes everyone." Which is mostly true.

Rebecca stands up and walks to the edge of the tent where the shadows end and the sun begins. I look around for Soldier, but he's nowhere to be seen. The wind is blowing as it always does at this time of the year, but right now it's not serious.

"My mother made this dress." Rebecca spins around. "Do you like it?"

"It's cool."

"She had to tear the cloth because they wouldn't let her bring her scissors."

"My mother's making a quilt."

"My father says we'll buy a good pair of scissors once we get to Oklahoma."

"Looks sort of like lace," I say.

"Feathers," says Rebecca. "I think the edges look like feathers."

"So, where are your folks?"

"Down there," says Rebecca. "They're watching the buffalo get shot."

The first corral is still there, but now a second corral has been built at the far end and the chute has been widened. The orange-plastic mesh has been stretched tight, and all along on both sides of the chute, junk cars have been set end to end to form a makeshift fence of metal and chrome.

"We heard they were killing the buffalo for their hides and leaving the meat on the ground to rot," says Rebecca. "But we didn't believe it."

I can see my father's U-Haul parked by the first corral and next to it is Franklin's maroon pickup. Farther on and out of sight, I can hear the rattle of a motorcycle, but standing there in the wind and the sun, I can't tell where the sound is coming from.

"There," says Rebecca, and as she steps forward into the wind and the light, she seems to shimmer for a moment and fade. "That's where you can shoot the buffalo."

The tourists stand in a knot, watching the buffalo in the corral. A couple of them have climbed to the top of the fence, their cameras at the ready. Above the wind, I can hear the motorcycle again, but all I see is the prairies and the late morning colours that pool up and flood the land. I shade my eyes. I know that the motorcycle is out there somewhere, and that if I wait long enough, it will leave the shadows and come into the light.

I figure that Rebecca can tag along with me until Lum shows up. Being from Georgia, she probably hasn't seen stuff like buffalo and mountains, but when I turn back to see if she's interested in any of these things, she's gone. I look in the tent but it's empty.

I hang around a while to see if she shows up, and then I drop down the side of the hill and head for the corral. The buffalo do not even turn to look at me as I walk by the fence. They stare stupidly straight ahead at the tourists. I could slip under the poles, slide through the grass on my belly, and slit their throats before they had a clue. Instead, I make low gruff noises and growl, but the wind is against me, and the buffalo are deaf to the danger behind them.

My father and Franklin are standing by Franklin's truck. Franklin has his finger aimed at my father's chest, and as he talks, he jerks the finger back and forth like a bird pecking at a worm.

"So, what the hell am I supposed to do?" says my father.

"Well, you sure as hell can't dump it here," says Franklin.

"We had a deal."

"Not for this kind of shit," says Franklin, and he gets in his truck.

"Grow up," shouts my father. "This is the kind of shit that pays." But Franklin is gone, fishtailing the truck across the flat, heading for the big tent.

The motorcycle appears out of nowhere. It comes in downwind, so I see it before I hear it. I watch as it loops across the prairies, and even before it is close enough for me to tell who's on it, I know that it's Lum.

"You're late, cousin," Lum yells at me as he swings in against the fence. The buffalo forget about the tourists for a moment and begin turning, following the motorcycle, as Lum circles the paddock. "My old man gone?" He stops the bike, swings a leg over the tank, and sits there like a movie star trying to sell aftershave or new cars.

"You just missed him."

"My lucky day." Lum pushes off the seat, limps over to the paddocks, and comes back with a short, thick rifle. He tosses it to me and jumps on the motorcycle. "You ever see one of these?"

"What's wrong with your leg?"

"It shoots paint pellets." Lum looks at me and smiles. "Get in." He kick-starts the engine. I step into the sidecar and put the butt of the rifle on the floor between my legs. "Okay," he says, and he drops the motorcycle into gear. "Let's go hunting."

"What do I do?"

"Just don't shoot me."

Lum circles around and rolls into the paddock. As soon as the buffalo see us, they begin backing up. Lum guns the engine hard. The tourists all have their cameras out and are draped over the fence, looking for a clear shot.

"We got to get them into the chute," Lum shouts.

The buffalo are reluctant to go. Lum charges at them, and each time he does, they back up a little more quickly. "All right!" Lum yells over the wind and the roar of the motorcycle. The buffalo break into a run and go charging down the chute. I've never seen buffalo run before, and they're faster than I would have imagined.

"Now!" shouts Lum.

"What?"

"Shoot them!"

Suddenly, everything is at full speed, the buffalo, the motorcycle, Lum, and me. The buffalo string out along the chute in two groups. Lum catches up to three of them right away, but as he pulls alongside, they veer off sharply, side-swipe the plastic mesh and the fence of cars, and crowhop to a stop. They turn quickly and face the motorcycle, ready to charge, but Lum ignores them, guns the engine, and passes them on the fly. Four other cows slide across the chute at a dead run, and Lum swings in behind them.

"Lock and load!" he shouts, and pulls alongside a large cow who is running with her tongue hanging out. Lum tries to hold her in against the fence, but each time he tries to close, she drops her head and angles in on the motorcycle.

"Shoot!"

I want to steady the rifle on the lip of the sidecar, but the ground is too rough, and I have to bring the gun to my shoulder and try to time the pitches and rolls.

"Shoot!"

The first shot is high and sails off into the grass. The second shot hits the cow in the butt. The third misses low and in front. The fourth and fifth shots hit her high on the hump.

"Way to go!" yells Lum, and he swings the motorcycle back to the centre of the chute. As soon as we leave her, the cow slows down and stops, the white paint dripping down her shoulder. She swings her head from side to side as if she's scolding me, and in that moment, she reminds me of my grandmother.

"Lock and load," shouts Lum. "Lock and load!"

We scream down the chute, Lum bent over the handlebars, his hair snapping out behind him. The wind whips my eyes, and all I can see is the motion and the blur of colour. Every now and then, I feel the motorcycle leap back as a brown shape flashes alongside the bike. Then I hear Lum yell and I duck deeper into the sidecar, point the gun at the sky, and pull the trigger.

We paint three buffalo before they escape to the far paddock.

"What'd you think?" says Lum.

"Great!"

"White man's wet dream," says Lum. "The tourists are going to love it."

"These the jobs?"

"What?"

"Driving the motorcycles."

Lum turns the motorcycle around and points it towards the open prairies. "You think my old man would let either of us near a tourist with one of these?" He rolls the accelerator back in short, quick bursts, and the engine sucks in air like someone out of breath. "You ever think about just taking off?"

"Sure," I say. "My mother and I were going to move to Toronto."

Lum looks at me.

"We still have the brochures."

I wait to see what he wants to do. He sits there on the motorcycle, staring off at the land. "Come on," he says at last, and before I can say yes or no, he kicks the bike into gear and we're roaring across the prairies. I look over my shoulder, but the corrals and the tourists and the buffalo have already disappeared.

We head west until we get to the river, and then we turn north and follow the Shield into the foothills. I don't know where we are going, and I'm not sure Lum does either. He runs the motorcycle along the coulee as close as he can get to the edge. It's not too bad for me because the sidecar is firmly on the prairies, and it's Lum who has to look down at the drop. Every so often, he speeds up, weaves out into the grass, and then leans hard left and pulls the bike back to the edge. Each time he does this, I hold my breath and pray that he doesn't surprise both of us and ride the motorcycle off the side of the coulee and into the open sky.

When we finally come to a stop, I pull myself out of the sidecar as fast as I can, in case Lum changes his mind. Lum throws a leg over the bike, limps out to the edge of the coulee, and looks down at the river.

"Look around," he says, and he takes his shirt off and tosses it into the grass. "This is the way it used to be."

"In the old days, right?"

Lum unbuckles his jeans and lets them drop in a heap around his boots. "You see any houses?"

"Nope."

"Any roads?" Lum bends over, takes off his boots, and steps out of his jeans. He's not wearing underpants, and even though I've seen him beat up before, the bruises are a surprise. Some of them are little more than abrasions. Others are yellow, the result of glancing blows. But the one that runs down his right hip is the colour of blood, dark purple and black.

"Jesus, Lum. Your dad do this?"

"No tourists," says Lum. "No railroads. No fences." He scoops up some dirt in his hand and spits in it. He works it around until it's mud, and then he draws his fingers across his face and chest.

"You been to the clinic yet?"

"You still dressed?" Lum turns to me and smiles. "Come on." At first, he limps badly, the right leg stiff and painful, but as we walk along the coulee, the hip loosens up and the limp begins to disappear. Every so often, I feel a piece of hard stubble or a cactus crunch under my foot, and I'm glad I have my boots on. If Lum steps on anything, he doesn't show it. I look back towards Bright Water, but all I can see is the motorcycle. From a distance, you could mistake it for a bear sitting down or an elk kneeling in the grass.

Lum squats down at the end of the point and waits for me. In the distance, where the river turns and swings back into the land, the edge of a coulee has collapsed and part of the face has slid down the cut into the river bottom. "Landfill economics."

I look again, and now I can see that it's not a slide at all. The coulee hasn't fallen away. It's been cut back and levelled off, the dirt pushed over the sides and down the hill. Along the edges of the cut, you can see thick tire ruts in the soft earth.

"Thought they shut it down," I say.

"They did." Lum stands up and holds his arms out and turns around in the sun.

I see the bulldozer before Lum does. It comes over the ridge silently, its blade held high. It catches the crest and hangs balanced on the edge. Then it lazily pitches forward, waddles down the hill, and wades across the flat.

"Thought they said it was too close to the river."

"It is." Lum stops turning. The mud on his face and chest has begun to cake and crack. "There," he says. "Follow the birds."

Behind the bulldozer and above, a wave of seagulls breaks over the hill and floods into the coulee. They rush over the machine and tumble into the shadows, flashing in the prairie sun like fire and ice. The machine follows them into the side of the hill, drops its blade, and begins to push at a dark mound. I look at Lum. He smiles and spits on the ground. "Garbage," he says, his voice hissing into the wind. "The new buffalo."

As we watch, the bulldozer drags the pile into the light, and for a moment, I can see the boxes and plastic sacks and the drifts of loose debris, and then the machine stretches, effortlessly, and shoves every-thing over the edge of the slide. The seagulls rise up in a cloud, scream-ing, and the bulldozer backs up, thrusts its blunt nose into the earth again, spreads a blanket of dirt over everything, and buries it whole.

"Shit." Lum drops down into a crouch, his mouth open. He raises his head, turns it to one side, and feels for the wind with his face. He looks wild and fierce squatting there on the prairies, streaked with mud, the river and the land and the sky rolling over his body, and I try to imagine what it must be like to be naked and not be afraid.

I wait by the motorcycle while Lum finds his clothes. He pulls his jeans up slowly, careful not to put any pressure on the bruise. He's calmer now, but the pain is back, and it makes him stiff and awkward. "I'm going to camp out at the river tonight," he says.

"She's not going to come back."

"Bring a sleeping bag."

I can feel the skull in my pack. I have forgotten about it and I hope that Lum has, too. "We'll be wasting our time."

"And bring some food." Lum reaches in his pocket and takes out the keys. "Want to give it a try?" He cups the keys in his hand and tosses them to me.

"I guess."

"Nothing to it," says Lum, and he limps around the motorcycle and shows me where the clutch is and how to shift up and down with my foot. "Don't try to steer it," he says. "Just lean in the direction you want to go."

It takes me a few tries, but I get the hang of it, and it's easier than my father's truck. I guess I expected that Lum was going to ride with me, but he doesn't. Maybe his hip hurts too much to allow him to sit in the sidecar or maybe he doesn't want to make me nervous. Whatever the reason, he turns away from the sun and walks all the way back to Bright Water, while I glide in circles through the prairie grass beside him.

CHAPTER NINETEEN

———

A few summers back, an older couple from Germany rented a Grand Cherokee in Missoula, crossed the line at Prairie View, and headed for Banff. Three weeks after the vehicle was supposed to be returned, the RCMP found it parked out on the prairies, the battery dead, the gas tank empty.

According to the newspaper, Helmut May was a famous fashion photographer and his wife, Eva, was a schoolteacher. When the police found the jeep, May's cameras were under the maps on the back seat along with a number of rolls of exposed film.

The story of the Mays made the front page of the *Calgary Herald*, and the paper printed some of the pictures from the exposed rolls. All of the photographs were panoramas, landscapes, the sort of thing that you would expect tourists to take. But the neat thing was that everything in the distance, the rivers, the mountains, the clouds, the prairies, was slightly blurry and out of focus, while everything in the foreground, the steering wheel, the windshield wipers, the hood, was crisp and sharp.

One of the curious things was where the Cherokee was discovered. It wasn't found in the mountains where, if you made a wrong turn, you could wind up getting lost in the web of logging roads and trails. And it wasn't found in the foothills where you could take a corner or a curve too fast, skid off the road, and slide down an embankment into a river.

It was found standing in the middle of the prairies. On high ground.

Even if you did get yourself lost, you could look out in any direction, whenever you wanted, and see exactly where you were.

When the RCMP finally found the jeep, the Mays were sitting in the front seat with their seat belts fastened. The windows were rolled up, the doors were locked, and there were no signs that they had ever gotten out.

Robbery was ruled out, and because there were no signs of foul play and nothing to indicate suicide, the cause of death was listed simply as "exposure."

CHAPTER TWENTY

═══

I don't see Franklin's truck at the corral and my father's U-Haul is gone, too. I pull the motorcycle up against the fence and wait for Lum to catch up.

"He's going to charge thirty-five dollars a run." Lum turns off the engine and pockets the keys. "Six shots."

"For a motorcycle ride?"

"He's already called the television stations in Calgary and Prairie View."

Most of the tourists have gone back to the RV park or have headed off to see the sights, but the buffalo aren't taking any chances. They stay in a circle at the centre of the corral, facing out. The only sounds are the seagulls squawking overhead and the wind cutting through the grass. The buffalo stand still as stone. They keep their eyes open and their heads low to the ground as they blow into the dirt.

"I have to help my grandmother get her tipi ready," I say.

"You bring the skull?"

"Yeah."

"Be sure to bring it tonight."

"You want to come along?"

Lum looks up at the tent and then he looks out at the mountains. "Time me," he says, and he hands me the stopwatch.

"You can't run with a bad hip."

Lum should be too tired from all the walking to go for a run. And he doesn't start off well. All the way across the flat, he carries himself tight and pulled off to one side. I figure maybe he'll loosen up, but by the time he gets to the first rise, he's still dragging his bad leg behind him. I climb to the top of the fence to see if I can spot him, but he's already dropped down the far side of the slope and disappeared into the landscape. I start the watch and leave it hanging on one of the poles in plain sight.

Soldier is waiting for me when I get back to the tent. "You missed all the fun," I tell him. He is on his feet and dancing around me. "Too late for that," I say. "It's time to go to work."

I think about getting on the motorcycle and going out onto the prairies to find Lum and bring him back, but he has the keys and there's no telling how far he'll go this time before he decides to turn around and come home.

My grandmother is in the yard cleaning a chicken. The air is full of white feathers. They settle over the garden like snow and stick to the tomato plants and the zucchini and the corn.

"Just in time," she says, and she hands me a chicken. The bird is still warm and feels as if it might survive if it gets quick medical attention. "Don't leave the pin feathers."

Plucking chickens is not my favourite job, and I'm not very fast. For every bird that I clean, my grandmother can clean four. "I don't like chicken all that much anymore," I tell her.

"No profit in being a romantic."

"No, I mean chickens sort of make me gag."

"Hand me the knife."

Soldier looks at my grandmother and the dead chicken in her hand. Behind her, in the coop, the live chickens are clucking happily, but as soon as they see Soldier, they back away from the wire, and the clucking turns hard and suspicious.

"We were just up at the big tent," I tell her. "You ought to see what Franklin is doing with the buffalo for Indian Days."

My grandmother gives me a wink and throws a handful of guts against the wire. Some of it gets into the coop, and the chickens forget about Soldier for the moment and stampede over and begin fighting over the intestines and organs. Soldier's eyes never leave the chickens. His head bobs up and down, and his tongue flops out of his mouth as he watches them climb over each other.

"Don't know which is dumber," my grandmother says.

Some of the larger pieces stick to the wire, and several chickens stuff their necks through the fence, lean around, and begin pecking at the guts from the outside.

My grandmother stands up and wipes her hands on her apron. "Come on," she says. "It's too windy out here." She drops the knife into the bucket on the table and heads for the house. "Carry it for me." Inside are four dead chickens, plucked and cleaned. I wave the bucket under Soldier's nose. He pulls his head back and rolls his eyes, until there is mostly white showing. "Leave him outside," she says as she opens the screen door. "And tell him not to chase the chickens."

"Come on," I say to Soldier. "We'll get the sprinkler." The minute we turn our backs to the chickens, the clucking becomes happy again.

I tie Soldier to the arbour near the garage and unroll the garden hose. The sprinkler that he likes the best is the small round one that sends the water up in a high arc. When Soldier sees what I'm doing, he gets happy and forgets about my grandmother and the chickens. I turn the water on, and Soldier barks and dashes into the sprinkler and puts his mouth over the spray. Then he turns around and sits on it.

My grandmother is standing at the sink, waiting for me. "Dump them in here," she says.

I sit at the table while she washes the birds. I can see Soldier through the window sitting on the sprinkler, the water bubbling up from beneath his butt.

"He still likes doing that?" says my grandmother.

"I guess," I say.

"Here," she says, and hands me one of the chickens. She takes the others, sits down at the table, and lights two short, fat candles.

"Don't burn the skin."

I can see the chickens in the coop. They don't look anything like what I'm holding. The only way you can tell it's a chicken is by its feet. The rest of it feels like a lump of cold, wet dough.

My grandmother slowly rolls her chicken in the flame, and the room is immediately filled with the smell of burning feathers. Little wisps of grey and black smoke spiral off the corpse and rise to the ceiling. I hold my chicken over the flame, but my heart's not in it.

"Mum's going to be in a play."

My grandmother starts to smile and then stops.

"*Snow White and the Seven Dwarfs*," I tell her. "Only, it's a modern version and they're going to do it with Indians."

My grandmother leans back in the chair and closes her eyes.

"Carol Millerfeather is going to use Indians instead of dwarfs."

Nothing.

"Mum may get to play Snow White."

My grandmother opens her eyes one at a time. She opens them slowly, and now she reminds me of an alligator. "Monroe Swimmer," she says.

I wait to see if she plans on saying anything else. "What about Monroe Swimmer?"

My grandmother gets the lemonade jar from the refrigerator and puts it on the table. "Maybe Monroe can play Prince Charming." She gets a glass from the cupboard and places it in front of me.

"Lum and me found a skull."

"All the girls liked Monroe."

"You want to see it?"

My grandmother has a peculiar way of making lemonade. At the beginning of the summer, she makes it with plenty of sugar. But each week, as she makes a new jar, she cuts back until there is hardly any sugar in the lemonade at all. Today it is cold and sweet. My grandmother goes to the sink and looks out the window. "What's he doing now?"

"Monroe?"

"I suppose if you're a dog," she says, "it probably feels good to have water sprayed up your bum." My grandmother wraps the chickens in brown butcher paper and sets them on the drain board. "What kind was it?"

"What?"

"The skull." My grandmother takes the chickens to the refrigerator and stuffs them into the freezer.

"Lum says it's human."

"Ah," says my grandmother. I like my grandmother. She doesn't say no, it's probably a coyote skull, and she doesn't look at me as if I made it up.

"It could be prehistoric."

"Bad luck to play with the dead," says my grandmother.

"The weird part was it had a ribbon tied to it." I take the skull out of my pack and put it on the table. "We saw a woman, too."

My grandmother goes to the door and takes her sweater off the hook. She wears it all the time, even in the summer. She puts it on now, settles in her chair, and lets the skull float in her hands.

"She had a short life," says my grandmother.

"Who?"

"And she died hard."

"So, is it prehistoric?"

"But she wasn't from around here," says my grandmother. "She's a long ways from home."

The burnt feather smell hangs in the air. I look to see if any of the soot has landed on me. My grandmother cradles the skull in her lap and begins humming to herself the way my mother does when she's thinking. Or when she's sad. "You boys find a lot of things."

"Actually, Soldier found it."

"Ah," says my grandmother, and she hands me the skull.

"Up on the Horns."

"Ah."

The kitchen is cool and dark. The refrigerator hums a little, and the wind makes little shrieks as it catches the corners of the house.

"Mom said I should give you a hand with the tipi."

"Don't need any help."

"I don't mind."

"You know what to do?"

"Sort of."

My grandmother reaches out and squeezes my hand. She doesn't do it so it hurts, but I'm not sure I could get my hand back without a struggle. "Before you go," she says, "take some lemonade to Cassie."

"She staying in the trailer?"

"Where else would she stay?" Wrapped up in her sweater, sitting in the dark, my grandmother looks like a bear.

From the garden, I can see that the outside door to the trailer is open. Auntie Cassie is sitting at the table with her back to me. The small black and white television is on. I rattle the handle so she won't be startled.

"Lemonade."

"Come on in." Auntie Cassie turns the sound down on the television.

"Movie any good?" It's probably not the question I want to ask, but it's what comes out.

Auntie Cassie shrugs. "See the guy with the gun?" On the table is the suitcase. It's open, and all around it the baby clothes are stacked in neat little piles. On top of one of the piles is a red ribbon tied in a bow. "He's that woman's brother, and he's going to kill the good-looking guy."

"Neat."

"Another American epic." Auntie Cassie closes the door behind me and takes the lemonade to the sink. "What brings you out here, nephew?"

There's a coffee machine that's too big for the trailer stuffed against the wall on the counter. Fresh coffee is slowly dripping into the pot. I watch it for a moment. At first, it is hardly amber and looks like thin tea. But as the pot fills, the coffee deepens down until it blocks out all light, and as the water rises, I imagine that if something were to slip into that pot accidentally, you might never find it again.

"You hungry?"

"Sure."

Auntie Cassie pours herself a cup of coffee. She puts it to her lips and sniffs. Each time she takes a sip, she squeezes her eyes shut, smiles, and hunches her shoulders as if someone she likes has just hit her.

"Refrigerator's right there," says auntie Cassie, and she sits down at the table and starts folding the clothes.

There isn't much in the refrigerator. I see a wedge of bologna, some packaged cheese, and a jar of mustard. "There's bologna," I say. "You want some?"

"It was here when I arrived," says auntie Cassie.

"I could fry it."

"God, no!"

Auntie Cassie holds up a tiny shirt. The whole thing would fit in my hand. It looks like something you would put on a doll. I cut off a slice of bologna, roll it into a ball, and stick it in the mustard.

"What's that sister of mine up to?"

"She's going to be in a play."

The bologna is greasy and a little on the rubbery side, and it takes longer to chew than it should.

"A play?" says auntie Cassie. She puts the shirt down and turns to me. "They've got a theatre in Truth?"

"Carol Millerfeather's going to direct it," I say. "*Snow White and the Seven Dwarfs.*"

When auntie Cassie picks up her cup and takes a drink, I can really see the tattoo. "It's a modern version." Each letter is thick and jagged and bent, as if they were cut into her knuckles with glass. They look like wounds, and they look as if they still hurt. "If you stayed long enough, you could be in the play, too."

Auntie Cassie looks back at the television. The guy is hitting the woman now. The good-looking guy is standing next to the door getting angry.

"I'd make a lousy Snow White."

"That's the part that mum wants."

"You think I'd make a good evil queen?"

I have forgotten that there are only two parts for women in *Snow White*, and I'm sorry now that I've mentioned it.

"Mirror, mirror on the wall," says auntie Cassie, and she drops her voice and lowers her eyes.

The good-looking guy is pleading with the woman to take him back. They're in an old, dark mansion. The only light comes from a candle, and as the woman cries and the man begs, I can see parts of auntie Cassie's face reflected in the screen.

"Maybe there isn't an evil queen," I say quickly. "Maybe in this version the queen turns out to be a good sister who saves Snow White."

"Saves her from what?"

"Bad guys?"

"All the King's horses and all the King's men," says auntie Cassie.

"That's Humpty Dumpty."

"Couldn't save Snow White."

Auntie Cassie puts her cup on the table, and as she does, she knocks over the stacks of baby clothes. The clothes fan out across the table, slide off the edge and onto the floor. The red bow winds up on auntie Cassie's lap. She looks at it for a moment, and then turns back to me. "This version have a handsome prince?" she says. "Every woman needs a handsome prince."

"I guess."

"Then I'll be the prince."

"You can't be the prince," I say.

Auntie Cassie bends over and picks up a pair of sleepers, folds them, and starts a new stack. "I thought you said it was a modern version." She's not smiling now, and I think that maybe I've hurt her feelings.

"Maybe," I say, "the prince is really a princess in disguise."

"One thing I do know," says auntie Cassie. "I sure as hell don't want to be Snow White."

"But it's the lead."

"Cleaning house for seven dwarfs."

"Indians," I say. "Carol is going to use Indians instead of dwarfs."

"Men," says auntie Cassie. She takes another sip of coffee. She squeezes her lips together and swallows hard.

"Were you ever married?"

"Don't believe everything you hear," she says. "If you want to know anything, ask me."

I'm looking right at the tattoo. Auntie Cassie catches me and puts her coffee cup down. "I did this when I was nineteen." She curls her knuckles into a fist. The letters stretch out and become larger.

"Neat."

The guy in the movie is still trying to convince the woman to take him back. He's promising that he won't drink anymore and that he'll be a good husband. All in all, it's a dumb movie. My grandmother would have chased him down and torn his throat out.

"Does it hurt?"

Auntie Cassie relaxes her hand and rubs her fingers over the tattoo. "Yes," she says. "Sometimes it does."

She walks me out into the garden. Soldier has had enough of the sprinkler and is rolled up in the shade against the garage. My grandmother is down at the chicken coop throwing feed through the wire.

"You going to stay?" I ask.

Auntie Cassie looks towards Truth. "I hear Monroe is painting the church."

"You should see it," I say. "He's making the church disappear."

"They do that all the time."

"Who?"

"Men."

"Do what?"

"Disappear," says auntie Cassie, and she turns and walks back to the trailer.

I untie Soldier and wake him up. My grandmother is in with the chickens. I wave, but she doesn't see me. I watch her as she slings the feed around the pen, her hand stroking the air as if she's trying to pet them. As soon as Soldier sees the chickens, he begins to whine and drool. I grab the chain and try to pull him around, but he's strong, and it's hard to get him turned towards Truth.

In the end, I have to drag him all the way out of the yard, but the minute he's into the grass, he forgets about the coop and the birds and begins sniffing his way from one ground squirrel hole to another.

At the top of the rise, I look back at my grandmother's place. There are no clouds, and the sky is the kind of blue you see in pictures of oceans and lakes in magazines, and the house and the coop and the trailer, on the far side of the garden, and my grandmother in her sweater, moving among the chickens, all seem to be under water.

CHAPTER TWENTY-ONE

By the time we get to the river, Soldier's neck has started bleeding again. The flies buzz around the cut, so I tie my handkerchief around his neck to keep them away.

"You okay?" I say, and I give him a couple of pats. When we get to the ferry, I put him into the bucket as gently as I can. I don't stop it in the middle of the river, and I don't swing it back and forth either. Soldier still pees all over the floor, but I don't yell at him.

"She's pregnant," I tell Soldier. "Auntie Cassie is going to have a baby." I figure my mother knows and that the two of them are keeping it a secret from my grandmother. "That's why she came home. That's why she wants my old baby clothes."

The lights in the shop are out, and the door is locked. I let Soldier go in first. "Mum?"

The kitchen is clean, and everything has been put away. I look in the refrigerator. There are some boiled potatoes and salad stuff and a large bowl of spaghetti that wasn't there this morning. On the counter under a bowl is a note that says, "Food's in the fridge." Under the note is twenty dollars.

"You hungry?" I ask Soldier, but he's already curled up on the couch with his head buried under his back leg. I pick up the twenty. With my mother off on her vacation, I don't see why I should be stuck eating left-overs.

Railman's is almost empty. Miles Deardorf is at the counter with Gabriel Tucker and Sherman Youngman. Skee is sitting on the ice cream freezer.

"Franklin bet on the bridge," Miles is saying, "and look what happened."

"You really think they're just going to let it sit?" says Sherman.

"Already too late," says Gabriel. "The decking's begun to warp. Once that starts, it's all over."

Miles stirs a chicken leg into the potatoes and sucks on it. "Sure has screwed things up," he says. "Hell, the only decent thing I've sold in the last while is the church."

Skee straightens up, drops the rag on the counter, and drags it down to where I'm sitting.

"Could have done us a lot of good," says Gabriel. "Bridge like that would have kicked the economy in the ass and got it jumping."

"I'll have a burger," I tell Skee. "Medium rare with fries. And a root beer."

"Real estate will manage okay," says Miles, and he looks out the window in the general direction of Bright Water. "But other businesses are going to wind up in the crapper."

"Happy Trails," says Sherman, "ain't going to be so happy."

"More like the end of the trail," says Miles.

Skee drops a handful of silverware on the counter in front of me and sorts through the pile. "Your old man hasn't been by for a while," he says. "He off on a toot?"

"Nope," I say. "He's fine."

"When you see him, you might mention that the cops were over at the shop looking for him."

"The police?"

"And they weren't looking to wish him happy birthday." Gabriel winks at Skee. "Elvin ever finish that chair for you?"

"He's still waiting for parts." Skee puts a glass under the pop machine and fills it until the foam pours over the top. "Ain't that right?"

Miles comes down to where I'm sitting. He slides in next to me and opens his newspaper. "You see this?"

It's a story about a research team from the University of Toronto travelling around Canada and the States, collecting blood from Indian people. There's a picture, too, of a doctor holding up a vial of blood and looking at it the way you see people looking at glasses of wine in those old black and white movies on late-night television. The project has something to do with genes and DNA.

"What do you think?" he says.

"Guy on the radio this morning called it the Vampire Project," says Sherman.

"Sure as hell wouldn't let them do that to me," says Miles.

"Bleeding people should come natural to you," says Skee.

Miles gets up and taps the paper on the counter. He buttons his blazer, and as he does, I see that there is a split opening up along a seam under his arm. It reminds me of the tear my father's truck put in Franklin's tent.

"They're trying to find out where Indians came from," says Miles.

"Don't need a blood test to see that," says Gabriel.

Miles stuffs the newspaper under his arm and pulls at the corners of his eyes so they slant back, and all of us have a good laugh.

"See your aunt's back in town," says Skee.

"That's right," I say.

"You tell her hello for me," says Miles.

"Give it up," says Gabriel, and he pours the rest of the cream into his coffee. "She's not that bored."

"She could do a whole lot worse."

"I don't know," says Gabriel, and he winks at Skee. "Who do you figure could be worse?"

"What about Swimmer?" says Miles.

"Monroe's rich," says Sherman. "Women like that."

"Probably queer," says Miles. "Most of those artists are."

Skee brings my burger over and drops the plate on the counter. The burger and the fries bounce and rattle around like coins in a can. The meat looks a little burned, but I don't say anything.

"So we got rich and queer versus broke and dull," says Gabriel.

"Anybody else in this room drive a Lincoln?" says Miles. "Anybody else in this room have a piece of recreational property?"

Skee takes a paper towel and blows his nose into it. "You talking about Parliament Lake?"

"It's lakefront property."

"It's a mud flat," says Gabriel.

Miles takes out a ten and drops it on the counter. "Soon as they fill the lake again, you won't be able to buy property like that for love nor money."

"You believe that," says Gabriel, "and I've got a bridge I can sell you."

We all have another laugh, even Skee.

"I'd watch out if those research boys show up here," Miles says to me as he goes out the door. "They sound like real blood-thirsty savages."

Skee goes to the machine and finishes filling the glass. "So, what about it?" he says, and he puts the glass down in front of me. "Where do you figure Indians came from?"

Soldier is waiting for me when I get back to the shop. He's stretched out in the middle of the shop floor. His eyes are open, and he's looking at me.

"I didn't leave you," I say. "You went to sleep."

I dig my sleeping bag out of the closet. It smells foul and musty, as if it has been buried under a pile of dirty socks. I dump the rest of the stuff into a plastic bag — flashlight, matches, toilet paper, and a water bottle. I get a box of crackers out of the cupboard and a couple of apples from the refrigerator and am looking for the peanut butter when I hear the bell on the front door jingle.

"Hello."

My father is standing in the shop next to Soldier's body. He's wearing a suit, and he's holding a handful of flowers twisted up in green paper. He looks a little wobbly, as if he's just jumped out of bed and now has to wait for his brain to catch up with his body.

"What's wrong with the dog?"

"He's pretending to be upset," I say.

My father smiles and looks down at Soldier, but I can see his eyes darting around the shop. He holds the flowers out in front of him like a stick, as if he expects that someone is going to leap at him from the shadows or come bounding out from behind a door.

"These are for your mother," he says.

"Great."

My father looks at the sink, and then he looks past me towards the back room. "She here?"

"You okay?" I say.

"Business," he says, and he unbuttons his coat and sits down in the chair by the sink. "Where is she?"

"Don't know."

My father drops the flowers in the sink and looks at Soldier. "You sure he's okay?"

"He's just looking for sympathy."

"She go shopping?"

"Don't think so."

"She and Cassie take off?" My father looks at me, and I know he thinks I'm not telling him everything there is to know. "Your mother and me were talking about Prairie View the other day," he says. "It's really growing."

"Is that where you've been?"

"Some good opportunities in that town for someone with a head for business."

"We moving to Prairie View?"

My father slides out of the chair and squats down next to Soldier and begins scratching his belly. "You know what's wrong with this world?"

"Sure."

Soldier sighs and slowly tips over on his back. "Just needs a little love." My father runs his hand behind Soldier's ears. "What happened to his neck?"

"Barbed wire," I say.

"Well," my father tells Soldier, "we're just going to sit right here and wait until old momma comes home, aren't we."

Through the window I can see that the sun is already in the mountains. I want to get to the flat before it's too dark. "I don't think she's coming home tonight."

My father stops rubbing Soldier. "She over at granny's?"

"I don't think so."

"She with him?"

I take a couple of steps back and feel for the wall. My father stays on the floor. Soldier rolls up on his side.

"Who?"

"She doesn't have a car."

"You haven't fixed it yet."

"What the hell is that supposed to mean?"

Soldier is on his feet. He circles my father and comes over and leans against me. I reach down and smooth the fur on his neck.

"Nothing. I didn't mean anything."

My father hasn't gotten off the floor yet, and this is a good sign. I try to remember if we have any beer in the refrigerator.

"Don't you lie to me!"

I can feel Soldier's neck muscles harden under my hand. "I'm not lying. Lum and I are going to camp by the river. I was just getting my sleeping bag and stuff."

"Sonofabitch!"

"You like to get away."

"That's business!"

"You want a beer?"

"Sonofabitch." My father rolls up on his knees. He sounds calmer, but you never know. "When's she coming home?"

"She said she was thinking about going to Waterton Lake."

My father frowns, and I'm sorry I've mentioned it. "Waterton? Why the hell would she go to Waterton?"

"I don't know," I say. "Another vacation?"

"And she didn't take you?"

"I didn't want to go."

My father begins roaming the floor between the sink and the window. "You can't get a reservation this time of the year. So, where the hell is she going to stay?"

"There's that big hotel."

"You think she can afford that?"

"No."

"Any of this make sense to you?"

"No."

My father takes the flowers out of the sink. "Women," he says, and he turns to me. "You'll figure that out soon enough." He peels back the green paper and holds them out so I can see them. They're carnations for the most part and a few daisies. They look weary and limp, but my mother has come home with worse.

"You want me to put them in water?"

My father drops the flowers back into the sink and shakes his head. Then he turns and opens the door, pulling it hard so that the bell snaps and makes Soldier jump. "The trouble with the world," he says as he steps out of the shop, "is women."

It's well into evening before Soldier and I get to the flat. I figure that Lum will be there already, but he's not. I throw my stuff in a pile under a cottonwood and lie down and wait. I take the skull out of the pack and prop it against the tree so it can see what's happening. Soldier watches the skull out of the corner of his eye. Every so often, he leans over and licks at it and then pulls away. He's waiting for me to do something interesting or fun, but I'm tired and just want to relax. He tries whimpering for a while and looking pitiful, but in the end, he gives up and goes to the river and sniffs his way up and down the bank.

I look up through the branches and the leaves, but I'm not trying to find the sky. I'm thinking about my father and what it would be like to move to Prairie View, and what's going to happen when my grandmother discovers that auntie Cassie is pregnant.

Soldier begins to bark. I can see him down by the water jumping back and forth. He stops and looks at me. His ears are up, his body all coils and springs, and I figure that it's a frog or a snake or something he hasn't seen before. There's always the chance that it's a bone, something to go along with the skull, but that's the sort of thing you see in movies and not in real life.

"What'd you find?"

The next thought catches me when I'm not looking. I'm still thinking about auntie Cassie as I roll off the sleeping bag, but as I stand up, I start thinking about that night on the Horns and the woman and how she stepped off the edge and disappeared. And as I walk towards Soldier, I know that what he's found in the water is a body, the body of the woman from that night, washed ashore.

"Don't touch it!"

I've seen those kinds of bodies in movies, and they never look very good, white and bloated with pieces missing, and as I hurry across the flat to the river, I'm sure that dead bodies in real life look even worse.

"Leave it alone!"

Soldier is bent over like a bow with his butt in the air. He barks and then jumps to one side.

"Soldier!"

I can see the body now. It glistens in the light, pale blue and swollen. I'm surprised by the colour, which is even worse than I imagined, and I stop for a moment and watch it as it bobs up and down in the water. Soldier looks back at me and growls.

"Get back!"

Instead, he charges into the water and begins dragging the body into the shallows. As he gets it to shore, I can see how you could be fooled. It's the evening light. It hangs along the tops of the mountains, slants down the slopes, and floods the prairies. In the glow, everything comes to life.

"That's not a body." Soldier wrestles it into the shadows of the bank. Out of the water and out of the light, it looks flat and dark and lifeless. "So, what are you going to do with it?"

It looks like one of those thin plastic tarps you see on the back of pickups, only it's much smaller. But when I try to lift it, it's heavier than I expect and it feels soft and swollen, as though it's been filled up with thick cream or jello. Soldier watches me as I turn it over. While the one side is blue and feels cold and slick, the other side is white and thick and feels more like cloth. There are stains on this side, yellow and brown bruises that float in circles and fans on the surface. It's a pad of some sort, but what it reminds me of most is a heavy blanket or a wet diaper.

"Maybe next time," I tell Soldier, "you won't say anything until you're sure."

Soldier flops down on the thing, and it squishes and rolls under him like a waterbed.

"Nobody's going to pet you," I tell him, and I head for the camp. I don't look around, but I can hear Soldier behind me, fighting the pad, growling, slowly dragging it back through the grass like a lion with a fresh kill.

CHAPTER TWENTY-TWO

——

Lum doesn't get to the flat until after dark. Soldier and I have a small fire going by then, and we are curled up on the sleeping bag, enjoying the smell of the wood and watching the sparks spiral up into the night sky.

"You advertising?" he says as he steps into the light. "I could see your fire all the way from the bridge." Lum's hip is still sore, and he limps as he crosses to the trees, but you can see he's in a good mood. Soldier folds his ears around his head and starts to tremble and shake with happiness. He rolls off the bag and goes wiggling over to Lum.

"Ever check his ass for a vibrator?" Lum drops his pack on Soldier's head, but he doesn't do it hard or in a mean way.

"Nobody's showed up yet," I tell him.

Lum looks up at the ridge. "Nobody's going to show up as long as you've got the porch lights on." He drags his boot through the pit and scatters the wood. The sticks flash bright for a moment and then everything settles back into hot coals and curls of grey smoke.

"I brought a flashlight."

"Won't need it." Lum pulls his sleeping bag out of his pack and throws it next to mine. "Moon'll be up."

"What if nobody comes?"

"What if they do?" Lum's pants and shirt are dirty. His hair is matted and you can still see faint traces of dried mud on the side of his neck. "You bring anything besides the mutt?"

Soldier is sitting by my sleeping bag, and I remember the pad and am wondering where it is when I hear Lum step on it. It makes a soft, low squish, like walking on wet snow or stepping on a fresh cow flop.

"What the . . . !"

Soldier trots over, grabs the pad by a corner, and drags it towards the trees.

"What the hell is that?" Lum picks up the flashlight. The pad is covered

173

with dirt and junk. He kicks it with his foot, and Soldier pounces on it and drags it off into the grass.

"Where'd he get that?"

"In the river."

"God," says Lum. "It's used."

"What is it?"

Lum follows Soldier with the flashlight. "They use them in hospitals," he says. "They stick them under sick people."

Solider is lying on the pad, chewing on one of the edges.

"Soldier!"

"Chez Mutt." Lum screws his face into a grin. "A real connoisseur."

"Soldier!"

"Probably just oozing with protein." Lum hands me the light. "If he were my dog," he says, "I'd let him finish his hors d'oeuvre. And then I'd shoot him."

Soldier stops chewing for a moment and watches Lum push the sticks and ashes around in the pit, but there is nothing left of the fire now except smoke and dust. "You bring the skull?"

"Yeah."

"So, why we hanging around here?"

"Where we going?" I know where Lum wants to go, but I ask anyway just in case he's still thinking and hasn't settled on it yet.

"Don't use the flashlight until we get to the top," says Lum. "Otherwise, she might see us."

"There's nobody up there."

While we haven't been looking, the fog has begun to form. It starts at the water's edge and works its way out over the river and back across the flat. It stays low, and we're above it before we even notice that it's there. By the time we get to the Horns, everything below us on the flat and on the river has disappeared.

"Okay," says Lum, "start looking."

"For what?"

"Clues," says Lum.

I go along, because there isn't anything else to do, and I'm not sleepy. We walk around on the Horns watching the ground, and while I don't think we'll find something that will tell us who the woman is, it is amazing how much stuff you can come up with when you're looking.

"Anything?"

"Crushed beer can and a pack of smokes."

"Empty?"

"Empty."

Lum finds a plastic bag from the Coast to Coast store, and we throw everything we find into it. We search the Horns for about an hour, and in the end, between the three of us, we find four crushed beer cans, two crushed soda cans, an empty pack of cigarettes, a postcard, a couple of popsicle sticks, a styrofoam cup, a flyer for free carpet cleaning, and most of a man's belt. All the writing on the postcard has been washed away, and you can hardly see the picture on the front. It looks like Banff, but there's no way to be sure. The man's belt is made out of thick leather with a heavy brass buckle. Lum wraps the belt around his fist and swings it through the air. "Could really do some damage with this baby."

We sort through the junk again, but there's nothing we find that even looks like a clue.

"Okay," says Lum. "Time for Phase Two."

"We go back to camp?"

Recreating the scene of the crime is Phase Two. Soldier and I get to be the truck, and Lum gets to be the woman.

"All right," says Lum, "put it in gear." Soldier and I walk out towards the Horns until Lum tells us to stop. Then Lum walks out to the Horns and stands on the edge. "This about right?"

I tell Lum that it looks good to us. Lum holds the skull in one hand and spreads his arms. "The woman with the suitcase full of bones stands on the cliff." He moves a little closer to the edge. "What will she do?"

Soldier stands up and takes a step forward.

"She's sorry for what she did!" Lum shouts into the night. "She's sorry, sorry, sorry, sorry!" And he takes another step.

Soldier is away from my side and on Lum in an instant. He grabs Lum's pant leg and jerks him backwards.

"The wonder dog wants to save the woman!" Lum pulls his leg free and tries to kick Soldier in the side. "But he's too late!"

"Soldier!"

Soldier grabs the other leg and begins dragging Lum away from the edge of the Horns. Lum tries to keep his balance, but he slips on the rocks and goes down hard. I'm on the run now, and I get there before Lum has a chance to get his gun.

"You okay?"

Lum lies on his back and catches his breath. "Cousin," he says, "you got to take this mutt out more."

Soldier rolls over on his back. Lum reaches out and scratches Soldier's belly.

"He thought you were going to fall," I say. "He was just trying to help."

"Is that what you were doing, you stupid mutt," says Lum, and he rubs Soldier harder.

"He didn't know it was just a game," I say.

The skull is resting against a rock. It has a small chip at the back, but other than that, it's okay. Lum brushes himself off, walks to the cliff, and looks down. Soldier follows close to his side. "Bring him here," says Lum.

At first, I think he's talking about Soldier, and I know I don't want Soldier with Lum that near the edge.

Lum takes the skull and holds it out. "What do you see?"

Truth and Bright Water have disappeared in the fog and all you can see is a soft grey swirl that floats on the water. Soldier backs away from Lum and gets ready to bark.

"Did you think she was going to come back?" Lum brings the skull close to his face. "Did you really think she was going to come back?"

"She won't be back tonight," I say. "It's too late."

"She throws you away, and you think she's going to come back." Lum rubs the skull against his face. "Silly baby," he says. "Silly baby."

"Probably should get back to camp."

Lum sticks his finger in the hole in the skull and spins it around. "Don't cry," he says, and he turns to me. "You hear the silly baby crying?"

"Sure."

"He's crying for his mother."

"My grandmother says it's a girl."

"Stupid baby."

Soldier stands up quickly and begins to bark. Lum tosses the skull into the air. "She's not coming back!" He catches the skull and throws it up again. "She's never coming back!"

Soldier and I hear the danger at the same time, but it's too late. Lum wheels around and grabs my shirt and pulls me in close. "Can you hear it?" he says. His eyes are black and slitted. His mouth trembles. I nod, but I don't say anything. Lum smiles and presses the skull against my ear. "Have you seen my mummy?" he says in his tinny voice and gently rocks the skull against my neck. "Do you know where my mummy is?"

I close my eyes and stand as still as I can. So does Soldier.

"Answer the baby!"

"Nope," I say, my eyes still closed. "I don't know where your mother is."

I don't think Lum is going to hurt me, but there's always the chance of an accident, of something happening when he's not paying attention.

"There," he whispers, and I feel him move past me. "There."

In the distance, the lights in the church have come on, and the tall windows glow in the night. Lum holds the skull up so it has a clear view of the church. "Oh, you think that's where she went," he says. "Is that what you think?"

I'm thinking we should go back to camp and go to sleep, but I know that isn't going to happen. Lum heads for the church and Soldier and I follow. As we move along the top of the coulee, the moon rises, and suddenly, everything is quicksilver and light. Soldier is calm now. He doesn't run after Lum, and he doesn't race down the side of the coulee. He walks beside me, silently, and keeps pace all the way to the church. We're halfway there when the moon goes behind a cloud, and the lights in the church go out, and for an instant, the building disappears in the night. I stop and wait for the church to reappear and to see what Lum is going to do now, but he keeps walking, as though he knows where he wants to go and what he wants to do.

When Soldier and I catch up with Lum, he's sitting on the tailgate of Monroe's truck. He smiles and bangs the side of the pickup. "You'd think that a big-time artist like him would be driving a BMW or a Mercedes," says Lum.

"Looks like he's gone to bed," I say. "We should probably get back to camp."

"Aren't you curious?"

"About what?"

"The lights," says Lum. "He turns the lights on, and then he turns them off."

"Maybe the woman will show up at the Horns with more bones," I say. "We don't want to miss her."

"Come on," says Lum. "No sense walking all this way and not saying howdy."

Monroe hasn't gotten to this side of the church yet, and it looks fine. I think about taking Lum around to the front to show him the part that's missing, but before I can say anything, Lum finds a thick board in the grass and leans it against the side of the building beneath one of the windows.

"What are you going to do?"

Lum begins working his way up the board sideways, his arms out for balance. I stand on the bottom of the board so it doesn't move or kick out from underneath him. The moon comes out again, and now I can see the window itself. It's the stained glass window of the man in the robes carrying the book. Soldier wants to follow Lum. He sniffs at the board and even puts one foot on it, but that's as far as he goes.

"All right!" Lum's voice is a low, enthusiastic whisper.

"What is it?"

"You won't believe it." Lum presses his face against the glass. "Monroe's got a woman."

"No way."

"You can see her tits!"

"Bullshit!" I say. "You can't see a thing."

"Suit yourself."

Getting up the board looks easier than it is. "Let me see." The plank is wide, but it rocks as I work my way up, and it's hard to keep my balance. The hardest part is near the top. Just before I get to the window, the board twists and Lum has to grab my shirt to keep me from falling.

He is smiling as we work to keep our balance. "Easy, cousin. You seen one, you've seen them all."

It's a little tricky, both of us on the board, but Lum shifts to one side and turns away from the window. "Hold onto the sill," he whispers. "Look through the book."

All of the glass in the window is dark and opaque, and even up close you can't see through it. But the glass that makes up the book is clear, like a regular window pane.

"What's happening?" Lum grabs my belt and tries to swing in behind me. "You see her?"

I can just make out the bed at the far end of the room. The blankets are messed up and piled in mounds, and if you didn't know better, you might think that there were a couple of people in bed under the covers.

"Very funny."

"What?"

"There's no woman."

"You blind?"

Lum turns back and leans over my shoulder, and both of us try to look in through the glass at the same time. Which is a mistake. The board twists suddenly and throws me against the side of the church. I hold onto the sill, and for a moment, I think I'm okay. Then Lum grabs my arm and we're both flipped off the board and land on the ground in a heap.

"Jesus, cousin. Wake up the dead, why don't you?"

The drop isn't far enough to hurt, but it does knock the wind out of me, and I have to lie in the grass until my head finds my body. "You think he heard us?"

"All of Truth heard us." Lum gets up smiling. "Not to mention Bright Water." He starts jogging away from the church. Soldier goes with him, and I limp along as best I can. Every so often, I look over my shoulder to see if the lights in the church go on. They don't, but Monroe could be standing at a window right now watching us.

When we get back to the camp, Lum starts a fire, and we eat the crackers and the apples. Lum goes on about the woman in the church. "She had nipples as big as my thumb."

"Yeah, sure." If Lum wants to play this game, so can I. "Hey, maybe it was the woman from the Horns."

"Hard to tell." Lum rolls up in his sleeping bag and turns away. "She was on her hands and knees most of the time." Soldier crawls over, crowds in against him, and starts snoring almost immediately. I stay awake and watch the fire until it's cold ash and dead coals, and I go to sleep thinking that maybe Lum wasn't kidding about Monroe's having a woman with him. But my dreams are about the woman on the Horns. She's pale blue, like the pad, and in the moonlight, as she rises out of the water and wades ashore, she looks cold and lonely.

In the morning, when I wake up, the world is soft and wet, and the fog clings to the sleeping bag like sweat. Soldier is snuggled up against me now, and his body feels warm and comfortable. I roll over to tell Lum about my dream, but he has already gone. The river bottom is quiet, and all along the banks, the shadow shapes of the cottonwoods lean out over the water like sad people weeping.

CHAPTER TWENTY-THREE

═══

It was my father who brought Soldier home. One night, he came back from work with a cardboard box under his arm. He put the box on the table and told me to guess what it was. Soldier was already crying his heart out, so I didn't have to guess much.

"A dog?"

"Nope," said my father. He was grinning, so I knew he was kidding. "It's supper."

"No, it's not," I said. "It's a dog."

My mother wasn't crazy about having a dog, you could see that right away, and Soldier didn't get off to a good start. My father took him out of the box, and the first thing Soldier did was pee on the table.

"Hey," said my father. "Look at that."

"Gross."

"The plumbing works."

My mother threw my father a cloth, and he wiped up the mess. The whole time, Soldier tried to climb up the side of the box and get back in.

"What kind of dog is it?" I asked.

"This," said my father, "is a boxer."

"Is he going to look like that when he's bigger?"

"And he's got papers," said my father.

"Newspapers," said my mother.

"Status papers," said my father. "He's a status boxer."

My mother picked Soldier up and looked him over the way you would check a tomato or a melon. "You might have asked me first," she said.

"Didn't cost us a thing," said my father. "Woman over in Prairie View breeds them."

"Why'd she give him away?" said my mother.

"Runt of the litter," said my father. "But in the long run, they're the best."

Soldier began whimpering as soon as my mother put him on the floor. I looked at him as he wobbled around.

"What happened to his face?" I said. "It's all pushed in."

"That's just the way boxers are." My father put his arms around my mother and gave her a squeeze. "You always wanted another baby."

"We going to keep him?" I hadn't really thought about having a dog. There were enough dogs around Bright Water to keep me and Lum busy for years.

"Would you like that?" said my father.

"I guess."

"Then you got to think up a good name for him."

I sat on the floor and looked at Soldier close up. He was tan with a flat black pushed-in face. All of him was about the size of a grapefruit. "What does he eat?"

"Milk, I guess," said my father. "When he's a little older, he'll eat anything."

Soldier staggered over to me and tried to get under my shirt. He began whimpering and moaning all at the same time, and licking my fingers, and I didn't have the heart to push him away.

"Should be a strong name," said my father. "Runts get off to a tough start."

That first night, my mother stuffed the box with old rags and put it next to my bed.

"He's sleeping with me?"

"He's your dog," said my mother.

"Puppies get lonely for the first couple of nights," said my father. "Then they're okay."

"But don't let him in bed with you," said my mother. "He gets used to that and you'll never get him out."

Soldier wouldn't stay in the box. Every time I put him in, he would crawl out and sit by the bed and cry. "Go to sleep," I told him, but he would just look at me and cry some more. I fell asleep somewhere between putting him back in the box and waiting for him to climb out again, and in the morning, when I woke and leaned out of bed and looked in the box, he was gone.

At first, I thought he had wandered out into the shop, but my door was closed. I checked around in the blankets in case he had found a way onto the mattress. I looked in the closet. No puppy. I looked under the bed. No puppy.

However, under the bed in the far corner was my favourite sweatshirt. I had been looking all over the place for it and was sure my mother had lost it or thrown it away. I got down on my stomach and reached out as far as I could, grabbed the sleeve, and dragged the shirt out. It was covered with dustballs, but wrapped up in the shirt along with a pair of dirty socks was Soldier.

The day after my father brought Soldier home, Lum came by and we played with the puppy until he threw up on the floor.

"Is he dying?"

"Naw," said Lum. "He's just not used to having such a good time."

"I'm supposed to give him a name."

"Call him Vomit."

"That's not a name for a dog."

"Oh," said Lum, and he picked Soldier up and held him high over his head. "Is that what this is?"

"He's a boxer," I told Lum. "And he's got status papers."

Soldier didn't seem to mind being rolled around on the floor or thrown into the air. He whimpered a little, but the minute you put him down, he'd waddle over and lick your hands until you picked him up again.

"How about Slobber?"

"Dad says it has to be a strong name."

"Stinky," says Lum. "Stinky is a strong name."

"You're going to hurt his feelings."

"Okay," said Lum. "But don't blame me if he winds up with a dumb name."

For the first two or three weeks, I spent most of my time cleaning up after Soldier. I put down newspapers the way my father showed me, and whenever Soldier peed someplace else, I'd rub his nose in it. Then he'd go and poop in the corner.

"I'm not sure I want a dog," I told my mother.

"Tell your father," she said. "Don't tell me."

"Maybe you could mention it to him."

Lum and I figured that Soldier would be more fun if he knew some tricks, so we tried to teach him a few, like how to roll over and how to sit up and how to count with his paw, but I guess he was too small.

"This is one stupid dog," Lum told me.

"He's just a baby."

"Hope he knows how to fight," said Lum. "Otherwise, he's in deep shit."

The amazing thing about Soldier was how fast he grew. The more you fed him, the more he grew. At three months, he was a good-sized dog, as big as many of the other dogs in Bright Water. And he was only half-grown.

And he was friendly. Lum would roll him around in the dirt and throw rocks at him. Once Lum hit him in the back leg with a baseball bat, and Soldier went down in a heap. He lay there whimpering and couldn't get up, and in the end we had to carry him home.

"Didn't hit him that hard."

"You almost killed him!"

"Dog's a wuss."

"You're really mean, Lum."

"You're a wuss, too."

My father thought the leg was broken. "I don't know what they do with dogs," he told me.

"What do you mean?"

"Well," said my father, "they shoot horses."

That night, Soldier crawled under the bed and curled up in his favourite corner. All night, I listened to him shift around and cry. I leaned over the bed and called to him and tried to get him to come up on the bed where I figured he'd be more comfortable, but he was hard into the corner and you could see he wasn't going to move.

Soldier was up the next day, limping badly. You'd think that he would've been angry, but when Lum came by to see how he was doing, Soldier wiggled and limped around after him as if Lum were his best friend.

"Hey, you're one tough puppy," said Lum.

"Dad says his leg might be broken."

Lum was almost two years older than me, so most of the time we did what he wanted to do. Which was okay with me, because he was always doing neat things. One day, we were down at the river fishing. I don't know what happened, but Lum slipped and fell in the water. By the time he got to shore, he was mad as hell.

"Sonofabitch," he shouted at me. "You pushed me!"

"No, I didn't."

"Fucking liar!"

"No way!"

I sat down on the bank and waited for Lum to cool off. He walked back and forth along the river, yelling at the trees and the sky. Then he bent down and picked up a stick and turned on me. He hit me once before I could move, but as he pulled back to take another swing, Soldier charged down the bank and jumped between us.

Soldier didn't make a sound. The hair on his neck sprang up, and he stood there with his legs braced and watched Lum and the stick.

"What're you going to do, doggy?" Lum took a quick step forward to see if Soldier would move. But he stayed put and began growling low in his throat.

"So, you think you're a dog soldier?" said Lum. "You think you're some big brave dog soldier?"

I knew if Lum had come at me with the stick again, Soldier would have stopped him, and I think Lum knew it, too. He stood there with the stick in his hand, watching Soldier. Finally, he cocked his arm and sent the stick sailing into the river.

"Fetch it, asshole," he shouted.

Soldier watched the stick land in the water, and then he turned back to Lum.

"Dog soldier saved your ass today, cousin," said Lum.

"I didn't push you," I said. "You just fell."

"Next time," Lum said, "you might not be so lucky."

After that day at the river, I began calling the puppy Dog Soldier. My mother didn't like the name much, but she said he was my dog and I could call him anything I wanted. My father liked the name and spent part of one Saturday telling me about dog soldiers, when I would rather have been at the matinee at the Frontier.

"They were the bravest men in the tribe," he told me. "The ones who stayed behind and protected the people from attack."

"So, they weren't dogs."

"Sometimes they would tie themselves to a stake or an arrow so they couldn't retreat."

"Why'd they do that?"

"Because they were brave."

"But why were they called dog soldiers?"

"No idea," said my father.

I don't remember when we began simply calling him Soldier. It just happened. It was as though it had always been his name, and had been waiting for him to find it. I thought it was a pretty good name, but Lum said he didn't care.

"I guess you got to call the mutt something."

Each night, Soldier would crawl under my bed and settle into the corner. As I went to sleep, I could hear him grunting and moving about, getting comfortable. And each morning, I would find him at the edge of my bed, watching and waiting for me to wake.

CHAPTER TWENTY-FOUR

All the way to the shop, I'm thinking about breakfast and have decided on sausage and fried potatoes.

"We're home!"

I don't know why, but I expect to see my mother at the sink, working on someone's hair. Instead, the shop is empty and quiet. I drop my stuff on the floor. Soldier trots into the back, just to make sure. When I get to the kitchen, he's waiting for me, curled up in front of the stove. It's strange not having my mother around. My father goes away all the time, but not my mother. She stays put. I look in the refrigerator in case something has changed.

"Cold food," I tell Soldier, and I pull out the bag of dry dog food and pour some in his bowl. He waits to see what I'm having, but as soon as I take the cereal box out of the cupboard and get the milk from the refrigerator, he gives up and begins picking at the food with his tongue. You can tell he's eating just to keep up his strength.

I jump in the shower and stand under the water until it runs cold. I'm not sure that helping Monroe is going to work out. He may or may not be crazy, but he's weird, and just to be safe I figure I better check out other possibilities for jobs. He hasn't paid me anything yet for the work I've already done, and I hope I don't have to ask or take an iron buffalo or a kite in trade.

The railroad yards take up most of the east side of the town. The job gate sits on the northeast corner. Just inside the job gate is a wood shack about the size of my grandmother's chicken coop. It's painted white with red trim, and on one side of the shack is an old sign advertising Washington State apples. There's a large picture of an Indian eating an apple and a caption that reads "Red and Delicious."

When Soldier and I get to the job gate, Wally is in his shack, sitting in his chair, reading a magazine. The windows are closed and the door is shut to keep out the heat, and the desk fan is blowing Wally's thin hair back into a point. Eddie Baton, Sherman Youngman, and Wilfred First Rider are sitting around in the sun outside the fence, waiting. My father is with them, and you can see right away that he's stayed with the drinking.

"Come and sit down," says my father, and he pats the ground next to the fence post. "I saved you the shady spot."

"Elvin tells us he's been giving you driving lessons," says Sherman.

"Did I tell you guys about how my boy here drove my truck into Franklin's tent?"

"No more than twenty times."

"Yeah," says my father, "but my boy hasn't heard me tell it yet, have you?" So my father tells the story, and even though he's added a few things here and there, I still recognize it, and it sounds a lot funnier now than when it happened.

"If you came for a job," says Wilfred, "you're too late."

"No, I'm looking for Lum."

"Wally's already passed out the apples," says Eddie.

"Nothing left but the skins," says Sherman.

It's an old joke, but we all laugh anyway.

"We heard they were running a string of fruit cars in," says my father, "so we thought we'd wait."

"You working for the railroad?"

"Work for anybody for the right money," says my father. "What about you?"

"Sure."

"Not too proud to get your hands dirty?"

"Nope."

My father and Wilfred and Eddie settle in against the fence. Sherman gets to his feet and walks over to the shack. Soldier has been waiting to see if there's any food to be had, and when Sherman heads for the shack, Soldier is right behind him. Maybe he can smell the doughnuts that Wally brings out to the shack every morning, or maybe he's just bored.

"Maybe you should ask Monroe for a loan," says Eddie. "You two used to be best friends."

"Another time," says my father. "Another life."

"High school, college," says Wilfred. "Spent so much time together, we thought they were hot for each other."

"Even used to dress alike," says Eddie.

My father stops Wilfred and Eddie in their tracks with a glance. "Lum hasn't been here," he says to me, and everybody takes a break from talking for a moment and just sits. Finally, Eddie lights a cigarette and passes one to my father. "Lum and his old man kiss and make up yet?"

"They don't get along too well," I say.

"Get along?" says Wilfred. "Hell, Franklin threw him out of the house."

"When?"

My father turns and looks at me. "Kicked the shit out of him while he was at it."

"Franklin's a real hard ass," says Wilfred.

"Losing the missus was rough on him," says Eddie.

My father bangs the back of his head against the wire, as if he's trying to move it around and make it more comfortable. "Franklin was a hard ass long before she died."

I watch Sherman standing down by the gate. The paint on the shack has begun to fade, and the apple on the sign has begun to peel. Underneath, there is nothing but grey metal. Sherman is waving his arms, trying to get Wally's attention. Soldier stands behind him, his tongue hanging out of his mouth like a wet sock. Beyond the shack, the boxcars wait in long lines for something to happen.

"When you see Lum," says Wilfred, "tell him me and Eddie said his old man is a hard ass."

Wally finally sees Sherman and comes out of the shack. They talk for a while, and I can see that both of them are smiling and laughing. Then Wally goes back in the shack, and Sherman wanders over to where we are waiting.

"No luck," he says. "Cars won't be in until tonight."

"Washing boxcars in this heat ain't what I call lucky anyway," says Eddie.

Sherman looks at me. "I told your dog to kill Wally, but all he did was fart."

"That's all Wally ever does," says my father. "We don't need a job anyway."

"That's right," says Eddie. "We're indigenous."

"What we need," says my father, "is something cold."

"So, who's buying?" says Sherman.

My father throws an arm around my shoulders. "You spend all that money already?"

I touch my pocket, and this is a mistake. The men stop talking and look at me.

"Put it all into stocks, no doubt," says Eddie.

"Hell," says my father, and he gives me a squeeze, "it's my money anyway, right?"

I want to tell him that I've left it at home, but it's too late to lie. Sherman stands up and dusts himself off. "That's one hell of a son, Elvin. I got seven kids, and none of them will give me the time of day."

I fish the money out of my pocket and give my father thirty dollars. He fans the tens out and holds them up to the light so you can see through them. I still have twelve dollars left from Railman's, and I try to slip this back in my pocket.

But my father stops me. "What about the rest?"

"Mom gave me this."

"I gave you forty."

"No," I say, "you only gave me thirty."

My father looks away for a moment, so I'm ready, and when I see his arm come forward, I duck, and he hits the fence instead.

"Getting slow, Elvin," says Wilfred, and he begins to laugh.

"Bad luck," says Eddie, "you cut your hand."

My father flexes his knuckles. The blood forms quickly and runs down his fingers.

"Remember?" I say. "You bought three votes. Ten dollars each."

My father wipes the blood on his jeans and turns back to me. "Thirty dollars isn't going to go very far in this heat," he says.

I hand him the twelve dollars.

"You holding out on me?"

"No," I say. "That's all I have."

"Come on, Elvin," says Sherman. "Anything beats the shit out of sitting in the goddamn sun waiting for Wally to share the wealth."

My father gets to his feet and starts moving towards town. "Pay you back as soon as I get ahead, all right?"

"Sure."

"Your mother's money doesn't count, right?" says my father. "I'll take the other ten out of what I owe you."

I watch my father and Eddie and Sherman and Wilfred until they disappear among the boxcars. Soldier comes over and lies down beside me and pushes his nose into my armpit. "It's okay," I tell him, but he has already started to whine, and all I can do is pet him until he calms down.

The walk out across the prairies to the church seems longer than usual, and it is probably because of the heat. The yellow grass crackles as if it's getting ready to shiver and burst into flames. Soldier plods along behind me, dragging his nose through the grass. The grasshoppers dance all around us, throwing themselves into the air like water from a sprinkler. Soldier doesn't even nod in their direction. I figure we'll go by the church one last time and see if I can get paid for the work I did the day before yesterday. That way, Lum and I can do whatever we want.

"It'll be cooler inside," I tell Soldier, and I make a straight line for where I figure the front door should be. It takes me a while to find the side of the building and work my way back to the doorknob. Even before I turn the knob and open the door, I can feel the cool air inside getting ready to rush out and greet us. "See?" I say to Soldier. "Much better." He takes eight or ten steps into the church and flops down on the floor, as if someone has shot him.

The stacks of boxes have all been moved to the far end of the church, and the place looks larger now and almost spacious. I don't see Monroe, but I get the feeling that he might be hiding somewhere and that, if I'm not careful, he'll come sailing down from the ceiling or roller skating out of the kitchen or tumbling through a window. I walk to the middle of the church and sit on the bentwood box.

"Soldier."

Soldier doesn't move and he doesn't open his eyes.

"Find Monroe."

Lum and I saw a movie once with this French detective and his Asian sidekick. Every time the detective came home, the sidekick would attack him, just to keep him in shape. Once, the sidekick was waiting for him in the refrigerator.

Monroe is not in the refrigerator, but there is a bottle of orange juice, and I pour myself a glass. There are fresh flowers in the vase on the counter, too. "You want some music?" I ask Soldier. I raise the lid on the piano and sit down on the stool. "Maybe you'd like something melancholic."

I work my fingers across the keys the way I've seen real pianists do on television, and even though the sound is all jumbled, I can hear that the piano is a good one and that, if I knew how to play, it would sound great.

"Maybe a little *Carmen*." I search around on the keys, and in no time at all, I've got part of the toreador song down pat.

"Can you sing?"

I turn around and see someone standing in the doorway. The prairie light is blinding, and at first, I can't tell if it's a man or a woman. But it's Monroe's voice. He steps into the church and closes the door, and now that I can see him clearly, I'm not sure it was a good idea to come unannounced. Monroe's wig has been braided and tied with red cloth, and his face has been divided in half. One side is painted black with red dots and the other side has been painted white with black dots. A thin yellow line runs across his forehead and there are long, thick blue marks on each cheek.

"Can you sing?" he asks again.

"A little."

"Write any poetry?"

"You okay?"

"Do you mean, am I crazy?" Monroe says, as if he's just read my mind.

"My mother can sing pretty well."

Monroe glides into the kitchen. Soldier gets up and follows him. "I'm not crazy," he shouts. "Do you know what a minstrel is?"

"Sure," I say. "It's a politician."

Monroe starts laughing, and he laughs so hard that I begin laughing, too. "Minstrel," he says, "is a medieval term to describe someone who sings songs or recites poetry."

"My auntie Cassie can probably sing, too." I watch Monroe to see if he wants to give anything away.

"Minstrels sing about heroes and great deeds," says Monroe. "You want to be my minstrel?"

One job with Monroe is plenty, but I'm curious. "Singing?"

"That's right." Monroe rushes over and sits down at the piano with me. "Here's how it works. I'm the hero, and you have to make up songs and stories about me so no one forgets who I am."

"What would it pay?"

Monroe begins to play the piano and hum a tune I think I know. Then he stands up, takes off his shirt, and begins to dance. "For instance," he says, "what am I famous for?"

"You're an artist."

"Doesn't count." Monroe takes off his pants. Soldier watches Monroe as he spins around the room. "What about great deeds? Can you name any of my great deeds?"

I think about the church, but I don't know if this is a great deed or just a trick that you do with paint.

"Exactly." Monroe stops dancing. "I haven't done any great deeds yet," he says. "But I will."

"You're rich," I say, in case he feels like paying me what he owes me. "Does that count?"

"And when I do," says Monroe, "I want you there."

"You could save a beautiful woman."

"They don't need saving." Monroe puts on his clothes. "In the old days, it was easy being a hero. And glamorous. All you had to do was slay a dragon."

"What about monsters?"

"Only monsters left in this world are human beings." Monroe goes to the stack of iron buffalo and begins counting silently to himself. "Did you bring a notebook?"

"No."

"Tape recorder?"

"Don't have one."

"Camcorder?"

"You're kidding, right?"

"Okay," says Monroe. "The oral tradition it is then." He pulls one of the iron buffalo out of the pile and begins dragging it towards the door. "Give me a hand."

For the next hour, I help Monroe load the buffalo onto the truck, while he tells me his life story. "I was born in 1952," he says. "June. Can you remember that?"

"My mother was born in January."

"When I arrived, my mother and father were happy to see me. Make sure you say that."

"Auntie Cassie was born in October."

"My favourite food is macaroni. With butter and ketchup."

We work our way along the ridge of the coulees. Soldier wants to sit in the front with me, but there's no room. He's a poor sport about this and tries to sit so that he blocks Monroe's rear view. Every so often, he squeezes his face against the rear window and drags his tongue back and forth until the glass is covered with thick slobber, and everything you see out the back looks distorted and bent to one side.

"My favourite colour is red."

We stop at the groups of buffalo we set up the day before. Monroe counts them carefully to make sure that every one is there and that none of the buffalo has wandered off and gotten lost.

"Little hard for them to wander off," I say.

"My favourite piece of music is 'Classical Gas.'"

"Especially since they're made out of iron."

"I like dark chocolate."

"Especially since they're nailed into the earth."

When we get to the long bluff overlooking the bridge, we stop. Soldier is out of the truck in a flash and launches himself into the grass.

"Soldier!"

It's no use. He's gone, and I know that I'm going to have to go after him.

"He run off like that a lot?"

"Every so often."

"I knew someone like that," says Monroe. "Always running away."

"What happened to him?"

"What always happens."

I help Monroe lift two of the larger buffalo off the truck. We drag them out to a small flat and face them so they can see the bridge and the river. And then we turn them so they face the mountains.

"Better go find him." Monroe sits down in the grass. "I'm going to have to think about this for a while."

I grab a piece of rope out of the back of the truck. If I find Soldier and he's having a good time, I may have to drag him back. He could be anywhere, but for the first little while, I can see where the grass is bent over and I have no difficulty following his trail. Every so often, I stop and listen just in case I can hear him ahead of me. It's kind of fun tracking Soldier, and as I make my way down the side of the coulee, I begin to imagine that I'm an old-time tracker on the trail of game. I take off my shirt and rub dirt on my body to kill my scent and to help me blend in with the landscape, and I get low to the ground and move through the grass as quickly and silently as I can.

I lose Soldier's trail almost immediately, but from the general direction he was headed in, I figure he's on his way to the bridge and the river. Maybe this is where he goes when he runs away. Maybe he has a secret place where no one can find him.

On top of the coulee, everything is sunshine and heat. But at the bottom, the air is cool and misty, and I have to put my shirt back on. The sun is beginning to burn away the fog along the river now, and there are long stretches where you can see the grey-green water floating low against the sides of the coulees. But among the cottonwoods and along the low runs of willow, the fog clings to the water, thin and silky, while in the shadows and the deep curves, it lies in dark pools so thick and heavy that nothing is going to move it.

Soldier is waiting for me by one of the bridge abutments. I'm a little disappointed that he wasn't harder to find, or that he didn't try to jump out at me from ambush or, at least, give me the chance to try to lasso him. Instead, he's lying in plain sight on a blue pad, and at first, I think he's found another one of those hospital things and dragged it out of the river.

"Soldier, get off that!"

But I'm wrong. It's a sleeping bag, and even before I see the backpack leaning against the concrete piling and the hockey stick and the basketball, I know that he's found Lum. Soldier wanders around the camp, sniffing as he goes. I squat next to the firepit and move my hand over the burnt sticks and the ashes.

Cold.

Soldier lies down next to the sleeping bag, buries his nose in it, and tries to look pathetic. I sit down next to him and tie the rope to his collar.

"Good boy," I say, which is only fair since he found the camp. "What a good boy."

Camping out is great as long as you have enough food and it doesn't rain or snow. Lum and I have done it lots of times. But part of the fun is knowing that you can always go home and get something hot to eat and watch a little television. I don't think I'd like it much if I had to do it all the time. The sleeping bag is damp. I pick it up and shake it off. Lum's blanket is rolled up in a ball underneath the bag, and I don't see it until I trip over it. Soldier sniffs at it, hard, and I can see he's hoping it's food.

"Forget it."

In addition to being wet, the bag also smells sweaty. I unzip it all the way and spread it out on the abutment so it can air. I hear Soldier behind me, and by the time I turn around, he's busy unrolling the blanket. "Leave it alone."

Inside the blanket, wrapped up like a baby, is the skull.

I pick up a stick and begin scratching at the ground near the firepit. "Where's Lum?" Soldier watches me as I write in the dirt. "Go find Lum."

Soldier creeps forward, puts his head on my leg, and begins to moan so it sounds as if he's singing. "It's not a baby." I wrap the skull back up in the blanket and set it next to the sleeping bag. "It's a bone."

I stand up and look at the message. Just to be safe, I push the stick into the ground as a marker, so when Lum comes back, he won't walk on the words before he has a chance to read them. I jerk on the rope to let Soldier know I'm ready to go, but he stays on the ground. His ears are tight to his head and the fur on his neck is curled up in folds.

"Calm down," I tell him, and as I speak, I feel something move at the edge of the camp. Something that flutters in the shadows of the bridge.

"Will he bite?"

Soldier lunges forward, barking, and almost yanks my arm off. I pull hard on the rope and fall over backwards.

"You okay?" It's the girl from the tent. I roll up on my side and snap the rope to let Soldier know it's not funny. "Sorry," she says. "I didn't mean to upset your dog."

I get up and brush myself off. Soldier bristles at my side. "He just likes to complain." I tighten the rope. I can see the collar cut into Soldier's neck, but his shoulders are set, and it's like trying to strangle a log.

"It's all right," says Rebecca. "He's just scared."

Soldier pulls his jowls up so you can see all his teeth. I don't know what's wrong with him, but I'm not happy with his manners.

"Here," says Rebecca, "I'll give you this if you and your dog will help me find my duck."

I have enough to do already, but it won't do any harm to keep my eyes open. And I figure that Rebecca will feel better if other people are looking for her duck, too.

She reaches up and undoes the red ribbon from her hair and holds it out. "It's almost new." The ribbon floats in the breeze.

"You can keep it," I say.

"No," says Rebecca. "You may need it. Maybe your dog would like it."

Soldier's fur is standing up now, and I can hear low rumblings rising out of his body like thunder. Rebecca looks across the river towards Bright Water.

"You and your folks staying for Indian Days?"

Rebecca nods. "Then we have to go." She looks tired, as if she's walked a long ways today and still has a long ways to go. I wonder if she is one of those girls who eat and then throw up after each meal in order to stay skinny.

"Your duck will probably be back by then."

"If she's not," says Rebecca, "Mr. Ross says we'll have to go without her. He says the soldiers won't wait for a duck."

"So, your folks are in the military?"

Soldier plants his legs and lurches forward. I see it coming and set my feet, and he winds up on his hind legs, his front legs dangling in the air. He's trying to bark but the collar presses into his throat and cuts off the sound. Rebecca kneels and looks at Soldier, as if she is trying to find something in his eyes, as if the two of them have a secret that they're not going to share with anyone else.

"Guess I'll see you at Indian Days," I say.

Rebecca smiles, turns her back to the camp, and heads for the river and the ferry. In her long dress, in the long prairie grass, she looks as if she is floating.

As soon as he can't see Rebecca anymore, Soldier calms down. "That wasn't very nice," I tell him. He nuzzles my leg. I reach down and scratch his ears, and when I look down, I can see that he has peed all over the ground.

By the time I get back to the truck, Monroe has finished setting up the last of the buffalo. "What do you think?"

They're all facing the river. Off to one side, Monroe has staked a small buffalo by itself, away from the rest, looking back towards the church.

"Is that supposed to be a baby?"

"Magic," says Monroe. "If you want the herds to return, you have to understand magic."

"Where's the mother?"

"Realism will only take you so far." He walks over and shakes the baby buffalo to make sure it's firmly anchored. "Every so often, a calf will get lost or separated from the herd."

"We've got a real herd of buffalo over in Bright Water."

"If the baby doesn't make it back to the herd in time, the coyotes will find it."

I look at the baby buffalo and wonder what the coyotes will think when they come out for an evening and find something like this stuck in the middle of the prairies. They might howl at it and they might pee on it, but I doubt that they'll try to eat it.

"It's sad." Monroe brushes his jeans off and throws the hammer into the truck. "But it happens all the time."

Soldier wanders out of the coulee and slides over to one of the buffalo and sticks his head through its body.

"You found him," says Monroe. "Where was he?"

"Down by the bridge."

Monroe shades his eyes and looks towards the river. "Well, would you look at that," he says.

At first, I don't see it. And then I do. A thick twist of dark smoke rising up beyond the bridge on the other side of the river. "Indian Days," I say. "Everybody's getting the camp set up."

"Not that," says Monroe. "Down there."

For a moment, I think that Monroe has spotted Lum on one of his runs along the river bottom, on his way back to camp, and I already have my hand up to catch his attention when the Cousins appear.

Monroe closes the back of the truck. "I was wondering where they went."

The Cousins follow the river and the line of cottonwoods, keeping to the shadows and moving among the trees like a long snake in three parts. They move slowly, fanning out along the shore, circling around the back water as if they're looking for something they've lost.

"When I was a kid," says Monroe, "I wanted to be a hero."

We're too far away to do anything about it, but I'm hoping Rebecca doesn't run into the Cousins since she and dogs don't seem to get along too well.

"Everybody wanted to be a hero," says Monroe.

I wave my arms and whistle to see if I can get the dogs' attention.

"Lots of great deeds left to do in this world." Monroe begins waving his arms, too. "But nobody wants to do them."

The Cousins disappear into the willows. I watch the trees and the deep grass for a while, and then I put my hands down. Monroe keeps waving. "You know what's wrong with this world?" He holds his arms out as if he's trying to feel for something in the air. "Nobody has a sense of humour."

Across the river, the smoke rises into the sky, thicker now and darker, and I can see that I was wrong. It's not coming from Bright Water or the Indian Days camp.

"Dragons." Monroe looks across the river at the smoke.

"No," I say. "It's the landfill."

"We spend all our time looking for dragons to kill."

"Sometimes they set it on fire in order to burn off the garbage."

"Dragons," says Monroe, and he shakes his head. "Even in the old days, they were never the problem."

CHAPTER TWENTY-FIVE

═══

Lucy Rabbit figures that Marilyn Monroe is an Indian because of pictures she saw of Marilyn when Marilyn was really young, before she dyed her hair blonde and became a famous star. "She was born on the first day of June," Lucy told my mother. "Same as me. What about that?"

My mother didn't say that Marilyn wasn't an Indian, but she said she was sure that there were other people born on the first of June who weren't Indians.

"Not many," Lucy told her.

Then there was the matter of Marilyn's father. "She never knew her father," Lucy said. "She was raised by her grandparents." Lucy had Marilyn's complete life story, from her birth in 1926 on the Curve Lake Reserve in Ontario to her murder by Mafia hit men working for the Kennedys. "She died young, of drugs. Sounds like an Indian to me."

Lucy worked for the band, and there wasn't much about a computer that Lucy couldn't explain. We didn't have a computer, but if we had and if we'd had any questions about it, we could have asked Lucy. That was how she found out that Marilyn Monroe was an Indian.

"You get on the Internet, and you can go to all these sites that have information on everything and everybody."

I was sort of intrigued by the Internet. I had heard about it, and sometimes I saw an advertisement on television for an Internet service, but neither Lum nor I had ever really seen the Internet in action.

"You type in a key phrase," Lucy told me, "and up pops everything on that subject."

"Neat."

"So I typed 'Marilyn Monroe,' and the first item was her biography."

"And it said she was an Indian."

"No," said Lucy. "It said she married a baseball player."

Even without a computer, Lucy was formidable. She knew everybody on the reserve and what they were doing. She could trace families all the way back to the old days before Whites arrived.

"When Marilyn's father left her mother, he went down to the States."

My mother liked to listen to Lucy, and so did I. She had some great stories and some good gossip, only she told us that nobody called it gossip anymore.

"The information highway," Lucy said. "That's what they call it now."

According to Lucy, Marilyn's father married a second time and had a son. "You ready for this?" she said. "Elvis Presley."

I knew more about Elvis Presley than I did about Marilyn Monroe, and I could see this because Elvis did look as if he could be Indian.

"Same sad story," Lucy told us. "If you put their lives side by side, you'd swear that they were twins." She brought some pictures of Elvis to the shop and laid them next to some pictures of Marilyn and told us to imagine Marilyn with dark hair. "What do you see?"

"What are we looking for?"

Lucy took a black marker and coloured in Marilyn's hair, and that made the looking easier. "Two peas in a pod," said Lucy, and I could see that they might be brother and sister. "You'd really be able to see the resemblance," she said, "if they had had the same mother."

When Lucy showed up with her Elvis pictures, I came up with what I thought was a pretty good idea. "Why don't you go back to your old hair colour?" I said. "Then you'd look like Elvis."

Lucy said it wasn't just the physical look she was after. "Marilyn was ashamed of being Indian," she said. "That's why she bleached her hair."

"A lot of people were ashamed of being Indian in those days," said my mother. "But they didn't all bleach their hair."

"And that's why I want to bleach my hair," said Lucy.

"Why?"

"So Marilyn can see that bleaching your hair doesn't change a thing."

Both Marilyn and Elvis looked pretty good in those pictures, and I was sure that both of them had someone like my mother to wash and cut their hair and to keep it from getting out of hand. Lucy liked to say that you could learn a lot about Indians and life in general by studying the lives of Marilyn Monroe and Elvis Presley. "All the women wanted to be Marilyn," she said.

"Like you?"

"And all the men wanted to be Elvis."

I don't think my mother saw much of a connection between Marilyn and Elvis and Indians. "Even if they were Indians," she told Lucy, "what difference did it make?"

"Elvis actually played an Indian in one of his movies," said Lucy.

"Lot of people who weren't Indians played Indians in movies," said my mother.

Lucy said that times change and that now everyone wanted to be an Indian. "Look at Adolph Hungry Wolf."

"The German guy?"

"He speaks good Blackfoot and lives in the woods."

"So?"

"It's a small world," Lucy would say. "It's a lot smaller than you think."

"Like Marilyn and Elvis?" I said.

"Everybody's related," Lucy told us. "The trouble with this world is that you wouldn't know it from the way we behave."

CHAPTER TWENTY-SIX

My mother doesn't come home that night or the next day. But when I get up the following morning, I hear someone turn the taps on in the shop, and the title song from *Oklahoma!* fills the room. And over the sound of the water and the music, I hear my mother's voice. She's standing at the sink looking as if she's never left. Soldier lies by the window in the sunshine. You can see he's happy to have her back.

Carol Millerfeather is sitting in the chair, a towel wrapped around her neck.

"Hi," I say.

"Hi," says my mother, and that's all she says.

"I'll bet you're proud," says Carol.

Carol has interesting hair. It's thick, for one thing, and looks as if it weighs more than it should. Most of it is grey and it sticks out from her head like an umbrella.

"I'll bet you're proud," Carol says again, and this time she looks right at me.

"You bet," I say, even though I don't have a clue what she's talking about.

"Who knows where it will lead."

My mother gets a comb and begins whacking at Carol's hair the same way she cuts vegetables on the cutting board.

"So, how was Waterton?"

"You need to put your sleeping bag away," says my mother.

"Did you stay at that fancy hotel?"

"And you forgot to knock all the mud off your shoes."

"I suppose you took the bus out to the lake."

My mother snips away at Carol's hair. I sit down on the sleeping bag and tie my shoes. On the chair next to me is a large envelope with *Snow White* written on the outside. "What's this?" I hold it up so my mother can see.

"The script," says Carol.

"Mom got a part in the play?"

"Your mother's the lead," says Carol.

"Snow White?"

Carol shakes her head and waves a hand. "No," she says. "Snow White is just another pretty face. Your mother is going to be the Queen."

"The wicked Queen?"

"She's not really wicked." My mother runs the razor around Carol's neck. Short hair is supposed to be the new fashion for women, but I don't think they had Carol in mind.

"The Queen is the best role in the play," says Carol as she slips out of the chair and does up the straps on her overalls. "Any fool can play Snow White."

The flowers my father brought are lying on the window sill. I had forgotten about them. They hadn't been in very good shape to begin with, but now they're dead. My mother heads for the kitchen. I gather up the flowers and follow her.

"Dad came by while you were gone."

My mother takes the eggs and sausage out of the refrigerator and puts the iron skillet on the stove. "You hungry?" she says, and she takes the sack of potatoes out of the bottom drawer.

"He left these."

My mother glances at the flowers, but I know there's nothing to save. I sit at the table and watch her cut the potatoes into thin slices and slide them into the hot skillet.

"He was surprised you got a room at the lake this time of the year."

"Was he?"

"He said the place is usually booked solid."

"Did he?"

"He thought maybe you changed your mind and went someplace else."

My mother reaches into her pocket and hands me a package wrapped in gold paper. "You want your eggs scrambled?"

Inside the box is a silver belt buckle with "Waterton Lake" written across the top and a lake and a bunch of trees carved into the metal. Sometimes the best way to get my mother talking about a particular topic is to change the subject and then work your way back to where you wanted to be. It starts her mind moving in a different direction, and after a while, she may forget about what she didn't want to tell me.

"So, what do you think auntie Cassie is going to do?"

This is the thing to say. My mother stops watching the skillet and looks at me. I can see she's trying to figure out if I know anything. "Cassie always does what she wants," my mother says, and she drops the sausage in the pan.

"Is that why she came home?"

"I see granny's lodge is up." My mother cracks the eggs and dumps in a bunch of pepper. "I hope you helped her."

Soldier comes over and lies down in front of the stove. My mother hooks her foot under his belly. He grunts but he doesn't get up or roll out of the way. He makes my mother nudge him across the linoleum floor with her leg, sliding him along like a sack of beans. "I'm going over as soon as I finish here," she says.

"Is it supposed to be a secret?"

"Indian Days?" says my mother.

"That she's pregnant."

My mother stops what she's doing and looks at me. "Who?"

"Auntie Cassie." I'm expecting that my mother is going to tell me that auntie Cassie's being pregnant is adult business. "I can keep a secret," I say. "Auntie Cassie knows I can keep a secret."

"Cassie told you she was pregnant?" My mother is wrestling with what looks like a frown, but she's losing.

"Sure," I say, but I don't know if I'm very convincing.

"Good," says my mother, and she shovels the eggs and potato and sausage onto a plate and hands it to me. "Now you know." My mother goes back to the shop and leaves me to eat alone, which I don't think is very nice, seeing as how she's been gone for the last two days. Soldier sits at attention and watches me. When I'm done, I put the plate on the floor and let him chase it around with his tongue. He corners the plate against the stove, licks everything off in a couple of swipes, and goes to work on the glaze.

I'm thinking I should go to the bridge and try to find Lum, see how he's doing, or I should stop by my father's shop to see if he's feeling any better. But both of them will be at Indian Days. My father always sets up a booth, and Lum is going to run in the race. So, I lie down on the couch and drag my mother's quilt out of the basket. The needles tinkle as I toss the quilt over my feet, and when I kick it into position, I can hear the washers rattle.

It's comfortable under the quilt, and I roll back and forth until I'm wrapped up like a baby. Soldier looks up from his plate and then he goes back to his grunting and licking. I don't plan on falling asleep, but I guess I'm tired from all the running around. And I guess I'm still thinking about the woman on the Horns, because that's what I dream about.

In my dream, the woman is standing above the river with her back to me. She's looking over the side of the Horns, and even though it's dark, down below on the water you can see a duck swimming back and forth. Every so often, the duck dives down and comes up with a fish in its mouth. But other times, the duck bobs to the surface with a bone or a beak full of baby clothes.

I keep trying to get the woman to turn around, but in the end she jumps off the Horns, and as she falls, the duck flies up and catches her and sets her gently on a suitcase that is floating on the water.

When I wake up, my mother is at the sink in the kitchen, washing her hands. I snuggle down into the quilt until just my face is showing. "Look at me."

My mother glances my way and shakes her head.

"I'm a baby."

"Get up, little baby," says my mother.

"I can't move. I'm too little."

My mother walks over to the couch, her hands dripping wet. I duck under the quilt just as she flicks her fingers. "Missed me." Which isn't the smart thing to say. My mother sits on my stomach and runs her cold hands under the quilt.

"No fair!"

"My," says my mother, "such a large vocabulary for a baby."

"You're going to squish the baby."

"Then I guess the baby better get up."

I'm nice and warm, and I'm not sure I want to get up. My mother goes back to the sink, and I lie on the couch and fiddle with the edge of the quilt. My mother has added some things to this area. She's linked safety pins in a semicircle around a yellow diamond so that they look a little like an old-time headdress.

"I don't mind if you give my baby clothes to auntie Cassie."

"What baby clothes?"

"The ones in the suitcase."

My mother wipes her hands. "You ready to go?" She kicks off her slippers and steps into her shoes.

"Really," I say. "I don't mind."

The more people on the ferry, the better Soldier likes it. I pull us across, and my mother pets him, so all he does is dribble on the bottom of the bucket. My mother is humming to herself, and I can see that if I don't do something quickly, she's going to burst into song.

"Tell me about the time you and auntie Cassie switched dresses in that restaurant."

"Where did you hear that story?"

"You and auntie Cassie."

My mother looks at me, and then she looks over the side of the bucket and watches the river flow beneath us. "Nothing to tell."

"I'll bet dad and uncle Franklin were surprised."

"Franklin?" says my mother. "Franklin wasn't there."

I've only heard the story a couple of times, and there's always the chance I am remembering it wrong. "So, who was with auntie Cassie?"

My mother pauses, and I can see that she is all set to tell me that it's none of my business. Then she nods and takes a breath. "Elvin."

"Dad?"

"They dated when we were at Wild Rose Community College."

"Then who were you with?"

My mother folds her arms across her breasts and turns her back to me. She stands framed against the clear prairie sky and looks out towards Bright Water. Even before I ask the question, I know the answer.

"Monroe Swimmer?"

"Another time," says my mother. "Another life."

Above the slide and roll of the ferry, you can hear the Indian Days drum now. It rises out of the land like the spring storms that appear on the prairies suddenly and without warning and catch you by surprise.

207

CHAPTER TWENTY-SEVEN

━━━━

Summers in Truth and Bright Water can be boring, but Indian Days are always great.

When we get out to the reserve that afternoon, my grandmother already has a bucket of tea on the boil. My mother and auntie Cassie lounge around on the mattress while my grandmother tells them who's already arrived and who's on their way.

"Don't let your father throw you for a loop," auntie Cassie tells me.

"Dad?"

"It was Lucy's idea," says my mother.

"What'd he do?"

"Just looking for attention," says my grandmother.

I sit in the lawn chair and wait to see if my mother is going to tell me what my father has done, but my grandmother is already working on who's getting married and who Edna Baton saw in Blossom with a woman who wasn't his wife. When my grandmother gets to who's pregnant, I look at my mother and auntie Cassie to see if either of them is going to mention what's happening in auntie Cassie's life. My mother closes her eyes. Auntie Cassie stuffs a pillow against her side and pushes her feet under one of the blankets.

The conversation is interesting for a while, but then the talk shifts to things like band politics and medical operations and how people should live their lives. When my mother and auntie Cassie begin to warm up on men, I get up and head for the door. I know they're not talking about me, but I have things to do and places to go, and I've heard most of this stuff before.

Soldier is waiting for me. I hold the flap open to see if he's stupid enough to go inside. "She was asking about you."

Soldier narrows his eyes.

When he was a puppy, Soldier followed me into my grandmother's tipi and wandered over to her, thinking he had found a friend. My grandmother wasn't mean about it. She didn't yell at him or chase him around the stove. She waited until Soldier forgot where he was, and as he turned his back to sniff at the cooler, she dropped out of the air like a hawk and snatched him up. He yelped once, more surprise than fear, and then he was out the flap on the fly.

"It's true," I say. "Go on in and check it out." But he doesn't budge. He sits back and shakes his head and scolds me for trying to get him into trouble.

The tourists who show up for Indian Days can get almost anything they want. Beaded belt buckles, acrylic paintings of the mountains, drawings of old-time Indians on horseback, deer-horn knives, bone chokers, T-shirts that say things like "Indian and Proud," and "Indian Affairs Are the Best." And all of it, according to the signs that everyone puts up, is "authentic" and "traditional." Fenton Bull Runner and his wife Maureen make dream catchers out of willow shoots and fishing line. Edna Baton runs a frybread stand. Lucille Rain and her sister Teresa do bead-work. Jimmy Hunt and his family sell cassettes of old-time powwow songs. My father brings whatever thing he's working on at the time.

Other artists come in from places like Red Deer, Medicine River, Hobbema, or from across the line, Browning, Missoula, Flathead Lake. Some of them rent the booths that the band puts up just below the big tent, and some of them sell off the back of their pickup trucks. A few just spread their blankets on the grass and wait for the tourists to wander over.

Lucy Rabbit is in my father's booth, hanging animal mirrors on the poles. A couple of women are looking at one of the turtle mirrors, and a guy in a pair of coveralls is picking through the coyote carvings.

"Where's dad?"

"You looking for the old hound dog?" says the tourist in the coveralls. It's my father's voice, but I don't recognize him right away.

"Love me tender, love me true." My father puts an arm around Lucy, and the two of them start to sing. He has a pair of sunglasses on and his hair has been slicked up so it looks like a large wave, the kind you see in travel magazines that curls up out of the ocean just before it hits the beach.

"Elvis Presley, right?"

"'Cause, my darling, I love you, and I always will."

The sunglasses are the mirrored kind, and when I look right at them, I can see everything going on behind me. Someone has painted sideburns on my father. They look okay, but he's sweating in the coveralls, and the sideburns are beginning to melt.

"It's Elllllviiiiin the Pelvis," sings my father, and he wiggles his hips around. Lucy holds her dress down as the wind swings through the booths and snaps the flags and the streamers.

"You guys seen Lum?"

"He'll be here," says my father. "Big race is today."

"Couple busloads of Japanese tourists just pulled in from Banff." Lucy looks over at the parking lot. "See those guys there?"

Three men are moving through the cars and the pickups. They're all dressed in buckskin shirts and fringed leather pants. One of them is wearing a good-looking bone breastplate. Their faces are painted so I can't see who they are, but they don't move as if they're from around here.

"Germans," says my father, and he takes out his comb and runs it through the wave. "They're from one of those Indian clubs in Germany."

"They want to talk to an elder," says Lucy.

"Bunch of wannabes," says my father.

"I think it's sweet," says Lucy.

"That's because you wannabe Marilyn Monroe." My father wiggles his hips at Lucy, and Soldier barks happily and jumps him from behind.

"Hey!"

"He just wants to play."

"When you see Lum," says Lucy, "wish him luck." She goes back to hanging the mirrors. My father takes off the glasses and squints in the bright light. "Got a surprise."

"What is it?"

"Have to get the booth set up first," he says, and he has to stop to wipe his eyes. "Meet me in the parking lot in half an hour."

"You and mom getting back together?"

"Who told you that?"

"Just guessing."

"And don't believe everything Cassandra tells you either." My father puts his sunglasses back on. "How do I look?"

Soldier and I wander over to Edna Baton's booth and get some frybread.

"You hungry?" she says when she sees me.

I give her my dollar and she finds the biggest piece of frybread in the basket. "How's your mother?"

"Fine," I say. "You seen Lum?"

"Saw Franklin."

The three German guys dressed up as Indians arrive at the booth, and Soldier goes over to make friends. They stand in a group and talk in low whispers, looking up every so often to see what Edna is doing. "They want to know the secret of authentic frybread," Edna tells me in a low voice. "The guy with the bones offered me twenty-five dollars."

"Did you tell them?"

"Naw," says Edna. "I've got my pride."

"Right."

"The Deutschmark is strong right now," she says. "So, I'm holding out for fifty."

One of the Germans, a tall guy with the bone breastplate, breaks away from the other two and comes to the stand. I keep my voice down. "How many times have you sold the recipe this year?"

"Twice, so far. But there's a woman from Montreal who's going to come back as soon as she finds her husband." Edna wipes her hands and winks at me. "Looks like it's time to do some fur trading."

Edna says hello to the German guy and the two of them start talking. The German guy keeps gesturing to the other men, who stay where they are. Edna has her Indian face on now. She points with her lips and makes elaborate signs like slapping her hands across one another and tracing a circle in the sky with her arm. The German guy crosses his arms on his chest. Edna nods, reaches down, and comes up with a small drum and starts singing a round dance. The German guy is suddenly all smiles and he can't get his hand into his pocket fast enough.

Soldier and I walk out to the buffalo run, and I can see right away that Franklin was right about tourists and shooting buffalo. There is a long line at the corral and people are gathered at the car fence two and three deep with their cameras. I can't see a thing, and all I can hear is the rattle of conversation and the rumble of the motorcycles. The speakers up at the tent suddenly come to life and begin blasting out powwow songs across the prairies, and for a moment, the people at the buffalo run turn back towards the tent.

"Hey, son," says one of the tourists. "You from around here?"

"Sure."

"This is Bill. I'm Rudy."

Rudy is a little taller than I am. He wears heavy glasses and has a beard that goes all the way around his face. Bill is skinnier with cold blue eyes and hair that looks more like hay gone bad.

"Hi."

"Bill here says that a buffalo can outrun a dog."

I don't have to look to see that Soldier is frowning at Bill.

"What do you say?"

"They're probably about the same," I tell Rudy. "A dog might be a little faster."

"What'd I tell you?" says Rudy

"Shit," says Bill. "Let's ask someone who knows."

I get to the parking lot early. It's quiet, and I don't see my father anywhere. Soldier and I walk up and down the rows until all the cars and trucks and vans and RVs begin to look the same. I'm just about ready to turn around and head back to the booth when I hear someone honk.

"Hey!"

It's my father. And he's driving the Karmann Ghia.

"What do you think?" My father pulls the car alongside and stops it.

"You fixed it."

"Where's your mother?"

Soldier jumps on the side of the car and looks around at the interior.

"She's at granny's lodge."

"Shit."

"Auntie Cassie is there, too."

My father smiles and runs his hand through his hair. He guns the engine a bit and looks in the rearview mirror a couple of times, as if he suspects that someone is sneaking up behind him. "Granny in a good mood?"

"I guess."

"Shit."

Soldier's ears go up. He gets off the car and turns back to the big tent. His body goes stiff and he begins to growl. I watch him out of the corner of my eye in case it's something serious like the Cousins.

"You want to do your old man a favour?"

It's Rebecca Neugin. She's standing by the side of the big tent but I can't see her clearly.

"Why don't you go tell your mother that there's a surprise for her in the parking lot," my father says. "Could you do that?"

"Sure."

"Great. Look, I'll park it down there. Don't tell her what it is. I want to see her face." My father starts to pull the car forward, and then he stops. "What happened with that girlfriend of yours?"

"Who?"

My father gives me one of his sly smiles. "The one we talked about at lunch the other day."

"Oh," I say. "No. That was nothing."

"I know," says my father, and he lets the clutch out. "Women are fickle as hell."

I watch my father pull the car into a parking space at the end of the lot. Soldier is still standing stiff and hard, but when I look again, Rebecca has disappeared.

We're halfway to my grandmother's tipi when Soldier slows down and begins angling off towards the tent and the music. I figure he wants to check things out for himself.

"Okay," I tell him. "But don't go getting lost."

I guess I'm expecting to find my mother and auntie Cassie and my grandmother sitting around drinking tea and talking, but when I step through the opening, the lodge is empty. This is a little annoying. I hang around for a while, but my mother and auntie Cassie and granny don't come back. I'm afraid to leave my father sitting in the car much longer, so I leave my mother a quick note and jog up to the parking lot to tell him that she's disappeared again. I half expect that he'll be gone like everyone else, but instead he's sitting in the car in the bright sun, shuffling his deck of cards.

"Hi," I say.

"Where's your mother?" There are four empty beer cans on the seat next to my father.

"She wasn't there."

"Shit," says my father. "Where'd she go this time?"

"Don't know."

My father reaches down and comes up with another beer. "It's a beauty, isn't it?" He runs his hand across the dashboard.

"Can I drive it?"

"You ought to hear the engine open up."

"Is it fast?"

"No," says my father, "but it corners pretty good."

"Mom's going to like it."

"I don't know," says my father, and he cracks the can. "If she doesn't show up pretty soon, I may just take it home with me."

"But it's mom's car."

My father finishes the beer and crushes the can against his thigh. "It's her car when I say it's her car."

"Why don't we both look for her?" I say.

My father shakes his head. "You can't go running after women," he says. "You go running after women, they won't respect you, and then you know what happens, don't you?"

"Sure."

My father holds up the deck of cards. "Pick one."

I pick the eight of spades and show it to him. He looks at it for a moment and I can see that it's not good news. "Shit," he says. "Tell your mother to hurry the hell up."

"Is it bad luck?"

"Sure as hell don't plan to sit here all day and die of sunstroke on her account."

Indian Days are going strong. Happy Trails is completely full, and there are RVs and trailers waiting to get into the park. The crowd at the buffalo run is larger now, and the line is longer. Even the big tent is jammed with tourists, and the dancing hasn't even started. I get a couple of glimpses of Franklin moving through the crowd, smiling, shaking hands, and I can see he's pleased with the turnout. Everybody has a T-shirt or a dream catcher or a beaded necklace. I'm having a good time, too, but it would be better if I could find Lum.

I stop by Edna's booth again. She and her daughter Shirley are making frybread as fast as they can. "You still hungry?"

"Nope," I say. "Looking for my mother."

Edna looks at the people flowing around the booths like water, and laughs. "Good luck," she says.

"Looking for Lum, too."

"Her and your auntie and your grandmother stopped by a little while ago, but they could be anywhere by now."

"Did the guy buy the recipe?"

Edna holds a finger up to her lips.

"How much?"

She smiles and leans across the booth. "All I can say," she says, "is that I've still got my pride."

On the rise behind Happy Trails, I can see people getting ready for the race.

"You seen Lum?"

"I hear there was trouble," says Edna.

"I guess."

"And generally speaking," says Edna, "things are always worse than what you hear."

By the time I get to the starting line, there are people all over the place, jogging and stretching and tying their shoes. In the old days, the race was just for the men of the tribe, but over the years, white runners, men and women, began showing up. At first, no one knew what to do with them. There was some talk about not letting them run, but that didn't seem friendly. Carleton Coombs wanted to make them pay an entry fee, but Franklin argued that letting them run was good for business. From the look of the crowd in their Nike sweatsuits and Nike shoes and Nike headbands, setting their Nike stopwatches, I can see where Franklin is probably right.

Lum wouldn't miss the race, but as I move through the runners, I don't see him. Out at the point, Franklin is standing on a stool by a red flag. He has a gun in his hand, and even though he's smiling, I'm not sure he's in a good mood.

"Have you seen Lum?"

"Nope." Franklin looks at his watch.

"If he doesn't hurry, he's going to miss the race."

"You going to run?"

"No," I say. "Lum's the runner."

"Then get out of the way," says Franklin. He raises the gun in the air, and the runners move to him. "Ready!" he shouts.

And for a moment, the world is quiet. Even the seagulls stop their squawking and ride the wind in silence. I back up a little and look through the runners. A couple of times I think I see Lum, but each time I'm wrong.

"Maybe you should wait for Lum."

"Maybe you should mind your own business." Franklin drops the gun and fires a single shot into the ground. The runners take a breath and spring away, and all you can hear in their going is the earth trembling beneath your feet. They plunge down the slope, a bright herd on the move.

I stand at the starting line and wait. In the distance, the runners begin to fan out across the flat on their way to the river. I keep expecting Lum to arrive any second, to come flying past me, lean and naked, and chase the pack down from behind.

Franklin shoves the gun into his pocket and picks up the stool.

"Is he hurt?"

Franklin brushes by me, carrying the stool like a club. "How the hell should I know?" He walks back to the big tent, and I watch him until he disappears inside.

"Hey, Chief. How much to take your picture?"

The guy behind me is dressed in a red Hawaiian shirt and a white cowboy hat. A nice pair of sunglasses covers his eyes and most of his face, and a large black camera hangs around his neck. I start to tell him that it'll cost him five dollars, but before I can say anything, he aims the camera at me and takes a picture.

"Stay calm," he says, and he pulls the dark glasses down just a bit so I can see his eyes.

"Monroe?"

"Shhhhh!" says Monroe. "I'm in disguise. Did I fool you?"

"A little."

"Good," he says, and he cocks the camera. "Smile."

I look around to see if anyone else recognizes Monroe. "Why are you wearing a disguise?"

"You wouldn't believe the number of people who want to shake the hand of a famous artist," he says. "Guess who I just saw."

"I don't think anyone is going to bother you."

"Marilyn Monroe and Elvis Presley," says Monroe. "You got a minute?"

I can't see the runners any longer, but I'm sure now that Lum is not with them.

"I could use your help."

"Sure," I say. "What's up?"

Monroe works his way through the crowd up to the parking lot. I follow, but I keep an eye out for my mother and Lum. The Karmann Ghia is where my father parked it. The beer cans are still on the seat, but my father isn't there. I figure he's gone looking for my mother so he can show her the surprise himself. Monroe doesn't stop until he's out of the parking lot and into the grass.

"Here we are."

I look around, but I'm not sure what I'm supposed to see.

"I finished painting the church," says Monroe. "What do you think?"

I know where the church used to be. Across the river and on the bluff above Truth. But even from this distance, I can see that it isn't there anymore. No roof, no steeple, no door. No church.

"Neat."

"So," says Monroe, "you think you can help?"

"With what?"

He takes off his sunglasses, tilts his head to one side as if he's trying to catch a glimpse of the church, and smiles. "Finding the church," he says.

I wait for the rest of the joke, but Monroe stands there rocking back and forth on his heels. "You lost the church?"

"That's about it."

"You don't know where it is?"

"I have a general idea."

"How could you lose the church?"

"I didn't lose the church," says Monroe. "I just lost track of it. Where's your dog?"

"Soldier?"

Monroe smiles some more and takes a picture of me with the parking lot in the background. "Bring him by tomorrow morning, okay?" he says. "He'll be able to find it."

"Soldier can't find his own butt."

"Dogs know about these sorts of things," says Monroe. He looks to see if anyone is watching and then takes a couple of shots of Truth and the bluff where the church used to be. "I better get going before word leaks out that I'm here."

I walk Monroe to his pickup. "What if he can't find it?"

Monroe leans against the truck and looks across the river. "I just wasn't thinking," he says. "I should have left the door alone until it was all finished." He slides into the driver's seat. He starts the engine and then hands me the camera. "Take a picture," he says. "'Famous Indian artist attends Indian Days on the reserve.' You can sell it for a ton of money after I'm dead."

I wander around the rest of the day, and even though I'm looking, I don't see my mother or my father or Lum anywhere. Soldier shows up that evening, excited and out of breath. I'm happy to see him, but I'm also upset that he's been gone for most of the day and hasn't even bothered to check in from time to time.

"You seen mom?" Soldier lies down and rolls over on his back. "What about Lum?"

When I get back to my grandmother's lodge, she has the propane lantern going and is bent over the stove dishing up plates of stew for Lucille and Teresa Rain. My mother is nowhere to be seen. I guess I look annoyed because my grandmother catches it right away.

"Gone," says my grandmother.

"Where's auntie Cassie?"

"Gone."

"So, I told him," says Lucille, "a beaded belt buckle will do the job just as well."

"And it's a lot cheaper," says Teresa.

"How's business?" I ask.

"Better than ever," says Lucille. "Going to sell out again this year."

"Never met a European I didn't like," says Teresa.

"Here," says my grandmother, and she hands me a plate of stew.

"Thanks," I say.

My grandmother looks over my shoulder. "It's not for you."

Rebecca Neugin is sitting on the cooler in the shadows of the tipi, out of the light. "Hi," she says.

"Rebecca's from Georgia," says Teresa. "She's Cherokee."

"We've never met a Cherokee," says Lucille, "so we invited her to have some of your grandmother's stew."

"Your grandmother makes the best stew on the reserve," says Teresa.

I hand the plate to Rebecca. I can see that she wants to be polite and take her time with the stew. But she must be hungry, too, because she never puts the spoon down until the plate is empty.

"All the Cherokee as skinny as you?" says Lucille.

"No, ma'am."

"Certainly are polite," says Teresa. "Some people around here I know could take some lessons."

"I was in Georgia once," says Lucille. "It was beautiful."

"That was very good stew," says Rebecca.

My grandmother takes her plate and fills it again.

"Now the rules are," says Lucille, "if you're a guest, we have to feed you, and you have to tell us all about the Cherokee."

Rebecca tries to smile, but she looks as if she's going to cry, too. Not so you can see unless you're up close.

"Do you speak your language?" says Teresa.

"Yes, ma'am," says Rebecca.

"Good," says Lucille. "Then you can tell your story in Cherokee."

"You guys don't speak Cherokee," I say.

"More to a story than just the words," says my grandmother. "You going to stay or go?"

I pick up a couple of pieces of frybread and two apples. "I promised Soldier I'd let him watch the dancers."

"You going to feed Edna's frybread to that dog?" says my grandmother.

"No," I say. "This is for me. For later."

"All right," says Lucille, settling into the chair. "Let's have that story."

Rebecca nods, and for the first time, she doesn't look unhappy. "Before the soldiers came, we used to live near Dahlonega in a really nice house," she says. "Maybe I'll start there."

"Start anywhere you want," says Teresa.

I open the flap. My grandmother leans back in the lawn chair and closes her eyes. Lucille and Teresa fold their hands in their laps and look up at the smoke hole, as if they expect to see something pass by in the night sky.

"Gha! Sge!" says Rebecca, and now her voice sounds better, too. "Hila hiyuhi u':sgwanighsdi ge:sv́i . . ."

"Ah," I hear my grandmother say. "A creation story. Those ones are my favourite."

Soldier is waiting for me at the side of the tipi. The hair on his back is up, and he is all snarls and bristles. "Cool it," I tell him. "You could have come in if you wanted to." Soldier moves on the tipi and jams his nose into the canvas. "It's just granny and Lucille and Teresa Rain," I say. "You know them."

Through the canvas, I can hear Rebecca's voice. It sounds almost as though she's singing. "That's Cherokee," I tell Soldier. "Sounds pretty nice, doesn't it?" I grab his collar and drag him off towards the big tent. He fights me all the way, whining and grumbling, and stares back at the tipi and the forms thrown off against the outside of the canvas by the lantern.

Up ahead, the big tent is ablaze with lights and sound. The drum is going pretty good, and the speakers send the song out to the mountains and back, and if you use your imagination a little, it sounds like thunder and rain.

Soldier calms down as we get to the tent. The place is packed. The tourists have taken all the benches and chairs, and they stand at the corners and the edges of the tent, with their kids perched on their shoulders. Everyone has a camera, and even though Soldier knows it's not lightning, he flinches as the flashes fill the night.

I keep a firm hold on his collar. If he gets loose and works his way through the crowd to the dance floor, I'll never find him. "No time for dancing," I remind him. "We have to find Lum." I pull Soldier around the side of the big tent and run into Lucy Rabbit, who is leaning against a pole having a smoke.

"What's up, Doc?" I say, before I see that it's not the right time for jokes.

"Ah," says Lucy. Her eyes are red, and her face is puffy. "It's one of the wascally wabbits."

"You okay?"

"Marilyn Monroe cried a lot," says Lucy. "Did you know that?"

"Where's Elvis Presley?"

In the lights of the tent, Lucy's hair almost looks blonde, and if she knew this, I'm sure it would please her.

"Out with his truck."

"Smuggling?"

Lucy shrugs and sucks on her cigarette. "You wouldn't believe the crap he's hauling these days."

"Soldier likes to watch the dancers."

"One of these times, they're going to catch him again," says Lucy. "And then it's *hasta la vista*, baby."

"Pretty good crowd," I say.

"You came too late." Lucy wipes her mouth. Most of the lipstick is gone and her lips look pale and cold. "No room left for the Indians." And she drops her shoulders, eases her way back into the crowd, and disappears.

Soldier turns and lopes off towards the river. I follow as best I can, bumping into people as I go. When he gets to the edge of the coulee, he stops and waits. Across the river, Truth is all lit up against the evening sky. "I know," I tell him. "The church is gone."

Soldier barks.

"Monroe doesn't know where it is either," I say. "Tomorrow, we're supposed to help him find it." But that's not what Soldier has found. I don't see it at first, and then I do. Along the river, the fog has begun to sneak out of the bushes, but by the bridge, the mist is light, and you can see the thin dark lines that rise out of the prairie and into the sky.

"Good boy," I tell Soldier, "good boy."

I can't see Lum's camp or his fire from this side of the river. Everything is too far away. But the smoke that hangs in the evening sky tells me he's come home.

CHAPTER TWENTY-EIGHT

Finding my mother turns out to be easy. As Soldier and I head for the ferry, I see her standing in the parking lot talking with my father. He's leaning against the side of the Karmann Ghia with his arms folded across his chest, and for a moment, he reminds me of the German guy who bought the frybread recipe from Edna Baton.

I grab Soldier, and we duck in behind a row of pickup trucks and work our way between the vehicles. I'm not trying to spy on them, but I'm curious to see how my mother feels about the Karmann Ghia. I'm excited about having a car, and I'm betting she is, too. We sneak in behind a red van with a herd of buffalo painted on the side. Soldier hikes his leg on the rear tire and just misses me.

"So, what do you want me to do?" I can hear my father's voice, and he doesn't sound happy.

My mother doesn't say anything. I get down on my hands and knees and look under the truck, but all I can see is their feet, and it doesn't look as if they're going to get back together right away.

"If you want to chase ghosts," says my father, "go right ahead."

I try looking through the windows of the van, but they've got that blackout film on them, and all I can see of my mother and father is dark shapes. I look around to see if Soldier and I can get to the next row of cars without being seen.

"Even if you do find her," I hear my father say, "you think she's going to be happy to see you?"

And then I hear a car door open. I drop down again, and now all I can see is my mother's legs in the grass.

My father starts the car. I expect he's going to drive off, but he sits there and revs the engine. Which is why I don't hear my mother until it is too late. I'm squatting by the tire when she walks right by the van on her way back to the camp. I freeze, but Soldier coughs, and it is only then, when she turns back and finds Soldier and me in the shadows, that

I see it isn't my mother after all. It's auntie Cassie.

My father is still revving the car, and even if auntie Cassie wanted to say something to me, I wouldn't have been able to hear it. But she doesn't. She just looks at me. She's not surprised, and she's not angry. I fumble with my shoelaces as if to suggest that that's the reason why I'm kneeling by the side of a van in the dark.

My father turns the radio on. It's loud, and I can hear him trying to sing along with the song. I keep my head down and tie both shoes, and when I look up, auntie Cassie is gone.

There is no moon tonight, and this makes it hard to see what you're doing and where you're going. Getting across on the ferry is easy enough, even though Soldier pees for the first part and cries the rest of the way. But as we head across the prairies for the bridge, the darkness really closes in, and the fog begins to rise, and I wind up floundering around in the grass, stepping into holes and walking into bushes. In the end, I have to hold onto Soldier and let him lead me across the prairies as if I were drunk or blind.

I smell the fire before I see the bridge or Lum's camp, and I'm debating whether to call out so I don't surprise him or to stay hidden until I can see that everything is okay, when Soldier stops and braces his feet.

"What is it?"

Soldier drops his head, and I can feel the fur on his neck roll forward.

"If this is about a rabbit," I whisper, "you can forget it."

Soldier moves forward cautiously, and I let him drag me along. The fog is thicker now, but as we come over a rise, I see the fire. Soldier grunts once and then suddenly, without warning, he bolts and disappears into the night.

The camp looks deserted. The fire has burned down until it's really just a glow, and the place feels cold and spooky. Soldier has already ruined the surprise, so I decide it's probably better if I announce myself.

"Hey, Lum!" I walk down the hill, trying to keep my footing. "It's me!"

The camp hasn't changed much, and I'm thinking maybe Lum has gone home and made up with his father. The hockey stick is lying in the same place and the sleeping bag doesn't look as if it's been moved. I wonder if the skull is still there, but I don't look.

"I brought some food." I hold up the frybread and the apples, and stand in the centre of the camp and wait and listen. When I hear the noise behind me, I don't turn around right away. It's Soldier. Sometimes he likes to play games like creeping up and jumping me. "I can hear you," I say.

The noises stop. And then they begin again. This time I turn, casually, so that Soldier knows he hasn't fooled me for a second. "You're going to have to do better than that." I'm expecting to see Soldier or maybe even Lum. I'm not expecting to see the Cousins. The dogs stand at the edge of the camp with just their heads poking through the fog. They fall back into the darkness for a moment, and then they reappear and slide out into the light.

"Lum." I back up slowly and move around the firepit so that it's between me and the dogs. "Hey, Lum! You home?" I take another step backwards and almost trip over the hockey stick. One dog stalks to the front of the campfire. The other two move around the edges of the light. I'm trying to hook my toe under the stick so I can raise it up without the dogs' noticing, but not having much luck, when something flashes out of the fog and the shadows and knocks the first dog down. I'm as surprised as the dog is, and I step on my own foot and go down in a heap. I roll over and grab the hockey stick just as I see Soldier pivot and plant his feet and go for the second dog's throat.

But the second dog has already seen the danger, and he turns and plunges into the night as Soldier's jaws snap shut on air. I'm on my feet in a second, the hockey stick at the ready. Soldier stands in front of the fire, his body sprung and swollen with rage.

"Way to go!" Soldier ignores me and watches the perimeter of the camp, in case the Cousins are waiting for him to make a mistake. "Good dog," I say. "That's a really good dog."

I feel the click and see the flash, before I hear the first explosion.

"Dead dog," says a voice, and the dirt around Soldier's feet erupts. Soldier stands his ground. He doesn't growl and he doesn't snarl.

"God," says Lum. "You can smell the mutt all the way to the river." He is limping badly, and I can see that the hip has gotten worse. He has the gun in his hand, and it's aimed at Soldier's head. But as soon as Soldier sees Lum, his butt begins to wiggle, and the tremor quickly moves up his body and gathers energy. Soldier bends himself in half and dances sideways towards Lum. "You miss me, mutt?" he says. "Did you miss me?" Lum tucks the gun into his waistband and squats down, and Soldier drops his shoulder and slides against Lum's legs like a baseball player stealing second.

I pick the frybread out of the dirt and dust it off. "I brought you some food."

Lum runs his hand under Soldier's front legs and scratches his chest. "That from Edna?"

"Nothing but the best."

Lum has cut his hair. It's short and uneven, as if it's been hacked off with a chain saw. And he's painted his face. Red on one side. Black on the other. He looks weird.

"I heard about what happened."

Lum shrugs. "What's to hear?" He takes the frybread and begins tearing it into pieces.

"My mother said you could stay with us."

Lum is naked to the waist. He has a red circle on his chest and long black marks on his arms. He looks like the Indians you see at the Saturday matinee.

"I'm fine here." Lum tosses a piece of the frybread into the fog. "Why don't you get your stuff? There's plenty of room here."

The Cousins emerge from the fog. Lum tosses the rest of the frybread to them. Soldier watches, but he doesn't growl or show his teeth. Finally, the first dog comes slinking over, and she and Soldier dance around each other, sniffing butts. The other two reluctantly join in, and for the moment, they're friends again.

Lum picks up the second piece of frybread, tears it in two, and tosses half to me.

You can't see across the river to Bright Water now, but the drumming from the tent cuts through the fog and fills the night. Lum listens for a moment, and then begins to sing. "How's Indian Days going?"

"Great," I tell him. "The buffalo run is a big hit."

"You see my father?"

"Yeah," I tell Lum. "He said he was sorry for throwing you out of the house."

In addition to looking weird with the paint and his hair cut like that, it's clear that Lum hasn't eaten for a while, and I'm sorry I didn't bring more food.

"She came back," says Lum.

"The woman?"

Lum squats down by the fire. He's not angry anymore. He's smiling now. Soldier crawls over and puts his head in Lum's lap. "It's my mother," says Lum, stroking Soldier's head and rubbing his ears. "She's come home."

I find a couple of sticks and throw them on the fire. I know Lum is waiting for me to say something. I know it couldn't be Lum's mother we saw on the Horns that night. And Lum knows I know.

"Jeez," I say. "I don't know. It was real dark."

"And that was her we saw at the church." Lum nods his head as if he's agreeing with himself. The Cousins are lying in a knot by the abutment. They look asleep, but I'm not going to bet on it.

"My father fixed up that car for my mother," I say. "He brought it out to Indian Days as a surprise."

"So, my old man's been lying to me all this time."

"It's in pretty good shape now."

"He tells everyone that she's dead," says Lum.

"Mom said I can drive it as soon as she breaks it in."

"That's the kind of fucking liar my father is." Lum has the gun in his hand again. He turns it over once, pulls the hammer back, and lays the barrel next to Soldier's ear. "You know what's wrong with this world?"

"We could go anywhere we wanted."

"I said, you know what's wrong with this world?" Lum stares at me. I try not to blink or turn away. Soldier twists his head around and licks at Lum's hand.

"Bullets," says Lum, and he begins to laugh. "There aren't enough bullets." And he slides the gun up under his chin and pulls the trigger.

The snap of the hammer on the empty chamber hardly makes any sound at all, but in my mind, I hear the bullet and I see Lum's head jerk backwards. He is still laughing as he sticks the gun back in his waistband. "You okay, cousin?"

"Fine."

"I was just kidding, okay?"

"Okay."

"We're still friends, right?"

"You could stay in my room," I say. "Soldier wouldn't mind."

Lum shakes his head. "He'll cool off once Indian Days are over."

"Sure."

"We fight all the time," says Lum. "It's normal."

"Same here."

"All in all," says Lum, "he's a great guy."

I can see why Lum likes it here on the prairies. The fog stays low and wraps itself around the camp like a quilt, while above us the sky is black and clear and bright with stars, and it's easy to imagine that you are at the centre of the universe.

"My grandmother has her tipi up," I say. "Got a big pot of stew."

"Sure," says Lum. "Your grandmother's cool."

"Auntie Cassie said to say hello."

"She's cool, too." Lum feeds a handful of twigs and grass into the fire. Soldier gets to his feet and nudges me, and I remember the apples.

"Brought these for you."

Lum takes both the apples and wipes them on his pants. "Who won the race?"

"That Cree guy from Hobbema."

"I can beat him."

"No contest," I say.

Lum turns his back and pokes at the fire with a stick. It flares for a moment, and he slowly stacks branches and pieces of cottonwood against the flame. Soldier and I walk to the edge of the camp. I look up at the stars and breathe the air, and I think about my bedroom in the shop with its windowless walls and starless ceiling and wonder why I ever expected Lum would want to share that with me. "So, I'll see you over at Indian Days?"

"Sure."

As we leave the camp, the fog sucks in around us. Soldier shakes himself as if he's just come up out of cold water, and then he pulls me into the darkness. When I get back, I'm thinking I should tell my mother that Lum is sleeping under the bridge and that he's not getting enough to eat.

You can't see a thing, and I begin listening for the river or the creak of the ferry as it hangs and swings on the cables to give me some sense of distance and direction. So, when Soldier pulls me around a hill, and I see the fire and Lum's camp in front of me, I'm surprised.

Soldier sits down and licks his face. You can see he's pleased with himself. I try not to make any noise in case Lum hears me and thinks I'm spying on him. I sit down on the ground next to Soldier. "You want to try again?"

But Soldier isn't listening to me. His ears are up, and all his muscles are cocked, and my first thought is that he's caught the scent of the Cousins sneaking up on us in the dark. Soldier whines and twitches his ears, and as he does, a low sound comes out of the fog, hangs in the air for a moment, and disappears.

I look through the camp. The fire is bright, and as it flashes and cracks, I see Lum. He's in the shadow of the abutment, sitting on the sleeping bag. Piled up around him are the Cousins. I count them just to make sure they're all there.

And then suddenly, the sound is back, and I realize that what Soldier hears is Lum singing. I can't hear the words, just a soft melody, and as I look, I see that Lum has something cradled in his arms and is rocking it gently back and forth.

Soldier stands and stretches. He looks up at the sky and opens his mouth. The fog floats in, and Lum and the Cousins and the camp disappear. I find Soldier's collar and pull him off the hill, but the singing follows us as we make our way down the coulees and across the cutbanks. And all the way back to the ferry, Soldier walks beside me, whimpering and humming along with the song.

CHAPTER TWENTY-NINE

Sleeping in a tipi is different from sleeping in a room without windows. For instance, in my bedroom at the shop, I don't have to worry about where the sun rises or just how bright it can be.

When I wake up the next morning, auntie Cassie is sitting on the edge of the mattress, feeding a piece of wood into the stove. "About time you got up," she says. "Coffee's on. Fruit's in the cooler. After that, you're on your own."

The whole east side of the lodge is golden and warm, and I have to squint as I roll out of the blankets. "Where's everyone?"

"Gone," says auntie Cassie.

"Where's mom?"

"Didn't come home." Auntie Cassie closes the door of the stove and pours herself a cup of coffee.

"Dad got the car fixed."

"So he did."

"She out with dad?"

"Wouldn't put money on that." Auntie Cassie sits on the mattress with both hands around the cup as if she is trying to warm her fingers up. The tattoo is darker now, more purple than blue. I'm not trying to stare, but she catches me looking. "Here," says auntie Cassie, and she tosses me a pen. "Give it a try."

I make a fist and print AIM in thick block letters on my knuckles. "Is this how you did it?"

Auntie Cassie ducks down behind her cup of coffee, but I can see she's smiling. "No," she says. "When I did this, I was drunk. And I did it in a mirror."

"But this looks pretty close, right?"

I'm just getting ready to ask auntie Cassie about the suitcase with the baby clothes when the flap is pulled to one side and my grandmother ducks in. She sees my hand right away and makes a noise like a whale coming up for air.

"It's just ink." I hold my hand up so my grandmother can see, but you can tell that it's not me she's after. I wet my knuckles and wipe them on my jeans, but the ink doesn't come off easily.

"Leave him out of it," snaps my grandmother.

"He's not in it," snaps auntie Cassie.

My grandmother hangs over the coffee pot like a weasel watching a trout. "We're going to need some more wood for the stove," she says to me. "Try to get the smaller pieces. They burn better."

"Don't worry," auntie Cassie says to me. "It's not serious."

"You talk to him yet?" says my grandmother.

"I guess that's my business."

"Suit yourself," says my grandmother.

"I will," says auntie Cassie.

Auntie Cassie and my grandmother settle in and square off like turtles. I'm a little nervous standing between the two of them.

"Better get the wood," snaps auntie Cassie.

"The skinny pieces," snaps my grandmother. "The fat ones won't fit."

I don't mind getting the wood, and with the current state of things, I plan on taking my time. I look around for Soldier, but he's off trying to impress the tourists. The fog is gone, and the sun is out, and everyone is walking around in shorts and colourful shirts, with black camera bags slung over their shoulders. They look like an army on the march.

I stop at Skee Gardipeau's booth just to say hello. Skee is scooping up potatoes and shiny corn, and fishing pieces of fried chicken out of a plastic bucket. "Who's got the special?" he shouts.

"Hi," I say.

Skee gives me a wink and drops the special in front of a tall man with glasses and a canvas hat, the kind you can fold up and shove in your pocket. "You hear about your father?"

"What?"

"He's getting pretty good at that."

"What?"

"Messing up."

A short guy and a skinny woman come up to the booth. They're wearing tan shorts, matching blue shirts with red parrots, and those sandals you see in the magazines my mother has in the shop. The sandals don't look like much, but they're really expensive because they mould to your foot and last for more than one summer. And, if you want, you can wear them with socks.

"Business calls," says Skee. "If you see your old man, tell him I'm still waiting for my chair."

I work my way through the crowd to my father's booth. "Hey, stranger," he says. "You're just in time." He still has the dark glasses on, but he doesn't look like Elvis Presley anymore.

"Lots of people," I say.

"And they've all got money," says my father. He spreads the wood coyotes out so you can get a good look at them. "You should buy one of the mirrors for your mother."

"She has one," I say. "A bear."

The mirrors look nice hanging from the top of the booth. The wind isn't crazy the way it sometimes is, and the mirrors turn slowly, flashing in the sun. When my father first started making them, he stuck pretty much to bears and buffalo and eagles. But there were a lot of calls for things like moose and beaver, too, and before long, he was making up turtles and rabbits and dogs and cats as well. He made up an elephant for one customer and a giraffe for another.

The three Germans dressed up as Indians come to the far side of the booth. The guy in the beaded leather shirt has one of Lucille Rain's medallions around his neck.

"Holy," says my father. "Those boys sure know how to dress." And he says it with a straight face.

"They're Germans," I tell him.

"No shit," says my father. "Boy, these days Indians are everywhere."

The Germans are looking through the coyotes, and my father is telling them how the coyote is a trickster and how coyotes are good luck and how a medicine bag isn't complete without one. Some of the stuff I've never heard of before, but if anyone knows about coyotes, it's my father.

I turn towards the mountains and let the wind pass over my face. It feels clean and powerful, and I'm thinking maybe Lum is wrong. That maybe Monroe and auntie Cassie didn't come home because they had no place else to go or because they were crazy, but because there was no place else in the world they wanted to be.

I watch the Germans wander over to Carleton Coombs's table and begin looking through the furs that Carleton gets from a white guy in Los Angeles.

"They buy anything?" I ask my father.

"Fussy assholes."

"They didn't like the coyotes?"

"Wanted them made out of turquoise," says my father. "The big guy had a vision."

"A vision?"

"Said he saw a blue coyote with ruby eyes."

"Neat."

"More likely something he ate." My father coughs and his whole body shakes a little, and I can see that he's still not feeling too well.

"How'd mom like the car?"

My father stops shaking and his eyes harden up. "You seen her?"

"No."

"She took off in the car," my father says. "Haven't seen her since."

"Must have really liked it."

My father reaches up and adjusts a couple of the mirrors. "I figured we could go for a drive," he says. "Maybe sneak over to Prairie View and stay the night. Like old times. I mean, you think she'd be a little grateful."

"Skee said there was trouble?"

"Nothing I can't handle."

A roar goes up from the buffalo corral. My father and I turn to see what's happening, but all we can see is the crowd of tourists packed in against the orange mesh and the cars and the long cloud of grey dust kicked up by the buffalo and the motorcycles.

My father rearranges the coyotes so that they are all pointing east. "Cops got nothing better to do than hassle small businessmen."

"Smuggling?"

"Hell, I'm public enemy number one." My father is smiling now. "Didn't your mother ever tell you that?"

A truck leaves the buffalo run and comes tearing up the hill towards the big tent. The tourists begin milling around and pressing against the cars. Some have their cameras held high over their heads. Parents with children on their shoulders are jostled out of the way.

"That a tattoo," says my father, "or you just practising?"

"What do you think?"

"Here," says my father, and he takes down one of the mirrors. "See for yourself." The mirror is shaped like a coyote or a wolf or a fox, and it's one of my father's best-sellers. I hold my hand up to the glass and make a fist. My father leans on the edge of the booth. "Those things are permanent," he says. "Not easy to get rid of."

It doesn't look too bad. I squeeze my fist so that the letters stand out.

"Feel tough, do you?" says my father.

I don't know why I don't see it right away, but it's only when I look a second time that I notice. MIA. It's supposed to say AIM, but what it says in the mirror is MIA. I pull my hand back and turn it around.

"I don't know," says my father. "If it were me, I'd probably get an eagle."

A couple of tourists come by at a dead trot. The man is red-faced and sweaty. The camera around his neck swings back and forth, thumping him in the chest like a rock on a string. The woman looks fresh and is pulling ahead as they get near the booth.

"Tell her to bring the van," shouts the man.

The woman runs on ahead, loping across the prairies like an ostrich. The man slows and grinds to a stop in front of us. He's breathing hard and has to bend over and brace himself on his knees.

"You're just in time," says my father. "All the coyotes are half-price."

While the man catches his breath, I look at my knuckles again, and now I can see what has happened.

"You should have seen it," says the man. "Christ, what a mess."

"If you buy three," says my father, "you get two dollars off."

"Real stupid," says the man, and he waves his camera at us. "That's what it was."

My father pushes the coyotes forward a little, but I can see he's starting to give up.

"Should have seen the blood," says the man.

"Coyotes are good luck," says my father.

"Never saw anything like it," says the man.

I look over at the buffalo run. The ambulance is just pulling up to the corral and is trying to work its way through the crowd, but no one wants to move.

"Anyone hurt?" I ask.

"Oh, hell," says the man. "They'll be lucky to live out the day."

I look at my father. He runs his hand through his hair and shrugs. The man straightens up and wipes his face with a handkerchief. "And I got it on film," he says, and he gives us a thumbs up and heads for the big tent.

As soon as the man is gone, I turn to my father. He's sorting through the coyotes again and turning them all to the south. "That doesn't sound too good," I say.

"What the hell do they expect?" says my father. "It ain't Disneyland."

I help my father at the booth for a while, and we sell six of the mirrors and a couple of coyotes, so he's a little happier and doesn't get back to complaining about my mother's running off with the car right away. I'm tempted to go down to the corral to see what happened, but the way things go, I figure I'll hear about it soon enough. My father starts talking and laughing with a family from Kingston, Ontario, who normally spend their summers on Prince Edward Island but decided to come west this year to find the real Indians.

"All the ones we hear about," says the woman, "are in the penitentiary."

I find Eddie Baton's truck without any problem. Eddie likes his trucks fancy, and he likes them red. He gets a new truck every year or so, and all of them have chrome running boards and chrome exhaust stacks that wrap around the bed and stick up in the air like ears or antennae. Eddie and Wilfred are sitting on the shady side of the truck having a beer. The back end is filled with cut poplar. "Help yourself," says Eddie. "You hear about your old man?"

Wilfred sips at the beer slowly as if it's the last one he's going to get for a while. "Cops," he says. "They love sticking it to Indians."

"It's not even our shit," says Eddie, and he drops the can on the ground and crushes it.

"Hell," says Wilfred, "the government should give us all medals for public service."

I load the wood into Eddie's pushcart.

"What the hell they want to bother Elvin for?" says Eddie.

"Right," says Wilfred. "He's just doing their dirty work for them."

The siren makes us all jump. Eddie and Wilfred stand up and shade their eyes. "Who the hell they after now?"

But it's not the cops. It's the ambulance that was down at the buffalo run. It swings up through the grass, skirts the big tent, hits the lease road on the fly, and disappears in a thick rooster tail of dirt and gravel.

"Couple of guys got hurt at the buffalo run," I say.

"Their own damn fault." Eddie shakes his head. "But they'll probably try to sue the band."

"Sherman saw it all," says Wilfred. "These two guys began fighting over one of the big cows."

"Then they began shooting at each other," says Eddie, and he starts laughing as he thinks about it. "Should see the mess one of those paint pellets can make on a nice shirt."

"Totalled both motorcycles," says Wilfred. "That's what happens when you think with your dick."

"You ought to know," says Eddie.

"That's what your wife said," says Wilfred, and he opens another beer and hands it to Eddie.

When I get back to the lodge, nobody's home. I unload the wood and help myself to some iced tea and wait. I want to talk to my mother about the car, and I want to ask auntie Cassie about the tattoo. I hardly get settled on the mattress when I hear Soldier outside the tipi, and he reminds me that we're supposed to be at the church helping Monroe.

"I remember," I tell him through the canvas. "I was just waiting for you."

Soldier complains until I come outside and scratch his ears and rub him all over. The crowd at the buffalo run has started to thin out. I can't see anything that looks like an accident, but I hear several of the cows bellowing, and I wonder if they can remember the good old days when they had the place to themselves, before they had to worry about Indians running them off cliffs or Europeans shooting at them from the comfort of railroad cars or bloodthirsty tourists in tan walking shorts and expensive sandals chasing them across the prairies on motorcycles.

CHAPTER THIRTY

H alfway across the river, I realize that we are in a little trouble. Soldier doesn't notice right away because he is concentrating on keeping the bucket from swinging, but by the time we get to shore and look around, he clues in.

"Where's the church?"

Seeing that it is gone is one thing. Finding it now that it has disappeared is something else. I try looking past the bridge, measuring out the church's approximate location, but the bluff above the river stretches out in both directions and the church could be anywhere along the way.

"Maybe we can find our old trail."

We try that and it doesn't work, and in the end, we're reduced to climbing to the bluff just below the bridge and then walking back along the ridge, keeping our eyes peeled. "If you see it, let me know," I say. "And watch out for the platform."

Soldier and I begin weaving our way through the grass. I hold my hand out in front of me like a blind person with a cane, just in case I find the church all of a sudden.

I look around for Monroe, but he could be anywhere, and if he's in the grass, swimming again, we could walk right by him and not even notice. I look back at the bridge every so often to try to keep my bearings, but it doesn't help much.

"It should be right around here."

Soldier is in front of me, and when I hear him bark and see him leap out of the grass, I figure that he's found it.

"Good boy!"

Soldier comes wiggling back to me with something in his mouth. At first, it looks like another bone, but it's just a piece of cut poplar, the kind my grandmother would like for her stove. Soldier drops it at my feet and waits for me to throw it.

"We're looking for the church."

Soldier turns and dives into the grass, barking as he goes. "That's right," I shout, and I toss the stick behind me. "Find the church." I look around, but everything is pretty much the same. It's as if the church has never existed, and I can see now why Monroe is so famous.

Almost immediately, Soldier is back with another stick in his mouth. This one is almost same as the other one, and for a minute, I think he's circled around and picked up the first stick, just to be cute. But this stick is thicker and fills Soldier's mouth. He drops it at my feet and sits down. It's a little weird to find firewood scattered about on the prairies, but I don't think much about it until we find the next piece and then the next.

The prairies can fool you. They look flat, when in fact they really roll along like an ocean. One moment you're on the top of a wave and the next you're at the bottom. Soldier and I walk up a slight incline, and when we get to the crest, I see it. Soldier leans up against my leg the way he does when he's done something good and I'm supposed to praise him.

"It's interesting," I tell him. "But it's not the church."

Below us, someone has cleared out a large circle of grass in the middle of the prairies, and at the centre of the circle is a pile of firewood. From the top of the rise, the pile of wood looks large enough, but it is only after we walk down and stand beside it that we realize just how enormous it really is. Soldier walks around the pile, drooling, trying to decide where to begin. "It's got to be Monroe," I tell him.

Soldier isn't listening. He turns his face into the wind and perks up his ears. He hears the sound before I do, but that's only because he's a dog. Monroe's truck comes over the crest of the hill and bounces its way along the ridge. In the back end is a load of wood.

I nudge Soldier with my foot. "What'd I tell you?"

Monroe is all smiles as he backs the truck up against the pile and gets out of the cab. "Just in time!"

He drops the tailgate and begins tossing logs onto the pile. Soldier jumps on the wood in the truck and begins passing pieces down to Monroe. I stand at the side and throw the smaller pieces as high up on the pile as I can.

"It's a pretty big pile of wood," I say.

"Yes, it is," says Monroe.

It doesn't take us long to empty the truck. Monroe is hot and sweaty and covered with sawdust, as if he's been cutting and loading and stacking for days. "That's the last load," he says.

"Neat," I say. "What's it for?"

"Now all we have to do," he says, "is find the church."

Yesterday, when Monroe told me he had lost the church, I thought he might be kidding, fooling around. But when he says it this time, I can see that he's telling the truth.

"Maybe we should drive around slowly, and see if we can find it that way," I say.

"Tried that already," says Monroe. "Didn't work."

"We could lay out a grid the way they do when they're digging for dinosaurs and prehistoric stuff."

"Take too long."

Monroe rubs Soldier's neck and talks to him until Soldier begins to moan and slobber all over Monroe's hands. "Okay," says Monroe, and he gives me a wink. "He says he'll do it."

Soldier jumps off the bed of the truck and begins sniffing through the grass. He sweeps to the east of the woodpile, works his way back, and then heads south. Every so often, he stops and pushes his nose into the dirt, and then he's off sniffing again.

"That's a great dog," says Monroe, and he sits on the tailgate of the truck. "Have I told you about why I'm famous?"

"You worked at museums. Restoring things."

"Did I tell you about the boxes and the drawers and the things tied together with string?"

"At the museums?"

Soldier is moving off to the west now, looking for all the world like a tan vacuum cleaner on legs. Monroe shades his eyes and glances up at the sky. "We have time," he says. "No point in starting too early."

Soldier starts barking and racing through the grass in long, loping runs as if he is chasing something.

"Aha!" says Monroe. "I think he's done it."

"Probably just a rabbit," I say. "He likes chasing rabbits."

"Does he ever catch them?"

"He caught a skunk once."

Monroe pushes off the back of the truck. He stands in the grass and sniffs the air. "It's not a skunk."

By the time we get to him, Soldier has stopped running and is rolling around in the grass. Monroe squats down next to him and rubs his belly and tells him what a good dog he is.

"So, where's the church?" I say.

Soldier gets to his feet, trots out into the middle of the prairies, and sits down.

"This way," says Monroe, and he stomps through the grass, swinging his arms as if there's marching music playing in his head. I tag along behind, but I know he's not going to have much luck following Soldier.

When we reach Soldier, Monroe turns around in a circle, looks at Soldier, and then thrusts his hand into space. "Hmmmmm," he says, and he feels around in the air. Soldier snorts. Monroe takes a step forward and feels around some more. "How about here?"

Soldier cocks his head to one side. I know he's guessing, but I have to admit that, over the years, he's been one lucky dog. Monroe takes a couple of steps to the left and slowly feels around with his hand. "Aha!"

I don't see a thing, but Monroe turns his hand as if he's twisting a knob, and he pushes, and the door swings open. "After you," says Monroe. He bends over at the waist, throws his arm out in an arc, and Soldier trots past him into the church.

I'm not sure what I'm expecting, but inside the church is pretty much the same. The paintings and the sculptures, the rugs and the bookcases, the couches and the chairs and the piano are all there. There are more fresh flowers in the kitchen. They stand up straight in the vase, full of colour and grace. My mother would be impressed.

Monroe looks around and rubs his hands. "Okay," he says, "let's get started."

"Doing what?"

"It's moving day," says Monroe.

"You're moving?"

"Just all the stuff."

"Where?"

"Outside," says Monroe.

"You're kidding, right?"

"We'll start with the big stuff," says Monroe, "so we don't wear ourselves out too soon."

The big stuff is the piano. "We going to try to move this?"

"Nothing to it," says Monroe. "It's got wheels."

Monroe and I each take a corner and brace our shoulders against the wood. It doesn't move right away, but as we lean forward and use our legs, the piano finally breaks free from the floor and begins rolling towards the front door.

"Now what do we do?" I say.

Getting the piano to the door is one thing. Getting it down the steps is another. I don't see any way that this is going to happen unless someone shows up with a crane. Monroe goes into the church and comes back with two long, thick planks. "You know how the Egyptians built the pyramids?"

"Lots of big guys?"

"Physics," says Monroe. "Grab a couple of those two-by-sixes."

He backs the truck up, and even though you can't see the porch, he gets the bed almost level with the top step. Then he lays the planks between the truck and the door. "Okay," says Monroe. "Time for some more physics."

I'm sure the planks are going to break, and the piano will wind up in pieces scattered about the landscape. The planks bow, all right, and they make angry noises, but they don't break, and Monroe and I push and sweat as we shove the piano onto the back of the truck.

"There," says Monroe. "The rest is easy."

The rest is not easy. Monroe drives the truck to the far side of the woodpile. At first, I think he's going to try to skid the piano off into the grass, but instead, he leaves it in the truck. "What do you think?" says Monroe. "This is fun."

We spend the rest of the day hauling everything out of the church and arranging it in the grass. We put the rugs down first and then the couches and the chairs. Monroe places the lamps among the furnishings so that if we had electricity, we could sit on a couch and read.

"Where should we put the bed?" Monroe asks me.

"Why are we doing this?"

Soldier curls up on one of the big Persians and goes to sleep. I know that there's not much he can do, but I'm cranky with him anyway.

"Could sure use some walls," says Monroe. "I guess all we can do is prop the paintings up in the grass." We lift and carry and sweat and grunt, and by the time we empty the church and Monroe finishes decorating the area around the woodpile, it is evening.

"We still have that bentwood box."

"Time for a break first," says Monroe, and he flops down on one of the couches.

The fog begins to form on the river, and it looks as if it's serious tonight. Overhead, the stars are beginning to show themselves. Monroe leans back and looks at the sky. "Don't see this in Toronto," he says.

"What if it rains?"

"You cold?" says Monroe.

"Wind comes up, and you'll get dirt on everything."

Monroe stands up and rubs his arms. "I'm a little cold."

Below us, you can see Truth all lit up. Across the river, you can see the lights at the big tent and the RV park. The drum is going, and it sounds like Red Bull. "Time to get started," says Monroe, and he walks over to the truck.

I'm hoping Monroe's not thinking of trying to move the piano, so when he comes back carrying a grocery bag, I'm relieved. When Soldier sees the bag, he scrambles to his feet and sucks his stomach in. I don't think it's food, but with Monroe you never know. "Here," says Monroe, and he reaches into the box and comes up with a handful of flares.

Soldier sniffs at them to make sure that they are not hot dogs.

"Stuff them in as far as they will go," says Monroe, and he heads for the woodpile.

Monroe and Soldier and I walk around the pile, cracking flares and wedging them under the logs until the stack is ringed with glowing red lights. When we're done, the whole thing looks a little like a spaceship getting ready to explode into the sky. Monroe wipes his hands on his pants and sits down on the couch. "What kind of music do you like?"

"My mother plays a lot of opera," I say. "Anything but that."

Monroe leans over and puts a CD into a portable stereo. "Don Ross," he says. "He's a great guitarist."

Soldier likes the music, and I have to admit that it's a lot better than opera. Monroe stretches out on the couch. I sit in the chair and watch the flares set the woodpile on fire. Soldier settles down on a rug.

In no time at all, the entire woodpile is ablaze. Soldier sits next to Monroe and we watch the sparks leap into the sky. "Come on," says Monroe, and he runs to the truck and comes back with two fire extinguishers.

"We're going to try to put *that* out?"

"No," shouts Monroe, and he jogs out onto the prairies and begins blasting the larger embers that have been thrown off by the bonfire. Actually, it's a lot of fun. Sort of like laser tag. An ember flies loose from the pile and floats into the grass, and I race over, level the extinguisher, and blow it to bits. We race around the fire like madmen, shouting, barking, chasing comets in the night. We only stop when the fire settles down and we run out of extinguishers.

"All right," says Monroe after we catch our breath. "Let's get the place cleaned up before company arrives."

The fog has closed in tight. I can still see part of the bridge, but Truth and Bright Water have all but vanished. Which is why I don't see the car until it pulls up next to the fire.

"Company!" shouts Monroe, and he and Soldier head for the car.

It's Skee and Gabriel.

"Skee, you old son of a bitch," says Monroe. "Where you been keeping yourself?"

I push off the tailgate and head on over to say hello just as Eddie Baton's truck comes out of the fog with my father and Wilfred in the front seat.

"We saw the fire," says Skee. "Figured we'd come over and say hello."

"You're just in time," says Monroe. "We're almost ready to start."

"Hello, Monroe," says Gabriel. "Damn nice fire."

More cars and trucks arrive, sliding out of the fog like ghosts. Lucille and Teresa Rain pull up in their Chevy. Sherman Youngman and Carol Millerfeather swing around the fire and park their cars at the edge of the light. Lucy Rabbit arrives with my grandmother and Edna Baton. I look to see if Rebecca is with them.

"Grab the brass turtle," Monroe yells at me. More people are pulling up in their cars, and at the far edge of the fire, I see the Karmann Ghia come into the camp. The top is down. My mother is driving. Auntie Cassie is sitting next to her.

"The antique ashtray." Monroe moves in front of the fire, his arms loaded with stuff. "Bring me the antique ashtray."

I look around to see if Lum has seen the fire and come into the circle, but I'm not surprised that he's not here.

"The kaleidoscope!" Monroe waves at me. "And the Navajo rug!"

I find a small bronze sculpture of an Indian running alongside an elk. It looks as if the Indian is going to try to bring the animal down with his bare hands. Or maybe he's just racing it to see who's faster.

"Can I keep this for a friend?"

"Absolutely!" yells Monroe as he rushes by me with a Northwest Coast mask in each hand. "Who wants the Japanese armour?"

Before long, everyone is standing around the fire, talking and joking and having a good time. Some of the older people sit on the couches and chairs. The kids run around the fire, darting in and out of the fog. I go over to see my mother and auntie Cassie. Auntie Cassie just has a light jacket on, and she looks cold. My mother has the quilt wrapped around herself.

"How's the car run?" I ask.

"So, this is where you went," says my mother.

"I didn't stay out all night," I say.

Auntie starts to smile and has to turn away. "Nice fire," she says. "You can see it all the way from Bright Water." And she reaches into the back of the Karmann Ghia and takes out the suitcase.

"Where's Lum?" says my mother.

"He's around."

"Is he okay?"

"I guess."

My mother turns and looks at the fire. "So, was this your idea?"

"What?"

"The giveaway," says auntie Cassie.

In no time at all, most of the people I know in Truth and Bright Water are standing around the fire or sitting on the furniture or lying around in the grass. Soldier trots around, saying hello to everyone, getting petted, begging food, and generally making a nuisance of himself. Monroe begins passing out all the stuff, and I help him. Skee gets a really nice painting of a woman on a beach for his café. Lucy gets a poster of Marilyn Monroe, and Lucille and Teresa get one of the big rugs. Monroe gives my grandmother a Navajo rug, and he lets Sherman and Wilfred and Eddie pick out turquoise and silver rings from a carved wooden box. Wally gets one of the two suits of Japanese armour, and Gabriel Tucker gets the other.

"What do you think your auntie would like?" says Monroe.

"I don't know," I say. "What do you think?"

There's still a lot of stuff left, and as we wander through everything, I can see Monroe making mental notes on who should get what. "Here," he says, and he picks up an Inuit sculpture of a woman with a child on her back. "We'll give her this."

I figure that Monroe is going to ask me what I think my mother would like, but he doesn't.

"Who did we forget?"

"Do you have anything that looks like a duck?"

It takes a long time for the fire to burn down, and as the pile begins to collapse into itself, the people begin loading their pickups or tying their gifts to the top of their cars. One by one, they back up into the fog and disappear. My mother stands by the fire with auntie Cassie.

"You want a ride back?" my mother says.

"No," I say. "I have to stay here and help Monroe clean up."

"Just be careful what you give away," says auntie Cassie. "There are some things you want to keep."

My father stands off to one side. My mother sees him, and at first I think she's going to ignore him, but in the end, the two of them walk out to the edge of the circle.

I stay with auntie Cassie. "Hi," I say.

"Hi, yourself," she says. The suitcase is lying in the grass. The Inuit statue is next to it.

"Nice, huh?"

"Beautiful," she says, but she doesn't sound happy or surprised.

"Monroe's pretty generous."

Auntie Cassie watches the fire. It's mostly a huge pile of embers now, red and yellow and black and glowing. I take the photograph out of my pocket. "Is this her?"

Monroe and Skee and Gabriel are trying to get the suit of Japanese armour onto the top of Skee's car. Auntie Cassie looks at the picture and then she nods towards the men. "I think they need help."

"You know . . . Mia?"

Skee has thrown a blanket on top of the car so that the armour won't scratch the paint. Gabriel is arguing that the legs should go up first. Skee wants to lift it all at once. Monroe is trying to figure out how it can come apart.

Auntie Cassie smiles as she watches the men struggling with the armour. "The Three Stooges," she says.

"Is she someone I know?"

"No." Auntie Cassie puts the photograph in her coat. "You never knew her."

I wait to see if auntie Cassie is going to finish the story, but I can see that she's gone as far as she wants to go.

"Another life," she says. "Another time."

In the end, Skee and Monroe lift the suit, and because I'm the lightest, I get on top of the car and guide it into place. Skee gets some rope out of the trunk, and we loop it through the car and around the suit, until it's tight and isn't going to go anyplace.

"All right." Skee turns to Monroe. "Don't be a stranger," he says. "Stop by the café, and your first special is on me." Skee and Monroe and Gabriel say their goodbyes. I stand on the roof of the car and watch the sky. It's still the middle of the night, but as I look east, I imagine I can see the first movements of dawn and feel the early coolness of morning air.

The fire has settled into a low mound. It's dying, but you can still feel the heat all the way to the car. My father is by himself now, and as I look around, I see my mother heading back towards the fire. My father stands up straight. My mother walks through the grass slowly, and by the look of everything, they've had one of their talks.

Auntie Cassie is still waiting by the fire. I wave to her, but she doesn't see me. She has her arms wrapped around herself, but I can't imagine that she's still cold, standing where she is so close to the flames.

"Tell your old man," Skee says to me, "he still owes me that chair."

Auntie Cassie opens the suitcase, takes out a small shirt, and holds it up to the light. Against the heat of the fire, the shirt looks soft and golden, and even though I'm watching, I almost miss it, the motion is so quick and casual. In the end, all I really do see is the shirt spread out and floating, bright against the night. It settles onto the embers, lies there in the fire for the longest time, and then slowly curls up at the edges, glows briefly, and is gone.

My mother circles the fire, the quilt dragging in the grass behind her. When she gets to auntie Cassie's side, she doesn't say a word, and she doesn't try to stop her. She opens the quilt and wraps it around her sister's shoulders, while auntie Cassie takes each piece of clothing out of the suitcase, deliberately, one at a time, and casts them all into the flames.

CHAPTER THIRTY-ONE

Everything is gone. The couches, the chairs, the suits of Japanese armour, the wheelchair, the paintings, the rugs. Everything. Except the piano. It's still on the back of the truck, and I have no idea what Monroe plans to do with it. I only hope he doesn't want me to help.

"That felt good," says Monroe. "How did that feel to you?"

"Whatever happened to that painting? The one you restored. The one with the Indians?"

"Which one?"

"There was more than one?"

"Oh, sure," says Monroe. "Lots."

"And you . . . restored them all?"

Monroe smiles and shoves his hands in his pockets, and when he does this, he looks sad. "I tried," he says. "But there were too many."

"How many?"

"And the museums kept firing me."

"What?"

"I don't think they wanted their Indians restored." Monroe picks up a stick and tosses it on the bonfire. "I think they liked their Indians where they couldn't see them."

Soldier wanders around the fire. I figure it's time I head back to Bright Water and my grandmother's lodge. "Skee really liked that painting," I say.

Soldier comes over and rubs up against my leg. He's happy, but he's tired, too. He yawns and I can see that all he wants to do is stretch out beside the fire and go to sleep.

"When you write the song about my exploits," says Monroe, "don't forget the giveaway."

"I won't."

"You don't have to say who got what," he says. "That's not important.

But it should be a ballad." Monroe is having a good time, and I hate to leave him because it's no fun having a good time by yourself. But it's late, and there's nothing left to do but stand around and wait for the sun to come up.

"You going to stay around here?"

"Don't know," says Monroe. "There's an old residential school for sale over near Medicine River."

"You going to paint it?"

"That's about all anyone can do."

And then I remember the bentwood box. It's still in the church, and if we don't get it out now, it might be hard to find the church again. Soldier was lucky this time. Next time, he might not be so lucky.

"What about the box?"

"What box?"

"The bentwood box," I say. "Remember?"

Monroe thinks about this for a moment. "The bentwood box."

"That's right."

He looks at me in amazement. "Of course," he says. "No wonder I couldn't find it." He has left the door propped open, so we have no trouble finding the church. Soldier leads the way, but I could have found it without him. "Can you see it?"

The inside of the church is dark, and all that comes in through the windows are shadows. "It should be right over there."

We stumble around, taking little sliding steps and keeping our hands out in front of us. I hear Soldier grumbling off to one side, and I slide in his direction just in case he's gotten lucky again.

But it's Monroe who finds the box.

"Sonofabitch!"

I've cracked my shin before, so I know how much it hurts. "You okay?"

We lift the box. It isn't really heavy, but it's clumsy and awkward, and we stagger about a bit. Soldier is waiting for us at the door, and now he is wide awake and wants to play.

"Go find a rabbit."

Soldier bolts out the door and down the stairs.

"You think your father would like this box?"

"He'd love it."

Monroe and I carry the box towards the truck. I don't hear Soldier and I don't see him, so when he careens into the back of my legs, it's a big surprise.

"Hey!"

I can't keep my feet under me. The box twists and gets away, and we hit the ground at the same time. By the time I get to my feet, Soldier has disappeared. The box is lying on its side and the lid has popped off. I figure we've broken it for sure.

"I got tripped," I say.

"It's okay," says Monroe. "These boxes are tough."

Just inside the box is Monroe's wig.

"All right." He seems happy to have found it. He picks it up and puts it on. I think it looks a little silly, but then it's not my wig. "Thought I lost this," he says, and he begins straightening the hair with his fingers.

Soldier comes out of nowhere, ambles over, and sticks his head inside the box. "Get out of there!" I yell at him. He shoves his head and shoulders all the way into the box and comes out with something in his mouth. "I'd drop that if I were you," I tell him. "You're in enough trouble already."

Soldier looks at Monroe, and then he looks at me. And then he opens his mouth, and I see something fall into the grass. Monroe walks over and picks it up. "Well, I'll be damned," he says. "I forgot all about you."

All along the eastern margin of the prairies, the sky has begun to lighten. It's still night, but I have no problem seeing what Monroe is holding.

A skull.

Monroe turns the skull around so they're facing each other. "Trying to hide, eh?" he says. The skull looks just like the one Lum and I found, and if I didn't know any better, I might think that Monroe has snuck into Lum's camp and stolen it. "Moving is a real pain," says Monroe. "There's always something left to do." He turns and starts walking to the truck, his long hair crackling in the light of the fire, and in that moment, I see what I should have seen before.

"It was you!"

Monroe stops and turns. "Ah," he says, "an epiphany," but I can see he hasn't got a clue.

"At the Horns." I'm not sure if I'm angry or not, but I am annoyed. "It was you that night at the Horns."

Monroe waits to see what comes next.

"You jumped into the river."

Monroe thinks about this for a minute, and then he smiles and scratches his wig. "You saw that?"

"Lum and me," I say. "And Soldier."

"Boy, am I embarrassed." Monroe sits down on the end of the tailgate. "I must have looked pretty funny. You know, when I was a kid, I could go off the top without making hardly any splash."

I'm all set for Monroe to deny everything, so I'm not ready for him to agree with me and I have to go back a bit.

"I must have looked like a sack of garbage when I hit the water."

"That's where we found the skull," I say. "On the Horns."

Monroe nods and then pauses for a moment. "Which one?"

"There were more?"

"Sure," he says. "The box was full. Took me years to collect them."

"This box?"

"You know how easy it is to sneak stuff like that out of a museum?" says Monroe. "Once I had a thigh bone in my lunch pail."

"You stole bones from a museum?"

Monroe nods his head and looks at Soldier. "I told them it was a soup bone from the cafeteria," he says. "A surprise for my dog."

Somehow the conversation has gotten away from me, and I'm more curious now than I am angry or irritated. "Why would anyone steal bones from a museum?"

"Oh," says Monroe, "I stole them from lots of museums. Toronto. New York. Paris. London. Berlin. You name the museum, I've probably been there." He stares into the distance and watches the sky clearing. He's more sombre now, and he slumps against the side of the truck as if he's just recalled a sad story or is dead on his feet.

"Children." Monroe turns his face away from the light and looks towards the river. "I found them in drawers and boxes and stuck away on dusty shelves. Indian children."

I sit on the ground. Soldier comes over and puts his head on my lap.

"Happens all the time," says Monroe. "Anthropologists and archaeologists dig the kids up, clean them off, and stick them in drawers. Every ten years or so, some bright graduate student opens the drawer, takes a look, writes a paper, and shuts the drawer." He stands up and rubs his hands on his thighs. "So I rescued them."

"How many?"

"All the museums wanted me. Famous Indian artist. The man who could restore anything!" Monroe pulls the hair out of his face. "It was wonderful. They'd invite me in and show me around."

"That box will hold a lot of bones."

"Where are you bastards keeping the children!" Monroe smiles and raises his hands. "Well, I didn't exactly say it like that," he says. "But I'd find them no matter where they had been hidden away. Sometimes those idiots had even forgotten where they had put them."

"And you brought them back here."

Monroe picks up the skull. "Look around you," he says. "This is the centre of the universe. Where else would I bring them? Where else would they want to be?"

The ride across the prairie is bumpy, and Monroe has to fight the wheel and take it slowly because of the piano. I let Soldier sit in front on my lap because he's still sad. He's also heavy, and the ride's not particularly comfortable, so it's a good thing that the Horns are not that far away. Monroe slows down when we get to the rocks and begins inching his way forward. It's not as dark as it was, and if it weren't for the fog, we'd be able to see just fine. "Better stop here," says Monroe. "Don't want to go over the edge with this load."

The fog is on the move, turning in currents and streams. Every so often it opens up, and you can see the Horns and the river. "Close enough," says Monroe, and he gets out of the truck. "What do you think about some music?"

"For what?"

"The ceremony," says Monroe. "For putting the bones in the river."

I've never heard of a ceremony for putting bones into a river. So far as I know, people who die get buried in graveyards. Monroe climbs into the back of the truck and sits down at the piano. "Classical or traditional?"

And he plays a piece that sounds particularly gloomy. Soldier and I wait around to see if it gets any better, but it doesn't.

"Okay," says Monroe, and he closes the lid on the keyboard. "Let's do it and go home."

We walk to the edge of the Horns, the three of us. Monroe carries the skull. Soldier walks beside him, his head hanging down. "Why do you throw them in the river?"

"No good reason."

"So, it's not traditional?"

"Don't think so." Monroe searches through his pockets. "You have anything we can use for the ceremony?"

"Like what?"

"I've been using ribbons," says Monroe. "But I ran out."

Soldier sits back and barks once. I've forgotten about the ribbon Rebecca gave me. I fish it out of my pocket. "What about this?"

Monroe loops the ribbon through the eye sockets and ties it in a bow. "What do you think?" He holds the skull up. The ribbon flutters out like wings. "If it was me," he says, "I think I'd want something pretty like this."

"Mum?" The voice comes out of the darkness, and Soldier and I turn at the same time. Monroe stays facing the river, talking to the skull, unaware of anything but his voice and the sound of the water below him.

"Is that you, mum?"

Lum stands in front of the truck in the fog. The Cousins stand at his side. I can't see Lum's face clearly, but I can see the gun. "Hi, Lum," I say.

Monroe turns around just in time to see Lum rock forward, level the gun, and pull the hammer back.

"No," I say quickly, and I reach out and take the wig off Monroe's head. "It's just Monroe, Lum. Monroe Swimmer."

Lum takes one step forward.

"It was Monroe we saw that night," I tell Lum. "It's a great story. You'll really enjoy it." I hold Monroe's wig up and shake it around so Lum can see that he's made a mistake. "See?" I say. "We thought it was a woman, but it wasn't."

"Hi," says Monroe.

"It could have fooled anybody," I say.

I make the mistake of lowering my arm, and as soon as I do, Soldier turns and snatches the wig out of my hand. I try to grab him, but I miss. He's got me really pissed off now, and if Lum doesn't shoot him, I might. I expect he's going to take off down the coulee, waving the wig around, pretending he's finally caught a rabbit. Instead, he carries the wig over to Lum and drops it at his feet.

Lum looks at the wig. The Cousins lean over and sniff at it. They're trying to look harmless, but they don't fool me.

"You missed a great giveaway," I tell Lum. "Everybody was here."

Soldier reaches up and begins licking the gun and Lum's hand.

"You probably saw the fire," I say.

Soldier whines and squeezes the gun with his mouth. He waits for a moment and then pulls on the gun gently. The Cousins fidget nervously now that Soldier is armed. They back up slowly and disappear. As soon as they are gone, Soldier lets the gun drop to the ground next to the wig and waits.

I don't know about Monroe, but I think waiting is a good thing to do.

Lum stares straight ahead. Soldier whimpers, leans in, and rubs his head on Lum's leg to try to get his attention. You'd think he'd fall over from all the love that my mother and I give him, but he's always look-ing for more.

"Hey, mutt," Lum says softly, and he bends over and gives Soldier a pat. "That your piano?" And Lum stands up and steps back into the fog.

I'm not sure that I want to stand on the Horns in the dark and wait for the sun to come up, but at the moment, it doesn't sound like a bad idea.

"That was exciting," says Monroe, and he walks over, picks up his wig, and puts it on. I wish that he would stay put until I'm sure that the coast is clear. "Here," he says, and he hands me the gun. "Dangerous thing to be lying around."

"Those dogs are a little unpredictable," I say.

"Don't worry," says Monroe. "I looked. It's not loaded."

"Sometimes they're friendly, and sometimes they're not."

"Friend of yours?" says Monroe.

"That's Lum."

"Franklin's boy?" says Monroe.

All across the high ground, the night has retreated. The sun hasn't appeared yet, but the sky is clear, and to the east, you can see the tops of the bluffs and the coulees rising out of the fog like islands. To the west, the river bottom is still buried, but you can see the mountains now, bright blue and white and purple in the morning light.

"Looks like a nice day," says Monroe. "Your friend going to be okay?"

"Franklin tossed him out of the house."

"Ah," says Monroe.

The air softens and swells and begins to move. Soldier leaves the piano and turns into the wind. He stands at the edge of the truck with his ears up, listening.

"He looks worried," says Monroe.

"He always looks like that," I say. I try to find what Soldier has found, but all I hear is the rush of the wind in the grass and the cries of seagulls floating on the wind.

"Well," says Monroe, and he holds up the skull. "I guess I better get back to this."

Soldier ignores the skull. He jumps down from the truck and heads off towards the bridge. I start to call him back, but I can see he's determined, and I know that I can shout until I'm hoarse and it won't do any good.

"Looks like he's on a mission," says Monroe.

Soldier trots down the side of a coulee and disappears into the fog. I'm fairly sure I know where he's going, and I'm not sure it's a good idea.

"You better go find him," says Monroe. "No telling how far he'll go this time." He leans against the truck and straightens the ribbon so it lies on the bone like lines of blood. "When you do," he says, "ask him not to bother the buffalo."

I don't catch up with Soldier. Even though I know where he's going, he has too big a head start on me. He's waiting for me when I get to Lum's camp. Lum is kneeling by the firepit, stirring the ashes with a stick. The Cousins are nowhere to be seen.

Lum doesn't look up. "They went home."

I want to believe this, but I'm not sure the Cousins would tell Lum the truth, even if he asked. The hockey stick is gone. So is the sleeping bag. I look around for the basketball and the frying pan and the sack of food.

"Where's all your stuff?"

"Here," says Lum, and he holds the skull out to me. "Think this belongs to your buddy."

"Monroe rescues them from museums," I tell Lum.

"Cool." Lum cradles the skull in his arms and smooths the bone with the sleeve of his shirt.

"Anthropologists stick them in drawers," I say. "Monroe steals them back."

"Cool."

It doesn't sound as interesting as it should, and I'm sorry I don't do a better job with the story. "Then he puts them in the river."

Most of the paint on Lum's face has rubbed away. You can still see some on his cheeks and on his neck, but he doesn't look as wild as before. "What do you think?"

It's good to see Lum smile again. "Sure," he says, "why not?" He dusts his jeans, walks over, and gives Soldier a nudge with his foot. "Let's do it." I guess I expect that we're going to go back to the Horns, but Lum heads for the bridge instead.

"Monroe throws all the bones off the Horns," I say.

Lum and Soldier walk on ahead. I trail along behind. When we get to the top of the bluff, I look back at the Horns, and if I squint, I think I can just make out the shape of Monroe's truck. But it could be a large rock, too, or a shadow cast by the rising sun.

The fence around the bridge has almost collapsed. It lies on its side coiled up in twists and bows, more a hazard than a barrier. I have never crossed the fence, and when I step on the wire, it sways under my feet, alive and dangerous. It would be easy enough to throw the skull into the river from here and that's what I'd like to do.

"Getting pretty windy," I shout.

"It won't hit the water," says Lum. "It won't hit the water from here."

On the far side of the fence, the plywood decking begins. It's weathered and split, and when we first step on it, it feels thin and flimsy, hollow, as if we are walking on a drum. I don't much like the sensation and neither does Soldier, but we breathe through our mouths and slide our feet along.

The decking only goes so far before construction stops and the planks and the plywood come to an abrupt halt. From here, as far as you can see, the bridge is nothing more than a skeleton, the carcass of an enormous animal, picked to the bone.

"You smell it?" says Lum. "The whole thing's rotting."

From the end of the decking, you can lean out and stare through the dead openings between the ribs and see the fog boil up off the river a thousand miles below. There's nothing to hold on to out here and the wind knows it. It grabs at my arms and legs.

"Lean into it," shouts Lum, and when I look at him, I see he's laughing.

"It's not funny!"

"Like hell it isn't!"

Soldier whines and starts edging back towards the fence. This is one of his better ideas, and I'm all for it. "Just drop it, and let's go back," I say.

"Back to what?" Lum shouts. He holds the skull up. "Look at you!" He steps off the planks and onto a girder. "You're pathetic!" He grabs a piece of rebar and begins bending it back and forth. "One useless piece of shit!"

"Come on, Lum."

"Useless!" The rebar snaps free, and in one motion Lum turns and whips it across his chest. "Where's your pride, son?" The rebar rips Lum's shirt, and I can see blood. Soldier tries to leap forward, but I hold him back. "Where's your pride?" Lum shouts, and hits himself again. And then again. "Where's your pride?"

"Come on, Lum," I say. "You're scaring Soldier."

"Hey, mutt." Lum raises the piece of rebar over his head. His chest is bleeding badly. "You want to chase something?"

Soldier growls and barks and tries to get traction on the plywood, but it's slick, and he loses his footing. "Then chase this!" Lum turns quickly and flings the rebar over the side of the bridge.

"It's not funny," I shout.

"Screw you!"

At first, I think it's just the wind rushing past the girders and the rebar and the wire. But Lum hears it, too, and so does Soldier.

The piano. Over the wind and the fog and the early morning stillness, you can hear the piano. Lum stands on the girder with the skull in his hand. He's quieter now, and I can feel the rage begin to drain away. "That was my mother's favourite song," he says.

"You okay?"

"He can't play it for shit."

Suddenly, I'm tired of standing on the bridge and letting the wind beat me. I've been up all night, and what I'd really like to do is have some of my mother's potatoes and go to bed.

"Hey, cousin!" shouts Lum. "Where you going?"

"Home."

"Come on back. I was just kidding."

"I'm hungry."

"Baby wants to say goodbye." Lum holds the skull out at arm's length. He slowly opens his hand and lets the skull roll off his fingers. "Bye-bye, baby," says Lum. "Bye-bye."

Movies are a lot better at this. In the movies, when something goes off the top of a building or off a cliff, you get to watch it fall all the way to the bottom. In real life, the skull only falls a few feet before it disappears between the girders, and all that's left is Lum standing there, his head down, his arms at his side.

"Did you see how easy that was?"

"Monroe couldn't have done a better job," I say.

"Nothing to it. All you have to do is let go." Lum looks exhausted. Soldier leans forward and pulls me along, and we go back out on the planks again to get him.

"Come on, man," I tell Lum, and I put my arms around him and coax him away from the edge. He feels thin and cold and weak, and I wonder if Soldier and I will have to carry him back to town. "How about we go to Railman's?" I say. "Skee makes a pretty good breakfast. We could even jog in if you liked and get ready for next year's race."

Lum nods. There's blood all over his shirt. His hair is matted and greasy, and he smells bad. But he's smiling now, and I can see that everything is going to be all right. "I can really run, you know."

"That Cree guy wouldn't have stood a chance."

"Here." Lum smiles and hands me his stopwatch. "Time me." He turns and faces Bright Water. "You know what I'm going to do when I hit the finish line?"

"Come on, Lum."

Lum starts across the planks, his arms against his side, his body leaning forward slightly at the hips. "I'm going to keep on going until I feel like stopping!"

"Lum!"

His first steps are heavy and taken in pain. He carries himself tight and pulled off to one side, his feet hitting the planks out of rhythm. But as he picks up speed, his body uncoils and stretches out.

"Lum!"

Soldier shifts his weight suddenly and tears the collar out of my hands. I try to hold him back, but he explodes out on the decking and sends me sprawling.

"Soldier!"

Lum is moving easily now. He glides along the naked girders gracefully, Soldier hard on his heels and closing, until the curve of the bridge begins its descent into Bright Water and Lum and Soldier disappear over the edge.

"Soldier!"

The fog swirls up through the holes in the bridge. I make my way through the maze of girders and steel I-beams, listening for the sound of running or the crack of Soldier's feet on the planks.

"Lum!"

I'm hoping that this is one of his lousy jokes, that I'll find Lum and Soldier crouched down and perched on a lower girder or resting on the wire mesh, having a good laugh. Or I'll spot the two of them safe in the river, chasing each other down the rapids.

But the bridge is empty, and all I see in the distance is the lights of Bright Water and all I see below me is the fog. And all I hear is the wind and the faint strains of the piano rising out of the land with the sun.

CHAPTER THIRTY-TWO

══════

Most everybody on the reserve showed up for Lum's funeral, and even some of the people from Truth came, too. My mother and my grandmother and Lucy Rabbit were there, of course. So was Skee Gardipeau, which surprised me. I didn't think he and Lum were friends, but Skee said that funerals weren't about friendship.

"You come on by afterwards," said Skee. "The special is on me."

Monroe showed up, and he stood with me and my mother and auntie Cassie. Franklin stood by himself in his black suit and never said a word. Two of Lum's aunties from Brocket drove to Bright Water for the service, but they wouldn't shake Franklin's hand or tell him how sorry they were for his loss.

It took the police a couple of days to find Lum's body. They went up and down the river hauling all sorts of junk out of the water. They found the usual stuff, tires, car parts, a lawn mower, a mattress. Farther on, they ran across a bunch of yellow barrels washed up on a sandbar.

They never found Soldier, but I don't know that they were really looking for him.

CHAPTER THIRTY-THREE

━━━

I'm sitting in the shop, finishing breakfast and watching my mother clean the sink, when Lucy Rabbit opens the door and sticks her head in. "All set?" she says to my mother.

My mother smiles, but all she really wants to do right now is clean the sink.

"Nervous?"

"A little," says my mother.

"Marilyn was always nervous," says Lucy. "Even after she became a big star."

My mother has carnations in the vase in the window. They're not my favourites, but they last longer than roses or daffodils or gladiolas.

"Nice piano," says Lucy. "When'd you get this?"

"Monroe Swimmer brought it by," says my mother.

Lucy cocks her head at me. "You play piano?"

"No."

"But he wants to learn," says my mother.

"What kind of music do you like?"

"Classical," says my mother.

"Forget that," says Lucy. "Rock and roll is more fun."

When Monroe showed up with the piano, I told him I wasn't sure I wanted one, but he said you couldn't refuse a gift.

"Bad luck?"

"Worse," he said. "Bad manners."

The piano wouldn't fit through the doorway to the back area, so we had to set it up in the shop against the wall. It looked pretty good there, and everyone who came by said nice things about it.

"Can you play anything yet?" says Lucy.

I shake my head.

"Go ahead," says my mother. "Show her what you can do."

"She doesn't want to hear."

"Yes, I do," says Lucy.

"I have to get going," I say.

"For me," says my mother.

Lucy shuts the door and sits down in the chair and waits. My mother stands against the sink with the scrub brush in her hand. You can see that both of them are determined. So, I play a little bit of what Monroe showed me. It isn't much, but I don't make any big mistakes. When I finish, Lucy and my mother clap.

"I know that song," says Lucy.

"Everybody knows that song," says my mother. "Monroe showed him how to play it."

I close the piano and head for the door.

"Where you going, honey?" She has that concerned tone in her voice again.

"Out."

"You going to the river?"

"Who knows."

My mother looks at Lucy to see if she's going to get any help. "Just be careful."

"And don't forget tonight," says Lucy. "Wouldn't want to miss the debut of your mother's new career."

My mother goes back to scrubbing the sink. Lucy stays in the chair, her hair bright and crisp, but she doesn't hum a song as she normally does, and she doesn't spin around in the chair.

"What's up, Doc?" I say.

"Ah," says Lucy, her eyes filling up. "It's the wascally wabbit."

My father arrived at the funeral late, and even though he did a good job of standing up straight, you could see he had been drinking. My grandmother stood next to my mother and snarled at him whenever he looked as if he might wander our way. When the funeral was over, he caught up to me.

"Figured I'd get you another dog," he said. "What do you think of that?"

"Don't want another dog."

"I don't mean right away."

"Don't want another dog."

"You got to feel sorry for Franklin," said my father. "You can't imagine how I'd feel if something happened to you."

Lucille and Teresa and Edna and Wally from the railroad all came over, and each of them told me a funny story about Lum. "You know what he used to say to Lucy?" said Lucille. "That always made me laugh."

I didn't see Miles Deardorf at the funeral, but when we got back to the parking lot, we found his business cards stuck under the windshield wipers of all the cars.

I walk the river bank from the bridge to the flat, just like the night Lum and Soldier and I went searching for the woman. I don't expect to find Soldier alive, but I am happy that no one has found his body either. There's always the chance that he survived the fall but was injured and lost his memory, and that one day he'll remember and come home. I saw a movie where that exact thing happened, only it was a man and not a dog.

I can see the buffalo on the sides of the coulees and on the bluff overlooking the Shield. A few of them have wandered off and aren't where they're supposed to be, but most of them have stayed put. Monroe said they might move around a bit and that it isn't a worry as long as they stay in sight.

The river is still high. But later in the summer, when the water drops and the gravel beds and sandbars appear in mid-stream, you'll be able to wade to the middle and never be in over your knees.

I get up to the Horns around noon and stand on the rocks. Below me, a flock of pelicans skims along the surface of the water, and farther out, flurries of seagulls beat their way towards Bright Water and the landfill. I stand on the edge of the Horns for a long time and look down. The water here is deep and black, and I wonder how it would feel to plunge such a great distance and have nothing to break your fall.

When I get home that evening, my mother is waiting for me. She notices that I am wet, but she doesn't say anything. "You must be hungry."

"I'm fine."

"I made some sausage and potatoes."

"We had that last night."

"Eat a little," she says. "And change your clothes."

I put some of the potatoes on my plate and sink into the couch. There's nothing on television, but I stuff a pillow under my head and watch it anyway.

It took Monroe and me and Skee and Gabriel Tucker to haul the piano off the truck.

"How the hell'd you get it on?" said Skee.

"Physics," said Monroe.

We tied ropes around the top and slid it off on planks. Halfway down, one of the planks cracked and the piano almost tipped over, but Skee used his bulk to steady it, and we were able to ease the piano down onto the sidewalk.

"This thing up to concert pitch?" said Skee.

None of us knew exactly what that was, and neither did Skee. He said it was one of the questions you were supposed to ask when you bought an older piano. "*Reader's Digest*," said Skee. "Never know what you're going to find in *Reader's Digest*."

We had to take the front door off its hinges, but that wasn't difficult, and then it was just a matter of pushing the piano into the shop.

"You know how to play?" Gabriel asked me.

"Middle C," said Monroe. "As long as you know where middle C is, you can play anything."

Monroe stayed around for a while after Gabriel and Skee left, and showed me how to play a couple of songs.

"You forgetting something?" he said.

"What?"

"Man's got to look out for himself," said Monroe, and he handed me an envelope. "Don't spend it all in one place."

When my mother came out of the back that morning, she was surprised to see a piano against the wall. I told her we could sell it or give it away, that I wasn't sure I wanted a piano, but she said no, it was a handsome thing, and even if I didn't learn to play, it was something nice for the customers to look at. I kept the sculpture of the Indian chasing the elk in my bedroom for a while, but it was dark back there, and in the end, I put it on top of the piano so it could be in the light.

Auntie Cassie comes by after supper.

"You go for a swim?"

"Come on," says my mother. "I don't want to be late."

Auntie Cassie squeezes one of my runners. Water leaks out and drips on the couch.

"Your father's coming by at seven-thirty to pick you up," my mother tells me.

"Do I have to go with him?"

"There's a party afterwards," says my mother, "so I won't be home until late."

"I'd rather come with you guys."

I can see my mother waver, but auntie Cassie comes to her rescue. "It's going to take me at least an hour to calm her down," says auntie Cassie.

"I'm fine!"

"Otherwise, she's going to pee her pants when she steps on stage."

My father shows up at seven. He's dressed in a blue suit and a red tie. "I got married in this suit," he tells me.

"You look great."

"That's what your mother said."

I get dressed, and we go down the street to Railman's. My father orders the special. I have the same, but I don't eat much.

"What's with the suit?" says Skee.

"We're going to the play," I tell him.

Skee looks at my father, reaches out, and runs his fingers along the lapel. "Pretty fancy," he says. "How's that chair coming?"

"Almost done," says my father.

"That right?"

"Absolutely," says my father. "You can count on me."

The day after the funeral, the people from Georgia loaded up their RVs and headed out. Lucille Rain said they were heading for Oklahoma, but that they were going to take their time and see the sights.

"That young girl was real nice," said Lucille.

264

"Did she ever find her duck?"

"And you missed a wonderful story."

I would have liked to have said goodbye to Rebecca, to tell her that I was sorry about her duck, that it might turn up yet, that I knew what it was like to lose things.

There are more people at the theatre than were at the funeral, but that doesn't surprise me. Dying on stage can be funny, and most people would rather laugh than cry. Monroe is sitting in the front row, right in the middle. He's dressed like my father and he's not wearing his wig. My father gets us seats in the tenth row. There's a post that's sort of in the way, but if you lean out and look around it, you can see fine.

"Aisle seats are always the best," he says.

The play is pretty good. My father tells me it's supposed to be a political satire about the federal government and Indians, but I've already figured that out.

"It sure as hell's not *Snow White*," says my father.

"Mom is great."

"That Carol Millerfeather," says my father. "Woman sure has a weird imagination."

When the curtain comes down, everyone in the theatre jumps to their feet and claps. Then the players come out on the stage, and someone from behind the curtain brings out bouquets of flowers. Standing there in the lights, smiling at the applause, my mother looks like an actress. She really does.

"So, what did you think?" my father asks me as we walk down the street.

"She was good," I say. "Didn't you think she was good?"

"Hell of a lot better than the bimbo who played Snow White."

My mother and auntie Cassie don't get back to the shop until late. I'm waiting for them on the couch. "Well," says auntie Cassie, "what did you think?"

"You were good," I tell my mother.

"Always did want to be an actress," says auntie Cassie. "And the good news was she didn't have to die of something that was contagious or embarrassing."

"You were the best," I say, but it doesn't come out clean or in one piece, and I have to put my tongue between my teeth and bite down hard to save myself.

My mother sits down next to me. "You know I love you," she says, and she touches my face with her fingers. Auntie Cassie sits down on the other side. "You know it wasn't your fault."

I'm trying to hold my lips in place, but my mother and auntie Cassie are sitting too close, and everything comes loose. And once that happens, there's no putting it back. "I miss Lum."

My mother pulls me to her and rocks me. "I know you do, honey."

"And I miss Soldier."

When I get up the next morning, my mother is out in the shop sweeping the floor and cleaning the combs. The carnations are gone and there is a large bouquet of purple flowers in the vase.

"You get those from Santucci's?"

"No," says my mother. "I got them after the play."

"What are they?"

"Freesias."

"Dad get them for you?"

"No," says my mother.

"Auntie Cassie?"

"No."

The next day, the freesias begin to open up and their fragrance fills the shop. It's a nice smell, like perfume, and I can see why women like flowers. They stay in the front window for a long time, and each day, my mother picks off the blossoms that have died, and carefully trims and cuts the flowers back until there is nothing left but the stems.

ACKNOWLEDGEMENTS

My thanks to the Canada Council for a writing grant that allowed me to work on the novel full time for a year, and my particular thanks to Alan Kilpatrick who once again came to my rescue in matters linguistic and who shares my views on the value of fame—ade:la ugv:wiyu agwadu:liha'.